UNTOUCHABLE

Titles by Jayne Ann Krentz

UNTOUCHABLE	SMOKE IN MIRRORS
PROMISE NOT TO TELL	LOST & FOUND
WHEN ALL THE GIRLS HAVE GONE	DAWN IN ECLIPSE BAY
SECRET SISTERS	SOFT FOCUS
TRUST NO ONE	ECLIPSE BAY
RIVER ROAD	EYE OF THE BEHOLDER
DREAM EYES	FLASH
COPPER BEACH	SHARP EDGES
IN TOO DEEP	DEEP WATERS
FIRED UP	ABSOLUTELY, POSITIVELY
RUNNING HOT	TRUST ME
SIZZLE AND BURN	GRAND PASSION
WHITE LIES	HIDDEN TALENTS
ALL NIGHT LONG	WILDEST HEARTS
FALLING AWAKE	FAMILY MAN
TRUTH OR DARE	PERFECT PARTNERS
LIGHT IN SHADOW	SWEET FORTUNE
SUMMER IN ECLIPSE BAY	SILVER LININGS
TOGETHER IN ECLIPSE BAY	THE GOLDEN CHANCE

Titles by Jayne Ann Krentz writing as Amanda Quick

THE OTHER LADY VANISHES	SLIGHTLY SHADY
THE GIRL WHO KNEW TOO MUCH	WICKED WIDOW
'TIL DEATH DO US PART	I THEE WED
GARDEN OF LIES	WITH THIS RING
OTHERWISE ENGAGED	AFFAIR
THE MYSTERY WOMAN	MISCHIEF
CRYSTAL GARDENS	MYSTIQUE
QUICKSILVER	MISTRESS
BURNING LAMP	DECEPTION
THE PERFECT POISON	DESIRE
THE THIRD CIRCLE	DANGEROUS
THE RIVER KNOWS	RECKLESS
SECOND SIGHT	RAVISHED
LIE BY MOONLIGHT	RENDEZVOUS
THE PAID COMPANION	SCANDAL
WAIT UNTIL MIDNIGHT	SURRENDER
LATE FOR THE WEDDING	SEDUCTION
DON'T LOOK BACK	

Titles by Jayne Ann Krentz writing as Jayne Castle

ILLUSION TOWN	SILVER MASTER
SIREN'S CALL	GHOST HUNTER
THE HOT ZONE	AFTER GLOW
DECEPTION COVE	HARMONY
THE LOST NIGHT	AFTER DARK
CANYONS OF NIGHT	AMARYLLIS
MIDNIGHT CRYSTAL	ZINNIA
OBSIDIAN PREY	ORCHID
DARK LIGHT	

The Guinevere Jones Series

DESPERATE AND DECEPTIVE
The Guinevere Jones Collection, Volume 1
THE DESPERATE GAME
THE CHILLING DECEPTION

SINISTER AND FATAL
The Guinevere Jones Collection, Volume 2
THE SINISTER TOUCH
THE FATAL FORTUNE

Specials

THE SCARGILL COVE CASE FILES
BRIDAL JITTERS
(writing as Jayne Castle)

Anthologies

CHARMED
(with Julie Beard, Lori Foster, and Eileen Wilks)

Titles written by Jayne Ann Krentz and Jayne Castle

NO GOING BACK

UNTOUCHABLE

JAYNE ANN KRENTZ

BERKLEY
NEW YORK

BERKLEY
An imprint of Penguin Random House LLC
1745 Broadway, New York, New York 10019

Library of Congress Cataloging-in-Publication Data

Names: Krentz, Jayne Ann, author.
Title: Untouchable / Jayne Ann Krentz.
Description: First Edition. | New York : Berkley, 2019.
Identifiers: LCCN 2018029359| ISBN 9780399585296 (hardback) | ISBN 9780399585302 (ebook)
Subjects: | BISAC: FICTION / Romance / Suspense. | FICTION / Suspense. |
FICTION / Romance / General. | GSAFD: Romantic suspense fiction.
Classification: LCC PS3561.R44 U58 2019 | DDC 813/.54—dc23
LC record available at https://lccn.loc.gov/2018029359

First Edition: January 2019

Printed in the United States of America
1 3 5 7 9 10 8 6 4 2

Cover photo by Karina Vegas/Arcangel
Cover design by Rita Frangie
Book design by Laura K. Corless

For Frank, with all my love

UNTOUCHABLE

CHAPTER ONE

———— ≋ ————

Fifteen years earlier . . .

She was fourteen years old and sleeping in yet another bed. The little house on Marigold Lane looked cozy and welcoming from the street—lots of curb appeal, as the real estate agents liked to say—but she had decided that she would not be there for long.

Every few weeks when she got tired of life on the streets she checked into the foster care system long enough to take some hot showers and score some new tennis shoes or a new pair of jeans or a new backpack. She had figured out early on that a backpack was essential to survival on the streets. The one she had picked up last month had a large rip in it, thanks to the junkie with the knife who had tried to steal it. The junkie was no longer a problem but the wounded pack had to be replaced.

She rarely stayed in a foster home for more than a few days. Sooner or later, there were issues. This time the problem would be the husband. His name was Tyler. She had privately labeled him Tyler the Creep.

She had seen the way he looked at her two days ago when she arrived with her ripped backpack containing all her worldly possessions: a few clothes, a hairbrush and a toothbrush, and the battered copies of *Winnie-the-Pooh* and *The House at Pooh Corner*.

Initially she had not been concerned; merely inconvenienced. She could handle Tyler the Creep but it meant that she could not go to sleep at night. Creeps like Tyler had a lot in common with roaches—they came out after dark.

The situation, however, had gotten a lot more complicated that afternoon when the social worker had arrived on the doorstep with another foster kid. The girl's name was Alice. All she had with her was a small rolling suitcase. She was eleven years old and she had been orphaned when her father's private plane had crashed on takeoff. Alice's mother had been a passenger. Both parents had been killed. Alice had been in school at the time.

Dazed and traumatized, she had said very little except her name and that her aunts would come for her.

Later, when she and Winter were alone in the bedroom, she had repeated the same thing over and over.

"My mom and dad told me that if anything ever happened to them, I should call my aunts. They will come and get me."

During her short stays in various foster homes over the course of the past year, Winter had heard similar claims. Mostly the tales turned out to be sparkly little lies told by well-meaning parents who had wanted to reassure their children that some adult family member would always be there for them; that they were not alone in the world. That they had family to protect them.

But after several months of floating in and out of the system, she knew the truth. There were no aunts, or, if they did exist, they weren't going to magically appear to rescue Alice. Sure, there might be a few distant relatives somewhere but there would be a thousand excuses why they couldn't take a kid into their household. *We're too old. We barely knew that side of the family. Our lifestyle won't allow us to take the child. We travel too much. We can't afford to take her. We have other children who would be upset. The child has severe emotional problems that we're just not equipped to handle . . .*

Winter sat on the top bunk, legs dangling over the edge. The new backpack was on the bed beside her. She wore the jeans and the hoodie that she'd had on during the day. She always slept in her clothes. It made for more efficient departures.

She had a penlight in one hand. In her other hand she gripped her copy of *Winnie-the-Pooh*. Earlier she had read some of the stories to Alice. Alice had said that she was too old for Winnie-the-Pooh, but the gentle stories had soothed her. She had eventually fallen into an exhausted sleep.

A few hours ago the new foster mom had been called away to deal with a family crisis involving one of her own aging parents. Tyler the Creep was now in the front room, drinking and watching television.

Winter had taken the precaution of locking the bedroom door but she had known that wouldn't do any good. The creep had the key.

It was another half hour before she heard the doorknob rattle. When Tyler the Creep discovered that the door was locked, he left. For a moment she entertained the faint hope that he would not return. But of course he did.

She heard the key in the lock. The door opened. The creep was silhouetted against the light of the hallway fixture, a balding, big-bellied man dressed in an undershirt and trousers.

He did not see her sitting there in the shadows of the upper bunk. He moved into the room, heading toward the lower bunk.

He reached down and started to pull the covers off Alice's thin, huddled body.

"Go away, Mr. Tyler," Winter said. She switched on the penlight and began to move it in an intricate pattern. "You're not supposed to be here. You don't want to be here."

She kept her voice calm; soothing but firm.

Startled, Tyler halted and instinctively averted his gaze from the narrow beam of light.

"What the hell?" In the next breath he softened his voice to a drunken croon. "What's the matter, honey? Couldn't sleep? I know it's hard adjusting to a new house and a new family. But you're in a good home now. There's nothing to worry about. I'll take care of you and Alice."

"Go away, Mr. Tyler," Winter said again. She kept the penlight moving, faster now.

Tyler was distracted by the light. He stared at it; looked away and then gazed at it again.

"I'm going to take poor little Alice to my bedroom," he said. "She's afraid to be alone."

"Alice is not alone," Winter said. "I'm here with her. Go away. You don't want to be in this room. It's hard to breathe when you come in here. You can't catch your breath. Your heart is pounding harder and harder. You wonder if you're having a heart attack."

Tyler did not respond. He was transfixed by the motion of the light. He started to wheeze.

"When I say *Winnie-the-Pooh*, you will realize that you can't breathe at all when you're in this room," Winter said. "You will leave. That is the only way to ease the terrible pain in your chest. If you stay in this room you will have a heart attack. Do you understand?"

"Yes." Tyler's voice was now that of a man in a trance, expressionless.

The rasping and wheezing got louder.

"Winnie-the-Pooh," Winter said in a tone of soft command.

Tyler came out of the trance gasping for air.

"Can't breathe," he said, his voice hoarse with panic. He swung around and lurched out into the hallway. "My heart. Can't breathe."

He staggered down the hallway and stumbled toward the kitchen. Winter jumped down to the floor.

"Winter?" Alice whispered from the shadows of the lower bunk.

"It's okay," Winter said. "But you have to get up and get dressed. We're going to leave now."

A heavy thud sounded from the kitchen. It was followed by an unnatural silence.

"What happened?" Alice asked.

"Stay here," Winter said. "I'll go take a look."

She went to the door. With the penlight in hand she moved cautiously down the hall. Alice climbed out of bed but she did not wait in the bed-room. She followed Winter.

Tyler was sprawled on the kitchen floor. He did not move. His phone was on the floor close to his hand. Panic arced through Winter. She won-dered if she had killed the creep.

Alice came up beside her and took her hand, clinging very tightly. She looked at Tyler's motionless body.

"Is he dead?" she asked.

"I don't know," Winter said. "I'll check."

She released Alice's hand and crossed the kitchen floor. She stopped a short distance away from Tyler and tried to think about what to do next. In the movies and on television people checked the throat of an uncon-scious person to find out if there was a pulse.

Gingerly she reached down and put two fingers on Tyler's neck. She thought she detected a faint beat but she couldn't be certain. He might not be dead yet but it was possible that he was dying. It was also possible that he was simply unconscious and would recover at any moment. Winter knew that neither outcome would be good for Alice or herself.

"Get dressed," Winter said. "Put everything you brought with you back into your suitcase. I don't know how much time we have."

Alice regarded her with big, frightened eyes. "Okay."

She turned and ran back down the hall. Winter followed. It did not take long to gather up Alice's few possessions. The little suitcase had not been completely unpacked.

On the way out Winter paused at the kitchen door. Tyler the Creep was still on the floor; still not moving.

"Hold on a second," she said to Alice. "I'm going to call a cab."

She used the phone on the kitchen counter. Tyler stirred just as she finished the call. He opened his eyes. He stared at her first in disbelief and then in gathering rage and panic.

"You did this to me," he wheezed. "You're killing me."

"Winnie-the-Pooh," Winter said.

Tyler gasped, clutched at his chest and collapsed again, unconscious.

Winter reached down into his pocket, took out his wallet and helped herself to the seventy-five dollars she found inside. She considered the credit cards for a moment and opted to leave them behind. Credit cards left a trail.

She dropped the wallet on the floor beside the phone and looked at Alice.

"Let's go," she said.

Alice nodded quickly.

A few minutes later they climbed into the back of the cab. The driver was obviously uneasy about picking up two kids in the middle of the night but he did not ask any questions beyond confirming their destination.

"You want to go to the bus station?" he said.

"Yes, please," Winter said.

She tried to think through a plan. She was accustomed to running away but in the past she had always been alone when she set out into the darkness late at night with her pack on her back. Tonight she had to deal with Alice.

Mentally, she started a getaway list. Even using cash, she would probably need an ID to buy bus tickets. It wouldn't be hard to find a street person and pay him or her to purchase the two tickets to Los Angeles.

The seventy-five bucks would not last long. They would have to use some of it to buy Alice a backpack. A suitcase, even one with wheels, was a problem on the streets, an environment where you needed to keep both hands free.

When the cash ran out she could always raise more doing the psychic-dream-reader routine. It was amazing how many people would pay twenty or thirty bucks to have someone tell them the meaning of their dreams.

She sat back in the seat, mind churning with plans. Alice huddled close beside her and lowered her voice to the barest of whispers.

"Don't worry," she said. "My aunts will find us. They'll take care of us."

"Sure," Winter said.

No need to make the kid confront the truth tonight. Alice would find out soon enough that no one was coming to save them. They were on their own.

"If anyone asks, we're sisters," Winter said. "Got that?"

"Okay," Alice said again. She gripped Winter's hand. "Are you a witch?"

Winter watched the lights of the house on Marigold Lane disappear into the night and wondered if Tyler the Creep was dead.

"I don't know," she said.

CHAPTER TWO

———≈———

Four months ago . . .

The dreamer followed the burning footprints through endless halls of fire. He knew his quarry was there, hiding in the shadows of the flames. From time to time he came across ghostly traces of Quinton Zane, faint clues that assured him he was not hallucinating.

The dreamer was ever vigilant. He followed every seething print, every trace of Zane, no matter how faint.

Tonight was not his first trip into the maze. He came this way often and not always in pursuit of Zane. He frequently hunted other killers in the same maze. On those occasions he was almost always successful. He was, after all, very good at what he did. But the calm he experienced in the aftermath of a successful search for a killer other than Zane never lasted long.

There would be no rest until he found Quinton Zane.

The dreamer was not oblivious to the risks he took in the fire maze. He was well aware that he paid a high price for his refusal to turn back from the hunt. But he could not abandon the search even though he feared that with each journey into the nightmare the probability of getting lost in the halls of flames increased.

The sense that time was running out drove him. He could not stop now, even though he was grimly aware that one night he would go too far . . .

The dream ended when the screaming started.

That was pretty much the story of his life, at least when it came to his relationships with women, Jack thought. But this time things were supposed to have a different ending. Then again, he'd hoped for a different ending last time, too. They said that the definition of insanity was doing the same thing over and over again and expecting a different result.

"Dr. Lancaster. *Jack*, wake up. *Wake up.* I'll have to call security if you don't wake up right now. Please, you must wake up."

Jack pulled himself out of the dream with a monumental effort of will. The urge to plunge back into the fiery maze had grown markedly stronger in recent months. It was getting harder to wake up.

But Dr. Margaret Burke was staring at him with the same expression of shock and poorly veiled fear that he'd seen on the faces of other women. The difference this time was that Margaret was not sharing his bed. She was the director of the sleep clinic that had provided him with the bed he had been occupying tonight.

He groaned when he realized he was no longer in the bed in question; no longer attached to the beeping, buzzing monitors. He was standing on the far side of the small room.

To buy himself a little time he went to the table and picked up his eyeglass case. He opened the case with great precision, removed the steel-framed glasses and put them on with both hands.

When he was ready he took a deep, steadying breath and risked a quick glance at the mirror on the wall.

One look was enough to confirm what he had already suspected. He was a very scary sight.

His hair was sticking out at wild angles. The shapeless hospital gown he had worn to bed had come undone, exposing way too much skin. Electrical leads that had connected him to an array of instruments and monitors dangled from the various places on his body where they were still attached with sticky tape.

Even if he ignored his eyes, he had to admit that he looked a lot like a modern-day version of Frankenstein's monster. *Make that Jack of the walking dead.*

He was never sure which frightened others the most—the sleepwalking or the weirdness in his gaze when he woke up. He had been informed by more than one bed partner that he looked flat-out crazy when he surfaced from the fire maze dream. Evidently he emerged with the vibe of a man who saw visions.

The modern world did not have a lot of room for people who hallucinated, let alone for those who could do it on demand.

It took a minute to regain what he knew Margaret would consider a normal expression. The glasses helped mute some of the effect. That was why he had taken the time to put them on even before he secured the hospital gown.

Margaret was at the door, one hand wrapped around the knob, ready to bolt to safety. She clutched her small computer as though it were a Kevlar vest.

After extensive research he had selected her clinic primarily because Burke had impressed him with her published papers on sleep disorders and her stated interest in exploring the phenomenon of lucid dreaming.

"Sorry," he said. He raised a hand to wipe the sweat off his forehead and came away with two electrical leads. Annoyed with himself and the whole damned situation, he tossed the leads aside and looked at Margaret. "I told you that if I dreamed the fire maze dream I might not be able to control it or the sleepwalking. You said you could help me."

Margaret made a valiant effort to regain her professional composure, but she maintained her white-knuckled grip on the doorknob.

"I thought I could deal with your unusual problem," she said.

"You mean you thought it would be interesting to run some experiments on me. That's what this is all about, isn't it?" He swept out a hand to indicate the sleep clinic. "I was just a lab rat as far as you were concerned. You were probably planning to write up my case for some journal."

"That's not true. Your dreams are unique, Dr. Lancaster. I've never met anyone who experiences lucid dreaming the way you do. But that nightmare you just had—"

"I told you, it's not a normal nightmare—assuming there is such a thing. It's a lucid dream that I constructed from scratch. I use it to do my work. But the maze keeps getting bigger. More convoluted. I'm losing control of it. I need to find the center."

"Do you even realize just how crazy that sounds?" Margaret's voice rose. "You're an academic, Jack. You've taught college-level classes on the subject of the criminal mind. You wrote a couple of books. Surely you understand that what you're describing is some sort of bizarre obsession. With fire, no less. I'm afraid it will only get worse, and if that happens you may become—"

She stopped very suddenly.

"May become what?" he asked quietly. "Dangerous? Paranoid? Mentally unstable? Is that what you were going to say?"

"Look, I really wish I could help you, but you need another kind of doctor. This is way out of my league. The truth is that the scientific study of dreams has not advanced very far. There is still so much we don't know. I would strongly suggest that you consult a psychiatrist, someone who will have a better idea of what kind of meds might help you."

"Been there."

He risked another glance in the mirror. He thought his eyes looked normal now. He hoped they looked normal. But they were his eyes, he reminded himself, so it followed that, naturally, they would look okay to him. The question was, what did Burke see?

She frowned. "You've tried medication therapy? You didn't mention that when you consulted me."

"Because it didn't work." He ripped off a couple more stray leads and went to the small closet that held his clothes. "Looks like we both wasted our time. I'll get out of your lab."

"Dr. Lancaster. Jack. I'm sorry. I really hoped that I could diagnose your sleep disorder and help you overcome it."

He opened the closet and took out the white button-down shirt he had hung there earlier that evening. It was one of a dozen white button-down shirts he owned. He only bought white shirts. That way he did not waste time figuring out which shirt to wear. White worked with both of his dark blue business suits and it worked with any of the six pairs of khaki trousers that constituted most of the rest of his wardrobe. He also owned four ties.

He found life complicated enough as it was. He tried to simplify wherever possible.

"I told you, I'm not looking for a diagnosis," he said. "I'm looking for a way to get better control of the damned dream. I can't make it work the way I need it to work anymore."

"I realize that when you go into a lucid dreaming state you are aware that you're dreaming," Margaret said. "I also understand that you feel as if you are manipulating some aspects of the dream."

"I don't *feel* as if I'm manipulating elements of the dream, I *do* manipulate them."

"A lot of people experience that sensation from time to time," Margaret said. "That's the definition of a lucid dream. The experience usually occurs when an individual is just starting to wake up. There is a very short period of time during which you realize that you are still dreaming. But what you're describing—this fire maze—that's more in the nature of a . . . uh—"

She broke off, flushing a dull red.

"More in the nature of a hallucination?" he finished. "A vision? I'm aware of that, Dr. Burke. I'm going to get dressed now. If you want to stand there and watch, that's up to you."

Margaret opened her mouth but evidently thought better of whatever it was she had intended to say. Without another word, she jerked open the door and hurried out into the hall.

Jack waited until the door closed.

"Shit," he said.

He ripped another lead off his chest and tossed the hospital gown aside.

Margaret Burke wasn't the first woman to flee a bedroom that happened to have him in it. Going forward he would resume his long-standing policy: Always sleep alone.

He found his precisely folded white undershirt on a shelf in the closet. He unfolded it and pulled it on over his head. All of his undershirts were white. They worked well with the twelve white button-down shirts.

CHAPTER THREE

———≈———

Several weeks ago . . .

The man who had once been Quinton Zane watched the fire from a safe distance. The vehicle was fully engulfed now, a blazing torch that lit up the desert night. The flames riveted him. They filled his world, obliterating the view of the glittering lights of Las Vegas in the distance.

He was alone. There was no traffic on the empty stretch of road at this hour. There was no need to suppress or conceal the electrifying excitement that flashed through him. He did not have to pretend to be appalled. There were no other witnesses to the spectacle. He was free to savor the glorious act of destruction.

Fire aroused all of his senses. Fire ignited an overwhelming sense of euphoria and sent shock waves of power through him. Fire was the most potent drug he had ever known; infinitely more satisfying than sex or cocaine.

Running a successful con was the only thing that even came close. True, he got a rush in that moment of triumph when he closed down a project and walked away with the money. It was gratifying to see the stunned expressions on the faces of the marks who were left to deal with the financial wreckage and the shattered lives. But not even a billion-dollar con could provide a thrill that was remotely close to the one he got from fire.

If he were normal—one of the weak members of the herd—he would probably worry about the quirk. But he wasn't normal. He wasn't weak. He wasn't a part of the herd. He was the predator they feared but never recognized until it was too late.

The flames were starting to fade now. He should probably leave. There was always the remote possibility that someone might notice the fire and decide to investigate. He did not want his rental car to be observed driving away from the scene.

Still, he hesitated. He could have stood there on the side of the road and watched until there was nothing left but blackened metal and a body that was burned beyond recognition. The thing about fire was that it had such a wonderfully cleansing effect. It could wipe out anything, including the past.

But he had not come this far only to start making mistakes. He forced himself to turn around and walk back to his car. Mentally he ran through the details of his grand project, making certain he had covered everything. It would probably take the authorities a while to announce a positive identification of the body. But soon they would conclude that the remains found behind the wheel of the burned-out Mercedes were those of the registered owner, Jessica Pitt. They would be right.

Jessica had been stunningly beautiful, smart and ambitious. Each of her three divorces had left her wealthier than the previous one. But, like everyone else, Jessica had craved something so desperately that she had believed him when he had promised to deliver it. She had, in turn, given him exactly what he needed in order to carry out the important first steps of the project.

Jessica had been quite talented, not only in bed but in far more crucial ways. He had enjoyed their time together but he no longer needed her. In the course of their relationship she had learned too much for her own good. He could not allow her to live. He was ready to move forward.

Jessica Pitt was just one more fiery sacrifice on the altar of his greatest project.

He got behind the wheel of the rental and drove away from the fire, into the night.

The exhilarating rush of excitement that had accompanied the explosion and fire was already evaporating. When it was gone he was left with only the old, familiar rage, one of the few emotions he could experience fully. He opened himself to the sensation. He knew that the inferno that burned at his core was the source of his strength.

He focused his attention on the next step in his plan. He had understood from the beginning that the smart way to pursue his objective was the tried-and-true strategy of divide and conquer. It had always been clear that when the time came to make his big move, Jack Lancaster would have to be taken out first.

Most people would have said that Jack Lancaster was the least dangerous of Anson Salinas's foster sons. Lancaster had spent a portion of his career in the academic world. These days he wrote books for a living. He did not have any military training and he had never worked as a cop. He could probably pull the trigger of a gun—hell, anyone could pull the trigger of a gun—but there was no indication that he owned a weapon, let alone that he was proficient with firearms.

Lancaster was not a martial arts expert like his foster brother Cabot Sutter. He lacked the profiling experience and the connections with the FBI and certain clandestine government agencies that his other brother, Max Cutler, possessed.

Lancaster had never even managed to hold a teaching position for very long, and he had never married. Over the years his name had popped up in the supposedly private online records of various psychiatrists and sleep disorder experts. There had been no clear diagnosis or even a detailed description of his problem. The term *delusional* had been used in some of the notes, however.

Whatever his sleep disorder was, it had evidently been enough to keep his personal life limited to a series of short-lived affairs. A year ago one ex-lover had even gone on social media to label him crazy.

But the man who had been Quinton Zane knew the truth about Jack Lancaster. A little over twenty-two years ago he had seen that truth in Lancaster's eyes.

Lancaster had been a twelve-year-old kid at the time but it had been clear even then that when he became a man he would not merely be dangerous. He would be downright scary.

So, yes, Jack Lancaster had to be the first of Anson's sons to go down. And he would go down in flames.

CHAPTER FOUR

———— ≈ ————

Present day . . .

Winter Meadows contemplated the hands of the client because it was distracting, even for a pro like her, to watch Jack Lancaster's face while he did his kind of meditation.

Jack did not close his eyes the way most people did when they sank into a self-induced meditative state. Instead, he fixed his gaze on the small chunk of black obsidian that he held. He focused on the stone as though it contained secrets and visions that only he could see.

Which, of course, was true, because Jack was not meditating. He was dreaming.

Technically speaking, he was in a lucid dream, a kind of dream that took place in the uncharted territory between sleep and the waking state. She had encountered lucid dreamers before—she'd had a few lucid dreams herself. Many people experienced them from time to time. But Jack's ability was highly unusual. He could dream on demand and he dreamed with purpose.

He had removed his steel-framed glasses at the start of the session and stowed them in a case. He should have looked more vulnerable, or at least more approachable, but the opposite was true. Without the lenses to mute the impact, his vivid green eyes exerted a compelling attraction—at least they had that effect on her. She found it difficult to look away. She did not *want* to look away. They were the eyes of a man who saw beneath the surface; a man who knew how to look deeply into things that other people never thought twice about. The eyes of a man with a mission.

His hands also intrigued her. They were strong and masculine but there was something sensual about the way he gripped the obsidian. Just watching him hold the rock sent a little thrill of awareness through her. One would have thought it was a diamond, not just an attractive stone that she had picked up on a morning walk.

The rest of the man went very well with the hands and the unusual eyes. Jack moved with the fluid grace of a natural-born hunter. His near-black hair was cut very short in a severe, no-nonsense style. His face was all edgy planes and strict angles. Everything about him was infused with an ascetic vibe. In another time and place he could have been a warrior-monk, she thought. Instead, he had a decidedly checkered job history.

He had taught classes on criminal behavior at various small colleges and he occasionally gave seminars on the subject to certain law enforcement agencies, including the FBI. But evidently he had abandoned that career path—or maybe it had abandoned him. All she knew for certain was that somewhere along the line he had left the academic world to write books on the subject of the criminal mind and to pursue what she sensed was his true calling—the investigation of the coldest of cold cases.

It was that line of work, or, rather, the aftermath, that had brought him to the front door of her small cottage a little over a month ago. She had just moved into the town of Eclipse Bay on the Oregon coast and set up in business as a meditation instructor. Jack had been one of her first clients.

She was well aware that requesting that initial consultation with her had not been easy for him. He had been extremely wary, downright skeptical, in fact. *Suspicious* would not have been too strong a word to describe his attitude toward her and her line of work. She had known at first glance that he had come to her because he had run out of options.

After a couple of sessions, however, he had become much more comfortable with what he called *the woo-woo thing.* But she was pretty sure that there was another reason why he had made the effort to overcome his skepticism and give her techniques a try: They had something important in common. They had both lost their parents while they were in their early teens and both of them had wound up with foster families. That made for an unusual but very real bond.

"Where are you now?" Winter said.

"Leaving the ice garden," Jack said. He tightened his grip on the obsidian. "Walking along the main boulevard toward the gates of the city."

He spoke in an uninflected, unemotional, trancelike voice. But unlike a person who had been hypnotized or someone in a true dream state, he maintained a degree of awareness of his surroundings.

The boulevard was a new addition to the dreamscape that he had been rapidly crafting under her guidance.

"Are you certain that you are ready to leave?" she asked.

"I identified the killer," he said in the same neutral voice. "The hunt is finished."

Only until the next hunt began, Winter thought. But she did not say the words aloud. When Jack was in a lucid dream he referred to his investigation as a hunt. But when he surfaced he was careful to call each dark venture that he undertook a case study.

Regardless of the terminology, they both knew that sooner or later he would be compelled to take on another investigation. That meant he would enter a new self-induced dream at the start and again at the conclusion. It was how he worked.

At the beginning of a hunt he used his talent for lucid dreaming to gather the evidence and weave it into a coherent story that would point him toward the killer. When the case was concluded he used another dream to process the emotional and psychological fallout.

And there was always fallout, because, as far as she could tell, Jack's cases never ended well. The best thing you could say about them was that they ended.

He seemed to be drawn primarily to old, unsolved mysteries that involved fire. She knew that there were those who would have described his investigations as an eccentric hobby. Others would no doubt label his work an unhealthy obsession. She was certain that what he did was something else entirely. Jack's cold cases were, in her opinion, quests.

She had understood from the start of their association that, like anyone with a gift, Jack could not thrive unless he used his abilities. But, as with any gift, there was a serious downside.

When Jack had first consulted with her, he had been struggling to find a way to deal with the psychological and emotional blowback that he endured in the wake of every case. Over time the accumulated weight of the aftereffects had become increasingly difficult for him to handle.

Initially she had taught him how to meditate. His lucid dreaming ability had made him a natural. Meditation had given him a tool that he could use to take a step back from the emotional and psychological aspects of a case.

After he had become comfortable with meditation, he had cautiously raised the subject of his lucid dreams. She had realized immediately that he was using the wrong imagery.

"Fire is counterproductive for you," she had explained. "It's getting in the way."

He had shot her a disbelieving look. "What, then?"

"Ice."

"You're serious, aren't you?" he'd asked.

"Trust me, I'm pretty good with this kind of thing."

"You don't think I'm hallucinating?"

"No, of course not. You are doing lucid dreaming. You just do it in a rather unusual way, that's all."

For a moment he had gazed at her as if he was wondering what planet she was from. Then something changed in his demeanor. He seemed to relax. She got the impression that a great weight had been lifted off his shoulders.

"Ice," he had repeated. He had mulled that over for a few seconds and then nodded once, very crisply. "An ice maze might work."

"Why limit yourself to a maze? Think big. Create a dreamscape with more options."

Within a week he had constructed an astonishingly detailed dream-scape in which to do his lucid dreaming. Now he hunted killers in Ice Town.

The fact that she'd had to convince him to abandon the fire imagery made her curious. The mind always clung tightly to strong visuals that triggered powerful memories. She had a hunch that at some point in his past, Jack had endured a terrible experience with fire. Someday perhaps he would tell her the story but for now he was keeping his secrets. She understood. She was certainly keeping a few secrets herself.

She was determined to practice patience with Jack but it wasn't easy. He was the most intriguing, the most mysterious, the most *interesting* man she had ever met, but she wasn't sure it would be smart to rush things.

"What are you doing now?" she said.

"I'm about to use my key to lock the gate," Jack said.

The "key" was actually a word that he said to himself when he wanted to end a lucid dream. Early on she had realized that, in addition to the radically different imagery, he needed his own private escape word to ease the transition from the dream state to the waking state. She had no idea what word he had chosen. It didn't matter. The important thing was that it worked for him.

Advising him to choose an escape word, one that had some deep, personal meaning to him, had been another simple fix. Nevertheless, Jack seemed to have been astonished by the results.

She realized that he was profoundly grateful to her for helping him get control of his unusual ability, but she was afraid that gratitude had become a huge problem in their relationship—or, rather, the lack thereof. She did not want him to see her as a convenient meditation instructor and dream therapist. She was determined to make him see her as a woman, preferably one to whom he might be attracted.

He blinked once and then he was fully awake. He looked up from the obsidian in his hands. She had worked with him often enough to know what to expect in the moments immediately after he surfaced from a dream. Nevertheless, she still got a thrill of awareness whenever he fixed his intense eyes on her.

She smiled. "Welcome back to the waking world."

"Thanks." He set the obsidian aside somewhat reluctantly and opened his eyeglass case. When he put on the glasses, the green fire in his eyes did not disappear, but it cooled a little. "You were right about ice. It's a lot easier to manipulate."

"For you. But that wouldn't be true for everyone. What you are doing when you construct a lucid dream is a kind of self-hypnosis. A trance of any kind usually works best when you use imagery that has a calming vibe. Fire is wrong for you because it arouses the part of you that needs to exert control."

His eyes tightened a little at the corners. She could not tell if he was amused or annoyed.

"You think fire arouses me?" he asked.

She had a bad feeling that she was blushing.

"Not in the sexual sense," she said quickly. "I meant that it calls forth the warrior side of your nature. When that aspect is ascendant, your logical, contemplative side is partially suppressed."

"I've been called a lot of things in my time, but never a warrior."

"Well, I suppose the right term, the modern word, would be *investigator*."

"Nope," Jack said. "I'm not one of those, either. Both of my foster brothers are private investigators and my foster dad is a retired cop but I'm the boring one in the family. I research cold cases and then I write books based on that research."

"Okay, so you don't solve those cold cases with a gun," she said, a little exasperated. "Instead, you use your ability to collect a lot of seemingly unrelated facts and link them together in a logical fashion."

"Some people would say that what you just described is the working definition of a conspiracy theorist."

She realized he was serious.

"That's ridiculous, and you, of all people, should know it," she said. "A true conspiracy theorist starts with the answer or the outcome he wants. Then he manipulates the facts to fit his theory. If some of those facts don't support the desired conclusion, he simply discards them."

Jack studied her for a long time, his expression unreadable. Then he appeared to brace himself, as though he was about to deliver bad news.

"I should tell you that, in the past, people have accused me of being a for-real, card-carrying conspiracy theorist," he said.

She smiled. "In that case, where's your tinfoil helmet?"

His eyes got a little more intense, as if he was processing some new information. Then he visibly relaxed.

"Must have left it back at my place," he said.

"Look, here's my take on your situation," she said. "You were exhausting yourself just trying to control your burning maze. You were like a firefighter trying to put out the flames while simultaneously analyzing bits and pieces of evidence of the arson that started the blaze."

Jack did not move. "How did you know?"

She widened her hands. "It's what I do, Jack. I understood your problem with lucid dreaming the same way you understand how to string clues together into a pattern that explains an arson scene."

Jack startled her with one of his rare smiles. "Amazing."

She leaned back in her chair and shoved her fingers into the front pockets of her jeans. "I do realize that you probably still have some doubts about my work. I'm well aware that you had to overcome a lot of skepticism just to book that first session with me."

"Well, I'm not going online tonight to order up a gong and a mantra. But I'm okay with your brand of meditation instruction and your dream therapy."

She raised her brows ever so slightly. "Just okay?"

"Better than okay. I'm fine with it."

"Your enthusiasm is a little underwhelming but I'm glad to know that you're fine with what you've learned from me, because I'll be sending you my bill at the end of the month."

"You'll get your money on time."

She wrinkled her nose. "That's good to know, because I have to tell you that trying to establish my meditation business here in Eclipse Bay is proving to be harder than I expected."

"I'm not your only client," Jack said. "I've seen some of the other locals stopping by your cottage."

"Between you and me, most of the people who have booked sessions have done so out of curiosity. But I have hopes that some of them will become regulars. My landlady tells me business will probably pick up when the summer people arrive. She says that bunch is a real yogurt-and-yoga crowd. She thinks they'll go for the meditation experience."

"Was that the kind of clientele you had when you worked at that spa in California?" Jack said.

She froze. "You never told me that you knew about my job at the Cassidy Springs Wellness Spa."

"Did you really think I'd book a session with a meditation instructor without doing some background research?"

Should have seen that coming, she thought. This was Jack Lancaster, after all. He was the naturally suspicious type and he knew how to do research.

Winter took a deep breath and told herself not to let Jack's comment rattle her. He was right. She should have expected him to look into her background before booking a session.

"You never asked me about my previous experience so I just assumed you weren't curious about it," she said, going for casual and unconcerned. "In hindsight, I guess that was rather naïve of me, wasn't it?"

"A little, given what you know about the kind of work I do." He paused. "Is there a problem here?"

"Nope," she said quickly. Probably too quickly. The *problem* was that, after a month in Eclipse Bay, she had allowed herself to let down her guard. She had begun to assume that she was safe. She tapped a forefinger gently on the table and tried to decide how to proceed. "Was it easy to find out about my previous employment?"

Jack made a small, somewhat apologetic motion with his hand. "I had a lot of data to work with. Your name. Your profession. The fact that you were from California. Your car's license plates."

She reminded herself that she had not been trying to hide from him. If Kendall Moseley was looking for her, which seemed unlikely, he would be forced to conduct a search from the Cassidy Springs end. She was quite certain she had left no clues to her destination when she fled that town in the dead of night. She hadn't even known herself where she was going. She had gotten behind the wheel and started driving.

But they said that you could find anyone these days, thanks to the Internet.

"Did you, by any chance, contact the Cassidy Springs Wellness Spa to ask about me?" she said very carefully.

"No," Jack said.

She allowed herself to start breathing again.

He continued to watch her with a shadowed expression. He was waiting for an explanation but it was clear that he was not going to demand one. She did not intend to provide one. It would not be right to drag him into the Kendall Moseley situation. There was nothing he could do about it. In any event, if necessary, she could take care of herself.

"The thing is, I left the spa without giving any notice because of a conflict with my boss," she said. "It's a long story but the upshot is that I'm pretty sure my former employer would not give me a good reference."

That was certainly true, as far as it went.

"I understand," Jack said.

She eyed him uncertainly. "You do?"

"I've had a few professional conflicts myself. Not everyone appreciates my work."

"But you do great work," she said. "You solve old murders. Who could possibly object?"

"Believe me, there are always people who are not thrilled when I start digging up the past."

"I see." She considered that briefly. "I hadn't thought about it from that angle. I can see that an investigation into a decades-old crime could disrupt the lives of those connected with the crime."

"Local law enforcement isn't always happy, either."

"Because you make them look bad?"

"Sometimes," Jack said. "Let's just say that, before I agree to accept a case, I try to make certain that my client is prepared for whatever answers I come up with. That's the most difficult aspect of a case for me, the part that I often get wrong."

"Trying to decide if the client can handle the answers?"

Jack turned his hands palms-up. "I'm very good at finding answers because, as you say, I can see links between facts. But old crimes have a tendency to send long shock waves down into the present. I've been surprised by the reactions of my clients often enough to know that I don't excel at reading them—not until it's too late."

"Probably because, when they hire you, they don't have any way of knowing how they'll react to the truth themselves."

Jack pondered that for a moment. "You're right. It's one thing to want to find out who murdered someone you loved a couple of decades ago. It's another thing altogether to discover that the killer was one of your own relatives or the person you later married or the neighbor across the street."

She shivered. "I think I see why your cases sometimes end badly."

"About those clients you used to work with at the spa. Can I assume they were all yogurt-and-yoga types?"

"A lot of them fit that description but while I was employed there we started to pick up some corporate business as well. Cassidy Springs is close to Silicon Valley. The intense twenty-four-seven work ethic in the tech world leads to a lot of stress, and that, in turn, creates a ready-made clientele for people who specialize in reducing stress."

Jack nodded. "People like you."

"Yep. Unfortunately, it turns out that there are not a whole lot of stressed-out tech workers here in Eclipse Bay, so I'm going to have to develop a different client profile."

"You need more clients like me?"

She smiled. "I doubt if there is anyone else here in town like you." She paused. "Well, maybe one other."

Jack grimaced. "Our landlady?"

"Uh-huh."

Jack's eyes were unreadable now. "Do you think I'm that weird?"

"No, I think you've got a talent. You just need to learn how to deal with the dark side of your gift. Because there is always a dark side."

"I've noticed." Jack glanced at the chunk of obsidian. "How did you know that rock would work for me?"

"I found it one day while I was out walking. I liked it but I didn't have any particular client in mind—not until you showed up. It just seemed to suit you."

"Frozen fire," Jack said quietly.

"What?"

"Obsidian. It's a form of volcanic glass that forms when lava cools very quickly. Frozen fire."

"Oh, right." She looked at the obsidian. "That description fits perfectly."

Jack uncoiled from the chair, stretching a little. He glanced at his watch. "I should be going."

She tried not to stare but the truth was she liked to watch him move. He was not a big man—he did not tower over her—but when they were in the same room he seemed to be the source of all the heat and energy in the atmosphere.

Jack glanced at her, one dark brow elevating a little. "Something wrong?"

"Nope." She summoned what she hoped was a bright, businesslike smile. "It looks like our time is up for today. Would you like to schedule another session?"

"Not until I need one. It's been a long day. What I need right now is a drink and then dinner." He paused briefly and then fixed her with his intense eyes. "Want to join me?"

She wasn't sure she had heard him correctly. "A drink and dinner? With you?"

"Is that a problem for you? I'm not sure what the rules are in your profession when it comes to personal relationships with clients."

She had always had a firm policy about personal relationships with clients: Never date one.

She cleared her throat. "Technically speaking, I'm not a certified meditation therapist. I consider myself a meditation *guide*. That said, it's never a good idea to get involved with a client."

"I see."

"You are, of course, free to fire me," she said smoothly.

He looked interested in that suggestion. "Fire you?"

"It's not like you need me anymore. Your dream problems have been resolved."

His smile was slow and surprisingly wicked. It sent a thrilling little frisson of heat through her entire body.

"In that case," he said, "you're fired."

She took a centering breath, giving herself a few seconds to think. *Don't get too excited.* Jack had just returned from one of his investigations. There were no happy endings in his work and now he was looking at a long night alone.

We're not talking about a relationship here. He just wants company.

So do I.

"You do realize that if we go out for dinner and drinks, the locals will conclude we're engaged in a torrid affair," she said.

Jack looked thoughtful. "I don't think I've ever had a torrid affair. Is it better than the non-torrid kind?"

She processed that for a beat and finally decided that he had made an attempt at humor. "I wouldn't know. I've never had one I would describe as torrid, either. Got a feeling they're rare."

"Probably one of those things you don't recognize until you actually experience it."

"Probably."

There was no point telling him that romantic relationships of any sort—torrid or otherwise—were rare for her. And like his cold cases, they never ended well. Jack was not the only one with a talent that included a serious downside.

"About dinner and that drink," Jack said.

She smiled. "What I was about to suggest is that we eat dinner here. Nothing fancy, I'm afraid. I was going to roast a big batch of cauliflower. There's enough for two. We can add a salad. I've also got some good bread and a bottle of wine from one of the small local wineries."

"You eat cauliflower and salad for dinner?" he asked with the polite curiosity of a tourist inquiring about odd local customs.

She flushed. "I happen to love roasted cauliflower. I chop it up into little pieces, toss it with olive oil and salt and then roast it until it's nice and crispy. Then I toss it with grated cheese."

"Interesting."

This wasn't going well, she thought.

"You're right," she said, trying to inject enthusiasm into her voice, "we should go out. Great idea."

"No," he said. "Dinner here sounds good." He looked pleased. "It sounds perfect."

CHAPTER FIVE

―――――≈―――――

"How bad was this last case?" Winter asked.

Jack stretched out his legs, leaned back in the shabby, overstuffed chair, drank some wine and contemplated the fact that he was spending the evening with a woman who should have scared the hell out of him. Instead, he was feeling damned good, better than he had in a long time; maybe in his entire life.

Winter Meadows had a witchy vibe that tantalized and intrigued and at the same time sent an unmistakable warning: *Touch at your own risk.* The impression was enhanced by the fact that she wore a lot of black. Tonight she had on a long-sleeved black sweater and black jeans. Over the course of the weeks they had known each other he had concluded that the combination was a uniform for her, just as his white shirts and khaki trousers were for him.

There was something strong and fierce about her, and at the same time utterly, devastatingly feminine. She struck his senses with the thrilling, disorienting impact of a wave crashing on the beach.

Dark fire burned in her shoulder-length auburn hair. Her amber-gold eyes gleamed with intelligence and mystery. She was petite, slender and gently rounded in all the right places. At the moment, she was curled into the oversized chair on the opposite side of the hearth, one slender ankle tucked under a lushly curved thigh. He really liked the way her snug-fitting jeans emphasized the curve of that thigh. He liked it a lot.

The meal had been surprisingly good, definitely the best he had eaten in a very long time. Cauliflower had never been one of his favorite vegetables but tonight he had discovered that roasting the stuff transformed it. Then again, he probably would have enjoyed canned stew just as much tonight so long as he was able to eat it in the company of Winter Meadows. And now they were drinking the last of the wine.

He forced himself to focus on her question. He rarely discussed his work with anyone except the members of his foster family. But Winter was different. Winter accepted him as normal.

"The case was bad enough," he said. "But I've had worse. The client seemed relieved by my analysis. I could tell that the answers made her sad, but she thanked me." He paused. "I never understand that part."

"The thanks from a grateful client? Why does that surprise you? You give people answers to questions that have probably kept them awake for years. It's no wonder they thank you."

"It doesn't always work like that," he said. "Sometimes clients get angry. They blame me for giving them answers they don't want to hear."

Winter rested her head against the back of the big chair and contemplated the flames. "I have a hunch that the real problem for the clients who get angry is that when you give them the answer they don't want to hear, you remove the last, faint sliver of hope."

He turned his glass in his hand and studied the play of the firelight on the wine while he considered the observation. He decided it rang true.

"That makes sense," he said. "Until I show up, the client can always hope that the body that was charred beyond recognition was not that of the missing loved one. Or that the killer was a stranger, not a trusted member of the family."

"Why did the client in this last case thank you?" Winter asked.

"Who knows? It's not like I was able to give her a happy ending. There was never any doubt but that it was her mother who died in the house fire nearly seventeen years ago. My client had always suspected murder but the authorities had concluded that the blaze was caused by an electrical malfunction."

"What made you believe that it was an arson homicide?"

"I used one of the oldest tricks in the world." He paused to swallow some wine and lower the glass. "I followed the money."

"Ah." Winter nodded approvingly.

"When I examined the files and looked into the backgrounds of the people who were connected to the victim, I discovered that one individual had profited from the death—the woman's second husband. He had taken out an insurance policy on his wife about a month before she died. No one else knew about the policy. He had managed to keep it a secret."

"How did you prove murder?"

"Basic research. Once I started digging, I discovered that the second husband had been married twice before. Each of those women died in suspicious fires as well. The husband collected insurance money on both occasions. He got away with it because he moved around the country and changed his name each time he remarried."

"Was he arrested?" Winter asked.

"No. He collapsed and died of a heart attack a few years ago."

"So your client did not have the satisfaction of seeing him put in prison."

"I could give my client answers but not justice."

"Yet the client thanked you," Winter said.

"Yes, she thanked me."

He drank some more wine.

Winter watched him from the depths of the big chair. "You did more than just confirm her suspicions, you know."

"I did?"

"I would be willing to bet that the reason she thanked you was because you believed in her enough to take another look at the case. Sometimes just knowing that someone thinks you deserve to be heard, that your opinion has merit, means everything."

He thought about it while he watched the flames. "You make me sound like some sort of therapist."

Winter said nothing. She just smiled.

He looked at her. "What?"

"It occurs to me that in your own way you are a therapist. You help people find closure."

He shook his head. "I'm more of a hired gun—minus the gun. People come looking for me online when they've run out of options. When they are desperate. I give them answers even if I know they won't like them. That's part of the deal. There is no therapy involved, trust me."

"Okay. It's your work, so you get to define it any way you like. I do have a couple of questions, though."

"What?" he asked, wary now.

"How did you get involved in the cold case work? I know you studied criminal psychology and that you taught it for a while. I also know that you wrote a couple of books on the subject. But here you are in Eclipse Bay. Evidently you've turned your back on the academic world. What made you walk away from teaching and research? I can't imagine there's much money in the cold cases."

He almost smiled at that. "There is almost no money in the cold case work—at least not the way I do it. Each case takes a lot of time. And the expenses add up fast. Very few of my clients have that kind of cash. No private investigator could make a living doing what I'm doing. And I'm not even a licensed investigator. Just a writer who is interested in certain kinds of crimes."

"Crimes involving fire."

"That's my specialty," he said. "Once in a while I get a client who can afford to pay me, but that's the exception, not the rule. I'm able to do the pro bono work because my first two books managed to cross over from the academic market into the mainstream and because I've got a contract for another one."

"How did you end up here on the Oregon coast? This is a very small town with zero nightlife and extremely limited social potential."

"I'm not a real social person," he said. "And I could point out that you seem to be in a similar situation—you're living in the same very small town. How did you end up here?"

She raised one shoulder in a graceful little shrug. "It just feels like the right place to be, at least for now. I don't know how long I'll stay. You?"

"Eclipse Bay works for now. Don't know how long I'll be here, either."

"Wow. Talk about a couple of people who know how to live in the moment, hmm?"

"Either that or neither of us is any good at long-term planning," he said.

"I tried long-term planning recently. I even bought my first piece of serious furniture, a gorgeous red sofa. But the plan did not go well. The sofa is now in storage."

He figured that meant there had been a man involved in her long-term plan.

"You want to tell me how you wound up here in Eclipse Bay?" he asked.

"Pure random chance."

"There may be such a thing as random chance," he said, "but if it does exist, it's damn rare."

"Yes, I know you're big on chaos theory," she said. "A butterfly flaps its wings on one continent and sets off a series of currents that eventually cause a hurricane on another continent."

"Something like that."

"When I decided to leave my job in California, I set out on a road trip. I followed the highway up the coast. I stopped at several places along the way but I kept moving until I arrived in Eclipse Bay. I like the energy here."

"The energy? Really? That's the reason you stopped in this place?"

She laughed. The sound sparkled in the room.

"I *love* the energy of this place," she said. "The surf during a storm. The amazing sunsets. The way the locals make me feel welcome even though I know they're wondering if I'm a refugee from another universe."

"They treat me that way, too. But so far everyone has been friendly."

"They're bound to be curious about us," Winter said. "We're the classic outsiders."

"Yes, we are." It was probably time for him to go. Reluctantly he got to his feet. "It's late. I should head back to my place. Thanks for dinner."

"You're welcome." She uncurled from her chair and stood. "You've had a long day. Make that several long days. You were gone for nearly a week this time."

"There was a lot of traveling involved in this last case. I had to talk to some people who had moved away from the town where the crime occurred."

"I understand." She crossed the room to the wall, took his windbreaker off the hook and handed it to him. He pulled it on while she opened the door.

They both looked out into the crisp, chilly night. The September moon was rapidly disappearing behind the solid bank of storm clouds rolling in across the ocean.

"The wind is picking up," Winter said. "I guess somewhere a butterfly flapped its wings and now we're going to get the results."

"The storm will make landfall in another couple of hours," he said. "According to the weather reports it's going to be a big one."

"The waves on the beach will be spectacular in the morning."

"Also dangerous," he said. "Every year a few people get swept out to sea on this coast because they decided to take a walk during or after a storm."

"Thank you for the advice," Winter said a little too politely. "I'll be sure to stay up on the bluffs."

He winced. "Sorry. Sometimes I can't help myself."

She laughed. "I know. It's all right. Truly. I appreciate your concern but I know the old rule about beach walking. Never turn your back on the ocean."

"Okay. Good. That's good."

He realized he was looking for an excuse to stay a little longer. No, not just an excuse to hang around. What he really wanted—what he craved—was an excuse to kiss her. He couldn't find one.

It's probably too soon. You do not want to screw this up, Lancaster.

He went out onto the porch and down the front steps before he could talk himself out of leaving. There were no streetlights to mark the unpaved trail along the top of the cliffs. It wasn't far to his place, the equivalent of a long city block. But for some reason it seemed like an endless journey tonight.

"I've got a flashlight you can borrow," Winter said from the doorway.

Jack took a penlight out of the pocket of his jacket. "I brought my own."

She smiled. "Of course you did. Were you a Boy Scout?"

"My foster dad was the chief of police in our town. He was big on being prepared."

"I see."

Jack studied her, wanting to store up the image of her for his dreams. Her hair glowed like a dark copper sunset in the light from the porch fixture. She watched him with her mysterious eyes.

"I enjoyed tonight," he said.

"So did I." She made no move to step back inside and close the door. "Can I ask you one more personal question?"

"Sure. Can't guarantee you'll get an answer."

"You specialize in cold cases that involve deaths by fire," she said.

Damn. He had known this was coming, he reminded himself; he'd dreaded it. She was bound to wonder about the fire thing. Sooner or later everyone who got close to him wondered about it—after all, it wasn't exactly normal.

"Yes," he said. "I do."

She folded her arms and propped one shoulder against the doorjamb. "Why fire?"

"It . . . interests me. No, that's not quite right. It's more accurate to say that the kind of people who use fire to commit murder interest me."

"Because of some personal experience?"

"My mother was murdered by a man who likes fire."

Shocked, she just stared at him for a long moment.

"I'm so sorry," she said finally. "That's . . . horrible."

"It happened a little over twenty-two years ago."

"I think I'm beginning to understand why you're interested in crimes involving arson," she said.

"Some people are of the opinion that my interest in crimes involving fire amounts to an obsession," he said. "Does that scare you?"

"I don't know. Should it?"

"Probably," he said. "There are times when it scares the hell out of me."

There was, he realized, such a thing as too much truth. Now she would be convinced that he wasn't exactly normal.

Nice work, Lancaster. For a guy with a couple of academic degrees after your name, you can be amazingly stupid.

"Good night," he said, quietly.

He turned and started walking toward the dark cottage at the other end of the path. If he hung around any longer he would have to tell her about his past, and he wasn't ready to do that. If she thought that his focus on arson crimes was not normal, she sure as hell would have a problem dealing with his history as a member of a cult.

Keeping secrets had long ago become a habit for him, just as it had for his foster brothers.

CHAPTER SIX

Winter closed the door and stood quietly for a time thinking about Jack's unnerving words. He had told her that his fascination with fire scared him but it wasn't fear that she had seen in his eyes—it was the expression of a man who has accepted the ghosts that whisper in the shadows around him.

She would have preferred the problem of fear. There were meditation strategies that could be employed to help a strong-minded person such as Jack cope with fear. She was not certain what to do with a man who kept company with ghosts.

A shiver of anxiety gave her pause. Jack was all right, she told herself. He had been calm when he left. Then again, he was always calm. Maybe too calm. She got the feeling that somewhere along the line he had learned to hold everything close inside.

There was no need to worry about him. Jack was all right.

But she could not shake the chill of dread. She realized now that it had been slowly coalescing throughout the evening, although there was no obvious reason for the uneasiness.

She went to a window and tweaked the faded flower-patterned curtain aside. She could just make out the narrow beam of Jack's flashlight. It moved steadily along the bluff path until it reached a point midway between the two cottages. There it stopped.

The ominous sensation intensified. Maybe it was just the energy of the oncoming storm that was rattling her. But there had been too many times in the past when she had survived because she had heeded her intuition. She could not ignore the feeling that something was very wrong.

She dropped the curtain, grabbed her jacket and a flashlight, and went quickly to the door. She was not sure exactly what she was going to do, but she could not let Jack stand alone out there on the cliff path, not at such a late hour. Ghosts were always most powerful at night.

She got the door open and rushed out onto the porch, adrenaline flooding her veins. She went down the front steps and stopped, aware that the freshening storm wind was tossing her hair and tugging at the bottom edge of her jacket.

She knew that Jack had seen her because his flashlight was once again in motion. He was walking back along the path, heading toward her cottage.

She stopped on the porch at the top of the steps and waited until he moved into the circle of light cast by the fixture over the door. He halted at the bottom of the three steps. Behind the lenses of his glasses his eyes were more unreadable than ever but it seemed to her that there was a lot of heat in his gaze.

"What's wrong?" he asked.

There was no mistaking the icy edge on his voice.

"Nothing," she said a little too quickly.

"Did you think I was going to jump?"

"No, of course not." She was horrified by the question. "I'm sorry. I was just a little concerned, that's all."

"I'm not going to jump."

"I never thought you would. I just got one of those weird little feelings. You know how it is."

There was a beat of acute silence.

"You're worried about me," Jack said.

She folded her arms. "You just concluded a difficult case. You need time to recover."

"What I said a moment ago—that sometimes my focus on cases involving fire scares the hell out of me—that's what made you nervous, isn't it?"

"Well, yes. Maybe. A little. But now I think I understand."

"Yeah? In that case, why don't you explain it to me? Because I'm not sure I understand."

"I realize now that, in your own fumbling way, you were probably trying to warn me that you might not be good relationship material."

"Fumbling?" he repeated, as if he was not familiar with the word.

"Awkward? Not very subtle?"

"Can I assume you got the message?" he asked.

"Message received."

He stood quietly for a moment as if he didn't know where to go with that information. He looked grim and resigned, as if she had now become just one more ghost.

"Is that it, then?" he said finally. "Just 'message received'?"

"I didn't say that I was going to pay attention to the warning."

"Are you going to pay attention to it?" he asked.

She smiled. "Nope."

She might as well have connected a couple of electrical wires. A fierce energy heated his eyes. And then he moved.

He dropped the flashlight into a pocket, vaulted up the three porch steps, gripped her shoulders and pulled her into his arms. She barely had a chance to catch her breath before his mouth came down on hers.

She thought she was prepared for his kiss but she was very, very wrong. Electricity arced across her senses, igniting a response that stunned her.

For a heartbeat or two she was overwhelmed by the intensity of the experience. Then an adrenaline-fueled excitement kicked in. She was suddenly shivering, but not because of the chilled night wind off the ocean.

She did not realize that she had dropped her flashlight until she heard it clatter on the wooden boards of the porch. Ignoring it, she gripped Jack's shoulders, anchoring herself against the onslaught of his embrace.

He dropped one hand to her waist and pulled her close, crushing her more tightly against his heavily aroused body. Everything about him was hard and intense. The rush of her response was as exhilarating as the energy of the oncoming storm. She tightened her grip on his shoulders.

Jack groaned and deepened the kiss.

A snort of amusement followed by a hearty chuckle broke the spell.

"Hey, you two, take it inside. Bit chilly out here for that sort of thing, don't you think?"

Winter yelped and tore her mouth away from Jack's. He loosened his grip on her but he did not release her. They both turned.

A woman dressed in faded camouflage and boots strode forward into the crescent of porch light. She was festooned with night-vision goggles, a military-grade flashlight and a camera. Her helmet of gray curls was tucked under a cap that matched the camo.

Arizona Snow was somewhere in her eighties but she projected the tough, wiry vibe of vigor and vitality. Probably all the exercise, Winter thought. Arizona took her self-imposed responsibility for keeping an eye on the town of Eclipse Bay seriously. She seemed to be always on the go. As far as Winter could discern, she did not sleep much.

"Evening, Ms. Snow," Jack said.

"Now, then, how many times have I told you to call me AZ?" Arizona said. "The only people who are supposed to call me Ms. Snow are tourists."

Winter smiled at her landlady. "Jack and I assumed we were still classified as outsiders. Neither of us has been here very long."

"Some folks belong here in Eclipse Bay, even if they don't know it yet," Arizona said. She winked. "Sorry to disturb you. Didn't mean to interrupt things just as they were getting interesting."

"It's all right," Jack said. He looked at Winter. "It's time I went home."

"It is getting late," she said. She knew she was turning red. "I'm sure you're exhausted."

"Strangely enough, I'm feeling a lot more energetic than I did this afternoon when I got back to town," he said.

There was still plenty of heat in his eyes. Another little frisson of awareness sparked through her. But she knew that it was probably best for Jack to leave now. She could tell he understood that, too. The kiss had been a turning point in their relationship but what was happening between them was too important and too fraught to be rushed. Relationships were complicated, especially in her case. She did not want to screw up.

Arizona glanced at the face of her thick black steel wristwatch. "Time I got back on patrol."

The faint edge of urgency in the words caught Winter's attention.

"Everything okay, AZ?" she asked.

"Things look okay." Arizona raised one black-gloved hand and rubbed the back of her neck. "But I've still got that weird vibe I told you about yesterday when you and I had tea and you had me talk to the rock."

"It was a piece of amber, not a rock," Winter said. "And I didn't tell you to talk to it, I just suggested that you hold it while you talked to me."

"Whatever." Arizona snorted and lowered her hand. "Felt like there was something going on between me and that rock. Reminded me of my old days when I was with the agency. Never mind. I've had that same vibe for a while now. It's like there's a real bad storm closing in on this town but damned if I can figure out what's wrong. The storm that's gonna hit later tonight looks pretty tame."

"Are you planning to patrol the town all night again?" Jack asked.

"Not like I've got anything better to do," Arizona said. "Never could sleep much at night."

"I'll walk with you as far as my place," Jack said. He turned to Winter. "I'll say good night. Again."

She smiled. "Good night."

She went into the cottage, closed and locked the door, and moved to the window. She twitched aside the curtains and watched Jack and Arizona walk off into the night. They looked surprisingly comfortable together, despite the decades that separated them. *Comrades in arms* was the term that popped into her head.

Maybe that was an accurate description, she thought. The battle they fought was the struggle to lead normal lives in a world that did not consider either of them normal.

Arizona and Jack each possessed an unusually profound ability to focus on small, seemingly unconnected details and then connect those tiny data points with the assistance of a vivid imagination.

Their ability was both a blessing and a curse. AZ and Jack were always at risk of being dismissed as conspiracy theorists, and they knew it. That, in turn, had a profound effect on the way they dealt with other people.

She let the curtain fall back into place and went through her customary routine, checking the locks on the doors and the windows. She switched off the gas fireplace and then turned off the lights, with the exception of the outside fixtures over the front door and the kitchen door. Last but not least she switched on the night-light that illuminated the tiny living-kitchen area and a portion of the hallway.

For a moment she stood in the hallway and studied the front room. It was a small space, but her beautiful red sofa was small. It had been designed for an apartment or a condo. It would definitely fit in the living room of the cottage.

Now all she had to do was figure out how to get it out of the self-storage locker in Cassidy Springs and haul it up to Eclipse Bay.

She undressed, pulled on a pair of cozy pajamas and then sat quietly on the side of the bed. Instead of meditating as she often did before sleep, she considered what she knew of Jack Lancaster.

She concluded it wasn't that he feared he had some sort of unhealthy obsession with fire. She was pretty sure that what really scared the hell out of him was that someday he would go into a lucid dream once too often—and get lost in a nightmare.

CHAPTER SEVEN

―≈―

"What's the problem, AZ?" Jack asked.

"Like I told Winter, I can't put my finger on it," Arizona said.

She spoke matter-of-factly, as if he were a colleague. She considered him a kindred spirit, Jack thought, someone who could relate to her unique view of reality. That probably did not bode well for his own future mental stability, but it was what it was.

"Go on," he said.

"You know how it is when you can almost see something in the shadows but you can't quite make it out?"

"Yes," he said, "I know."

Now that he was no longer holding Winter in his arms he was more aware of the chill of the night wind coming off the ocean. The storm was going to be a big one. Winter would probably find it exciting.

"Most people think I'm a little crazy," Arizona confided.

"Is that so?"

Arizona chuckled. "It's okay. Folks around town have known me forever. They're not afraid of me. I'm kind of like a cat that everyone in Eclipse Bay has decided to adopt. Know what I mean?"

"I think so. I'm sort of adopted, myself."

"Sort of?"

"I've got a foster dad and a couple of foster brothers."

"Well, there you go," Arizona said. "You could say that Eclipse Bay is my foster family. Every year someone decides to give me a birthday party and the whole damn town shows up. It's real sweet."

"I'm surprised you told anyone the date of your birthday. I had the impression that you try to live off the grid as much as possible. I would have thought you'd be reluctant to give out personal information like a birth date."

Arizona snorted. "'Course, I didn't tell anyone my real birthday. Had a lot of different sets of ID's over the years. The outfit I used to work for handed 'em out to the agents like candy. When the head librarian here in town asked me for the date of my birthday, I had a hunch what was going down so I picked one of the old ID's and used the DOB on it."

There was no way to know if Arizona actually had worked with a clandestine government agency. Most of Eclipse Bay doubted the rumor. But in a sense it didn't matter, Jack thought, because AZ had woven the information into a coherent personal history and a worldview that worked for her. Oddly enough it worked for him, too. The longer he knew his landlady, the more he was inclined to believe the story about the agency.

He wondered if he should be worried about the ease with which he could step into AZ's version of reality.

"Weren't you afraid that the librarian would do a search on your date of birth and come up with a few questions about your past?" he asked.

"That particular ID is rock solid," Arizona assured him. "One of my favorites. It's just close enough to the truth to sound good. People never question it."

"The best lies always contain just enough truth to sound real."

"Yep."

"So, what did you see that set off the alarm bells and made you decide to double down on the night patrols?"

"You know what it's like," Arizona said. "You can't always be sure what it is that rings that damn bell in your head. But you can't ignore the vibe."

He exhaled slowly. "Yes, I know. Frustrating."

"Damn frustrating."

"It either keeps you awake or it gets into your dreams."

"Yep."

It was comforting to know that someone else experienced the same sleep issues he encountered when he got the sort of disturbing ping that Arizona had described. He couldn't rest until he found the butterfly that had flapped its wings.

"'Course, it's easy to see how things fit together when you look back," Arizona said.

"Providing you have enough information."

"Right. But at the start you usually don't have all the data you need," Arizona continued. "Sometimes you can't make out the damn pattern until it's too late to do anything about the situation."

"That's why I stick to the old cold cases," Jack said. "The damage was done years ago. I'm not working against a ticking clock, trying to save the next victim. All I have to do is look back with the advantage of having a couple of decades' worth of information. Most of the time it's easy to see the connections."

"Back in the day I could usually identify whatever it was that set off my internal alarm bells immediately. That gave me something to work with, know what I mean?"

"It's like identifying true north on a compass. Once you nail it you can figure out where everything else fits and then you can navigate the connections."

"Exactly." Arizona sounded satisfied.

"Maybe it's the storm that's giving you the uneasy vibe," he suggested.

"I've been through a lot of storms. This feeling is different. You know, it's good to talk to you, Jack. Been decades since they shut down the agency. Lost track of most of the agents I worked with. The smart ones all tried to disappear, of course. That's what I did. Some died, though. A few by their own hand if you believe the death certificates."

Talking with AZ was a lot like working a multidimensional puzzle, Jack reflected. He had understood from the start of their association that the most comfortable way of communicating with her was to go with the flow and embrace her reality.

"You have doubts about the causes of the deaths of some of your old colleagues?" he asked, choosing his words carefully.

"You bet I do." There was a rare anger in Arizona's voice now. "We were all potential problems for them, so they tried to hunt us down and terminate us."

"Why?"

"Because we knew too much about the agency and what was going on in that secret lab of theirs. And don't even get me started on the drugs and radiation they used on us. Hell, if any of us had ever gone public, we could have ruined a few careers, and that's a fact."

"What do you mean?"

Arizona grunted. "If you're a politician running for high office, you sure as hell don't want the media to find out that once upon a time you were responsible for funding an off-the-books government operation that conducted paranormal research. And you damn sure wouldn't want it getting out that the agents you recruited were used in black ops work."

Jack felt as if he had just taken a body blow. For a couple of seconds he could not say a word. Memories of his own very private, very secretive research into the realm of psychic phenomena momentarily overwhelmed him. It was his most closely guarded secret, because that kind of academic interest was a surefire career killer, to say nothing of what it did to professional and personal relationships.

He had not mentioned his investigation into the paranormal to anyone, not even Anson and his foster brothers, Max and Cabot. His family already considered him a little weird. They were okay with the weirdness but he had known instinctively that it would not be a good idea to burden them with that bit of information.

The fact that he, an academically trained professional, had taken the psychic thing seriously enough to delve deep into the literature and chase down rumors in the darkest corners of the Internet might make Anson, Max and Cabot conclude that he was more than just a little out there. It might convince them that he had lost it altogether.

Arizona seemed unaware of his stunned reaction.

"That's one of the reasons why I like talking to you, Jack," she continued. "Over the years I've only met a few other people who see things the way I do."

The possibility that he saw things the way Arizona Snow did was more than a little unnerving, but he figured that as long as he could question his own sanity he was probably still on the right side of the blurry line between normal and not normal.

They arrived at the front steps of his cottage. He stopped and looked at Arizona.

"If you figure out what gave you the bad ping, will you tell me what it was?" he said. "I'd really like to know."

"Yep. Not like anyone else will listen to me. Well, except for Winter, of course. She'd pay attention but I doubt that she'd know how to deal with whatever's coming down. Got a feeling we're looking at a real serious situation developing here."

Great. Now he was getting the unpleasant vibe.

"You're sure?" he asked.

"The problem is, Winter is a civilian," Arizona said. "She doesn't have the skill set to deal with real trouble. All that positive thinking and meditation crap works great right up until it doesn't."

"True," Jack said.

Arizona nodded once, decisive. "That means it's up to you and me to keep an eye on things around here, Jack."

"Okay," he said.

Evidently Arizona had decided he was not one of the "civilians." It was disconcerting, but he was surprised to discover that he was warmed by his new status.

Arizona raised a gloved hand in farewell. "See you tomorrow."

"Right," Jack said.

He started to go up the steps but stopped halfway, thinking about the conversation with Arizona.

Her logic could be difficult if not downright impossible to follow, but as far as he had been able to tell she did not invent facts from

scratch. There was always some solid basis for her observations and conclusions.

"AZ, wait," he said.

Arizona paused and looked back over her shoulder. "What's the
problem?"

"You said that Winter would pay attention if you talked to her about
the bad vibe."

"Right. She's smart."

"I agree. You also said that she wouldn't have the skill set to deal with
a serious situation."

"Figure she'd be in way over her head," Arizona explained.

He chose his next words with exquisite care.

"Why would Winter be the one who would have to deal with a crisis
here in Eclipse Bay?" he asked.

"Because I'm pretty sure that the nasty vibe I got a couple of days ago
is linked to her."

Arizona turned on one booted heel and started to march off into the
darkness.

"Shit," Jack said. He went quickly down the steps. "AZ, wait. We need
to talk."

"Sorry," Arizona said over her shoulder. "That's all I've got for now.
But I'll work on it while I'm on patrol tonight. I always think more clearly
at night, know what I mean?"

He halted at the bottom of the steps.

"Yes," he said. "I know what you mean."

Night meant dreams for him—dreams that were infused with riddles,
clues, shadows and ghosts. Night was when he did his best work. Evidently
it was the same for Arizona.

"If I come up with anything solid, I'll swing by your place and tell
you," Arizona promised.

"I'd appreciate it," Jack said. "Anytime, night or day."

"Understood," Arizona said.

She disappeared into the night.

CHAPTER EIGHT

Jack stood watching Arizona until all he could see was the faint beam of her flashlight. When that vanished behind a vacant summer cabin, he went back up the steps, crossed the porch and unlocked the front door of his cottage.

Not that there was much point in locking doors in Eclipse Bay, he thought. The small town was as safe as a small town could be. But he had no intention of abandoning the habit. *Call me paranoid.*

It occurred to him that Winter would not approve of the negative self-talk.

In that case, call me cautious, not paranoid.

Cautious sounded a bit more positive.

He moved across the threshold and flipped a wall switch to turn on a lamp. For a time he stood there, contemplating the interior of the rustic one-bedroom cottage. Something was wrong with the space but damned if he could figure out what it was that bothered him.

The cottage was nearly identical to Winter's rental, right down to the ancient floral drapes and the well-worn furniture. But tonight her place had felt different; it had felt cozy and comfortable, almost like a real home.

His cottage, on the other hand, looked like exactly what it was—one more rental in a long string that, with one notable exception, stretched all the way back to his early childhood.

The exception had occurred during his teenage years. He and his foster brothers had spent that volatile period of their lives growing up under the guidance of their foster father. Anson Salinas' house had been small but it had been home, at least for a while.

He peeled off his jacket, hung it on a wall hook and crossed the room to a window. He pulled the curtain aside. Winter's front porch light glowed at the far end of the bluffs but as he watched, most of the other lights in the house winked out. She was on her way to bed.

He wondered if she understood what a priceless gift she had given him. The new skills she had taught him had helped him find the calm center in the chaos.

At the start of a case he always got an adrenaline rush, but when it was over he invariably sank deep into the darkness for a time. It had been that way from the beginning but lately the blowback had been getting worse. The downtimes had been lasting longer and longer.

Until Winter. She was his butterfly. Because of her the currents of the storm inside him had been changed.

She probably assumed that he went into the dark because none of his cases had happy endings. That was true as far as it went but it was not the whole truth. It was not the reason why he found himself standing on the edge of a cliff, gazing into the abyss, after every successful investigation.

The truth was that each closed cold case ultimately reminded him of his one blazing failure. Quinton Zane continued to elude him.

It was too soon to tell Winter why he was drawn into the dark place in the wake of a case. Or maybe he was too much of a coward to tell her.

He thought about the incendiary kiss on her front porch a short time ago and wondered if she would conclude that he had developed a crush on her because he was grateful to her. She had, after all, quite literally changed his life.

She probably got gratitude from a lot of her clients. He did not like the possibility that even now she might be adding him to a list of previous clients who were attracted to her positive energy; clients who were grateful to her.

He wondered what she would say if he told her that he had chosen her name as his escape word. *Winter.*

It was her name that made it so much easier to surface from one of his dark lucid dreams.

He tightened his grip on the windowsill. He was going to drive himself nuts if he didn't focus on something else. He glanced at the cupboard that held the whiskey bottle and decided against a nightcap. He'd had enough to drink tonight. But he wasn't going to be able to sleep right away, thanks to Arizona's cryptic warning, so he might as well occupy himself with some useful task, like organizing his notes from the latest case.

He sat down at the table, opened his laptop and went to work. The investigation had been surprisingly straightforward once he had identified the key element that had set events in motion. But, then, as Arizona had pointed out, they all looked simple once you had the key.

An hour later he finished the notes and filed them under *Closed.* Time to call it quits and try to get some sleep, but there was one more thing he had to do before he shut down the laptop. He opened the folder labeled *Recent Suspicious Fires.*

He had not attempted to log the details of all the fire-related deaths that had occurred since Anson and Cabot had closed the Night Watch case a few months earlier. It would have been an overwhelming task. According to the latest government statistics, there were, on average, as many as three thousand deaths linked to fire each year in the United States alone.

The Recent Suspicious Fires folder was a carefully curated file. It contained only cases that had occurred since the Night Watch case and that appeared to have Quinton Zane's signature.

Officially, Zane had died over twenty-two years ago, shortly after torching the compound of the cult that he had founded. The inferno had killed several of his followers. Jack's mother had died that night. So had the mothers of Cabot and Max.

Zane himself had supposedly perished in a fire at sea while attempting to escape the country on a stolen yacht. The body had never been recovered.

Jack had never believed that Zane was dead. Anson, Cabot and Max had never bought the story, either.

Every arsonist had a style, Jack thought. For years he had been collecting and analyzing reports of fire-related deaths that whispered of Zane's signature. The investigations had become increasingly refined as the online search engines grew more efficient and sophisticated. As a result, he was now able to exclude the vast number of cases that otherwise would have landed in the Recent Suspicious Fires file. But there remained a handful that, for one reason or another, he could not dismiss.

If Zane was alive, then he was still a pyro, still obsessed with fire. Guys like that did not change. But the fact that he had escaped detection this long meant that he had some control over his obsession.

If he was still alive—if the ghostly footprints online and in Ice Town did belong to him—then little had altered in Quinton Zane's pattern over the years. His process remained the same: set up a clever financial scheme, con and manipulate people into doing exactly what he wanted them to do, make a lot of money, ruin a lot of lives and then burn down the whole project and murder the witnesses.

Jack paused over a brief report that had pinged when it had been swept up by a search engine a few weeks earlier. He had looked into it at the time and concluded that it should probably be moved to the Inactive file. Nevertheless, for some reason he hesitated.

Las Vegas: A fatal car crash on a rural desert road took the life of the driver late last night. The vehicle caught fire and the body was badly burned but the authorities have tentatively identified the victim as Jessica Pitt of Burning Cove, California. It is believed that Pitt was smoking and may have fallen asleep at the wheel.

Pitt was married and divorced three times and was single again at the time of her death. She had no children . . .

Fires happened in vehicle accidents but not nearly as often as television and the movies made it appear. Still, a vehicle fire was hardly a rarity.

"What were you doing out there alone on an empty desert road, Jessica Pitt?" Jack asked softly. "And why won't you let me move you to the Inactive file?"

There were no answers.

He needed sleep.

He shut down the computer, got up and headed for the lonely bed at the end of the hall.

He was still awake when the storm made landfall shortly before midnight. He got out of bed and went to the window. He could no longer see the light over Winter's front door. That worried him for a few seconds. Then he pulled the chain on the lamp beside his bed. The light did not come on. The heavy winds had knocked out the power.

He wondered if the storm was making Winter nervous. Probably not. She had told him that she liked the energy. The window-rattling wind might keep her awake, though. If she was awake, was she thinking about that red-hot kiss?

After a while he stopped thinking about Winter. He wondered if the tempest had caused Arizona Snow to abandon her patrol. He hoped so. He did not like to think of her outside, battling the elements as she walked her lonely patrol for the citizens of Eclipse Bay.

The more he thought about Arizona outside on her own, the more concerned he became. She was tough and accustomed to the wild weather on the Oregon coast, but she was in her eighties, after all.

He turned away from the window and got dressed.

CHAPTER NINE

———≈———

Winter awakened from the chase dream gasping for breath. Her pulse skittered wildly.

The unnerving nightmare took various forms but each version had two things in common—she was always on the run and she always knew that, sooner or later, the monster would find her. On some nights she ran through a dense forest, seeking a cave in which she could hide. In other variations she struggled to swim to safety through a gelatinous sea.

Tonight, however, the dream took a new and disturbingly different dreamscape. She had found herself racing through a fiery maze, desperately searching for the way out but knowing all the while that she was only going deeper.

Crap. She had adopted a dreamscape that had been constructed by a client. It was the first time that had ever happened. She had her own nightmares. She did not need to borrow Jack's old, well-used dreamworld.

Meditation guide, center yourself.

Lightning crackled outside, strobe-lighting the night for a few seconds. The wind sang a song that sounded as if it came from another dimension.

The storm had made landfall. That was probably what had awakened her.

But for some reason that didn't feel like the right explanation.

She pushed the quilt aside and swung her legs over the edge of the bed. The room was cold. The comforting glow of the porch lights and the plug-in night-light had disappeared. That meant that the power had been knocked out.

There was a battery-operated camp lantern in the kitchen cupboard. Arizona had given her instructions on how to use it. There was also a powerful flashlight in the kitchen drawer.

But first she had to navigate the darkness of the bedroom and hallway. She fumbled for her cell phone. It was right where she had left it—on the end table. She gripped it and tapped the flashlight app. The narrow beam of bright light illuminated the path into the front part of the cottage.

She slid her bare feet into her slippers and stood. She was surprised and more than a little annoyed to discover that she was still struggling to calm her breathing and her pulse. *It's just a storm. You enjoy storms. The energy is exciting.*

She focused on her breathing and told herself that there was no good reason to still be on the edge of panic.

If your body is fighting your mind, there will be a reason. There is always a reason. It may not be a good reason but it will, nevertheless, be a reason. Listen to your senses.

She stopped focusing on her breathing technique and went through her senses one by one. She could not have seen anything because she had been asleep. Perhaps she had heard some small, unusual sound. She listened intently but the storm was still in full roar. The rain slammed against the windows. The wind shrieked and wailed. Underlying it all was the endless boom and crash of the surf at the foot of the bluffs.

She went down the hall.

She was crossing the living room area, heading for the small kitchen, when she heard the muffled groan and snap of metal and wood being wrenched apart. Shock flashed through her.

She turned toward the front door just as it slammed open.

Cold, wet wind howled into the cottage. A man loomed in the doorway, silhouetted against the glare of a lightning strike. The beam of a flashlight speared the darkness, sweeping the small space. She could just make out a long object in his other hand.

There was a loud thud as the crowbar he had used to gain entrance hit the floor.

Instinctively she looked to the side to avoid being temporarily blinded. She fumbled with the cell phone. It slipped from her fingers and clattered on the wooden floorboards. The narrow ray of light angled uselessly across them.

There was no time to retreat to the bedroom and lock the door. Her only chance was to make a run for the kitchen door. But even as that realization hit she knew the odds of escaping into the night were nonexistent. The dining counter that marked the border between the living room and the kitchen was in the way. It might as well have been a brick wall.

Lightning flashed again in the night. She watched in shock as the intruder yanked a long knife out of a sheath.

"I told you not to run from me, Winter," Kendall Moseley said. "Now I'm going to have to punish you."

CHAPTER TEN

———— ≈ ————

"What the heck are you doing out here in this storm?" Arizona asked.

"I wanted to make sure you were okay," Jack said. "I went to your place first to see if you were home. When you didn't answer the door, I figured you were probably still out on patrol."

He had intercepted Arizona just as she was in the process of checking the lock on the front door of a vacant cottage. They were now standing in the limited shelter provided by the porch roof of the small house. Arizona was attired in full storm gear—a voluminous military-style poncho, a billed cap and sturdy, waterproof boots.

Jack was wearing his heaviest rainproof jacket with the hood pulled up to partially shield his face. His glasses were safely stowed in a pocket. There was no point trying to wear them. The rain would have sheeted off the lenses, effectively blinding him.

"Can't let a little wind and rain keep me from making my rounds," Arizona said. "But I vary the patrol route every night, so how did you know where to look for me?"

"Everyone develops patterns," Jack said. "I've been in town long enough to pick up on some of yours."

Arizona nodded appreciatively. "You're pretty sharp, you know that?"

"Sometimes," Jack said.

"Sometimes is as good as it gets. Nobody gets it right every time. Well, thanks for checking up on me but as you can see, I'm fine. We get storms like this one all the time. I'm used to 'em."

"It's bad out here, AZ. Why don't you go home?"

"I told you, I don't sleep much, leastways not at night. You run along now. Don't worry about me. I'll be fine."

There was not much point arguing with her, Jack decided. Arizona was tough and she was stubborn. She was also an adult who had every right to make her own decisions.

"All right," he said. "If you're sure you're okay."

"I'm sure," she said.

He went down the porch steps, stopped and looked back at her. "You said you usually remember things best late at night, AZ. Have you figured out what it was that made you think that Winter might be in trouble?"

"Been thinkin' about that a lot tonight. Pretty sure it had something to do with a vehicle."

Jack did not move. "What kind of vehicle?"

"One that didn't belong here in town. It came through a couple of days ago while you were away on that last cold case job."

"A lot of cars come through town," Jack said. "What was different about this one? Out-of-state plates?"

"Nope, Oregon plates. I took a photo and checked. Car was a rental."

He realized he was fascinated. "You photographed the license plate on a tourist's vehicle that was just passing through town?"

"I photographed that one."

"Why? The most logical explanation is that the driver was just a visitor who got curious and left the main road to check out Eclipse Bay."

"Yeah, that would be the usual story," Arizona said. "But the thing is, tourists who end up here in Eclipse Bay usually head for the beach. It's pretty much our only scenic attraction."

"At this time of year?"

"We get some real spectacular sunsets in the fall. And then there are the folks who come to dig for clams or just to walk on the beach. No one with a lick of sense tries to swim in that surf at any time of year. Got a real mean riptide just offshore."

"Yes, I know."

"Once the tourists get bored with the beach they usually head for a coffee shop or a gas station or a gift shop. But that's about it. This guy didn't bother to check out any of those things. He didn't go to the beach. Didn't get coffee or gas."

"What did he do?"

"Stopped at the real estate office."

"Well, there you go, then," Jack said. "He was interested in property. Maybe looking for a place to rent."

"We don't get a lot of year-round renters here."

"What about Winter and me?"

"You two are different. You're locals."

He and Winter were not locals but there was no point trying to convince Arizona of that. It was not important, not at the moment. He felt compelled to inject some logic into Arizona's story, however, because he needed to figure out what had alarmed her.

And, okay, maybe it gave him some comfort to offer up a few bits and pieces of reality in an otherwise very strange conversation. As long as he was capable of injecting some logic into a discussion, he could always tell himself that he was still on the right side of normal.

"I had a little chat with Marge McDonald," Arizona continued, her tone darkening.

"The real estate broker?"

"Yep."

"Did she have anything interesting to tell you?"

"She said the driver of the vehicle asked her for a list of rental properties."

"Is that all?" he asked.

"Yep. Marge gave him the list. He got back in his car and left town."

This was going nowhere.

"What made you connect the driver of the vehicle to Winter?"

"He didn't ask Marge to show him any of the vacant rentals," Arizona said. "Most folks who are interested in summer places want to take a look at a few. This guy just drove straight out of town."

"That concerns you?"

"Yep. See, that list that Marge gave the guy?"

"What about it?"

"Marge told me that he wanted to know which of the properties was currently rented. Not a lot of cottages are this time of year."

"Damn," Jack said. He said it very softly. "If you happen to be searching for someone in a small town like this and if you have a list of rentals with the currently occupied cottages marked on it, you'd have a very good idea of where the person was living."

"Yep, you wouldn't have to take the risk of asking questions at the local grocery store or gas station," Arizona said.

"Winter and I are both recent arrivals here in Eclipse Bay and we're both renting cottages from you."

"Right, but you've been here nearly three months now," Arizona pointed out. "She's only been here about a month."

"You think that someone might have come here looking for her?"

"People move here for one of two reasons. They're either looking for something or—"

"Or they're hiding from someone," Jack finished.

"I like the way you think," Arizona said.

CHAPTER ELEVEN

"Winnie-the-Pooh," Winter said.

She spoke in a cool, calm, authoritative voice.

Kendall Moseley froze.

He was still in the doorway, knife in one hand, a flashlight in the other. The rain and wind continued to sweep into the room. But Moseley was now oblivious.

Winter reached down and grabbed her cell phone. Straightening, she managed to drag in a ragged breath. She was shivering with adrenaline and fear but for the moment she was safe. The hypnotic command that she had implanted weeks ago had stopped Moseley as surely as a bullet. He had gone straight into a trance.

The problem was that, unlike a bullet, the command was not a permanent solution.

"You should not be here," she said. "Following me was a dangerous mistake. Do you understand?"

"Yes. Following you was a dangerous mistake."

The words were uttered in a monotone.

"The knife is very heavy," she said. "You cannot hold it any longer. You must let go of it."

Moseley unclenched the hand that gripped the knife. Winter was still partially blinded by the beam of his flashlight but she heard the weapon clatter onto the floor.

"The flashlight is also very heavy," she said. "It is a great weight that you can no longer hold. You must let go of it."

The flashlight dropped to the floor and rolled a short distance. When it came to a stop, the beam angled across the small living room, splashing across one leg of the heavy coffee table.

She directed the light of her cell phone directly into Moseley's eyes.

"You cannot look away from the light," she said.

She pinned Moseley with the beam and cautiously closed the distance between them. She had to get the knife. She could not afford to take the chance that he would emerge from the trance. If he did, he would pick up right where he had left off.

She used the toe of one slipper to send the blade skittering across the floor. Retreating quickly out of range, she reached down and scooped up the heavy weapon. It felt both lethal and unnatural in her hand, as if some malevolent force was infused into the metal. She gripped it very tightly.

Kendall Moseley was a lot bigger and stronger than she was. If something shattered the hypnotic trance, the knife was all she had to protect herself. It was clear she could no longer rely on the power of hypnotic suggestion. She had to find out why the one she had given Moseley had failed.

"How did you find me?" she asked, struggling to hold on to the calm, firm tone.

"My chat room friend told me where you were hiding," Moseley said without inflection.

She was dumbfounded. That was the very last thing she had expected to hear. She had been prepared to learn that Moseley had tracked her down online but not that someone had helped him locate her.

Questioning someone in a hypnotic trance was more complicated than most people assumed. A person in a trance answered questions in a very literal manner. She groped for a line of inquiry that might lead to some useful information.

"Who is your friend?" she asked.

A bolt of lightning shattered the storm-filled darkness behind Moseley. He gave a violent start.

"You *bitch*," he snarled. "Did you really think that I'd let you fuck with my mind? You're *dead*. You hear me? I'm gonna gut you and then I'll kill the guy you're fucking, too."

He lunged at her, big hands outstretched.

The lightning strike had broken the trance.

Winter dropped her phone and fell back, instinctively wrapping both hands around the hilt of the knife. She brought the blade up in front of her in a warding-off gesture, not a conscious act of self-defense.

Between the cell phone and Moseley's flashlight there was enough ambient light in the small space to reveal the blade in her hands. Moseley was enraged but he was not suicidal.

He scrambled to a halt a short distance away from her.

"Mind-fucking bitch," he screamed again. He reached inside his jacket and pulled out a gun. "One way or another, you're going to die tonight."

Footsteps thudded on the front porch steps.

"Winter," Jack shouted.

He swept through the doorway, a violent force of nature that seemed to have been generated by the heart of the storm.

Moseley started to turn to meet the new threat but Jack slammed into him. The two crashed against the dining counter. The impact sent a bowl of sea-washed stones to the floor. Glass exploded somewhere in the darkness. Winter thought she heard the gun fall.

She bent down and waved the cell phone light in a frantic arc, searching for the gun. In the glare of another burst of lightning she caught dazzling, black-and-white images of the two men locked in mortal combat. The sickening thuds of fists striking human flesh seemed unreal.

The cell phone light finally glinted on metal. She put the knife down on the floor and grabbed the pistol. When she straightened, she saw Moseley struggling to get to his feet. He appeared wild-eyed and desperate, intent only on escape.

Jack, still on the floor, grabbed one of Moseley's ankles and yanked hard. Moseley cried out and toppled backward. He managed to stagger a few feet and then went down hard.

There was a terrible crunch when his head struck the edge of the big wooden coffee table.

Moseley collapsed on the area rug. He did not move.

An unnatural stillness gripped the interior of the cottage for a few heartbeats. The surreal silence was broken only by the sound of Jack's rasping breaths. Winter knew that there would be blood—probably a lot of it.

She aimed the flashlight at the very still form. There was, indeed, blood. It came from Kendall Moseley's head and it was soaking into the old rug.

Jack got to his feet and came to stand beside her. She was vaguely aware of him peeling her fingers off the gun. When she looked at him, she saw that he was not wearing his glasses. He had probably lost them in the course of the savage hand-to-hand combat.

"Are you all right?" he asked.

The heat of battle radiated from him.

"Yes." Her voice sounded thin and fragile. Crystalline. She took a deep breath, centering herself. It had been a while since she'd had to deal with violence but some skills you didn't forget. "Yes," she said again, infusing strength into the word. "You?"

"I'm okay." Jack took the flashlight from her. He shone the beam squarely on Moseley's unconscious face. "Do you know him?"

"Yes," she said. "His name is Kendall Moseley. Former-client-turned-stalker. But he should not be here."

"No shit," Jack said.

"I don't understand what happened. I thought . . ." She broke off and took another centering breath. "I thought I had the situation under control."

"Evidently not," Jack said.

She watched him reach down and use two fingers to check Moseley for a pulse.

"Is he—?" she whispered.

"He's not dead." Jack straightened. "Not yet, at any rate. He's bleeding fairly heavily from the head wound, though."

"I'll get a towel to use as a bandage."

Jack took out his phone. "I'll call the police. They'll need an ambulance for Moseley."

Winter grabbed a clean bath towel out of the linen cupboard and returned to the living room. She crouched beside Moseley and pressed the thick towel to his bleeding head. He did not stir. His eyes did not flutter.

She listened as Jack spoke to the local emergency operator. She was adjusting the makeshift bandage on Moseley's head when she heard another set of footsteps on the front porch. A few seconds later a powerful flashlight lit up the living room.

Arizona spoke from the shadows.

"Had a feeling this was gonna be a bad night," she said.

CHAPTER TWELVE

"I should have figured it out sooner," Arizona said. "In the old days I would have put it together a lot faster. Are you okay, Winter?"

"Yes," Winter said. "A little rattled, but okay. Jack's the one who got beaten up."

Jack ended his call to the emergency operator and clipped his phone to his belt. He took an eyeglass case out of the pocket of his windbreaker and opened it.

"I'm all right," he said. He slipped on the glasses and dropped the case back into his pocket. "The cops and an aid car are on the way."

He and Arizona moved to stand looking down at Moseley.

"How long has he been stalking you?" Jack said to Winter.

"It started a few months ago when I was still working at the spa," Winter said. "Moseley booked an appointment with me. I could see right away that he was going to be a problem. After that first meditation session I made excuses not to take any more appointments with him. He complained to my boss, who got mad at me. Moseley was a valuable client, you see. He spent a fortune on massages and various treatments. Then Moseley started showing up in places where he knew I would be."

"That sort never quits," Arizona announced, grimly authoritative. "Only one way to deal with 'em."

"AZ is right," Jack said. "Obsessive stalkers don't stop. They tend to escalate."

"I thought about trying to get a restraining order," Winter continued. "But Moseley was very careful not to give me any solid evidence. Nothing I could take to the police or a judge."

"Can't depend on a restraining order, anyway," Jack said.

"Just a piece of paper," Arizona said.

"In the end, I realized I had to disappear," Winter said. "I knew Moseley might try to search for me but I thought I had come up with a way to deal with that problem. Obviously I was wrong. I'm so sorry the two of you got dragged into this mess. I never meant for that to happen."

Jack looked at her. "Just to be very clear, I've been involved since the day you and I met."

"Same here," Arizona said. "You're a neighbor and a tenant. 'Course I'm involved."

Winter looked at each of them in turn. Their faces were set in hard, determined lines. The atmosphere around them shivered with a very strong vibe.

These people are my friends, she thought. *I'm not going to have to deal with this on my own.*

"Thank you," she said.

She wanted to say more but she could not find the words.

Sirens wailed in the distance, rising and falling above the whipping wind and the restless waves.

Jack switched his attention to Arizona. "Is this the man you saw coming out of the real estate office, AZ? The one who wanted a list of vacant rentals?"

"Nope, that's not him," Arizona said. She sounded very sure of herself. "That guy was a little older. Midthirties, I'd say. Moved well, like a man who kept himself in good shape. But he looked downright scruffy. Brown hair that was so long it touched his collar. Almost completely bald on top. Tortoiseshell glasses. Old gray parka and baggy jeans. But the boots looked new. And expensive."

Winter stared at her. "You remember all those details about a man you saw leaving the real estate office?"

"A good memory for details was what you might call a job requirement in my old line of work," Arizona said. "I paid attention because I didn't like the look of the man. For one thing, those boots didn't go with the rest of the getup."

"I see," Winter said, nonplussed.

Jack's jaw tightened. "This is not good."

"Nothing about this situation is good," Winter said. "What, specifically, are you referring to?"

"The fact that this is not the same man AZ saw coming out of the real estate office a couple of days ago."

"You're right," Arizona said. "This definitely complicates things."

She and Jack exchanged somber, knowing looks.

"Whoa," Winter said. "Just a minute here. What are you two talking about?"

"Later," Jack said. "Before we get to that we need to have a real quick, real private conversation before the police arrive."

"That sounds like you want us to get our stories straight," Winter said.

"That's the general idea," Jack said.

"But why do we need to do that?" Winter asked. "It all looks straightforward to me. A stalker pursued me to Eclipse Bay and attacked me. My neighbor on the bluff interrupted the assault. There was a fight. Moseley was injured."

"Doesn't look that simple to me," Jack said. "You left out the part about how you were so sure Moseley would not follow you to Eclipse Bay."

There was a short, tense silence.

"It's hard to explain," Winter said finally.

"Try," Jack said. "And make it fast. I need to know what I'm working with here."

"He's right," Arizona said. "Better give us the facts."

Winter thought about it for approximately one and a half seconds. What the hell. She was tired of keeping her secret from Jack and Arizona. Or maybe she was too unnerved by the violence to think clearly.

"You probably won't believe me," she said. "But the truth is that I'm a hypnotist. A very good one. Before I quit my job at the spa and left Cassidy Springs I did one last meditation session with Kendall Moseley. In the course of that session I put him into a trance and gave him a very strong post-hypnotic suggestion."

Jack studied her. "You told him that he should not follow you?"

"I told him that he did not *want* to follow me," Winter said. "But that kind of suggestion can wear off over time. It needs to be reinforced fairly often. I knew I wouldn't be around to do the reinforcing, so as a backup, I implanted a post-hypnotic command—three words. The idea was that if I ever spoke them to him, he would go straight into a trance. I figured that, if he did attack me, the command would give me time to escape."

Arizona whistled softly. "Looks like something went wrong with both the suggestion and the command."

"Obviously the post-hypnotic suggestion wore off," Winter said. She looked down at Moseley's unmoving form. "Which surprises me, to be honest. It should have lasted longer. I really am a good hypnotist. The emergency backup command worked, at least long enough for me to get the knife away from him. I was questioning him, trying to find out how he had found me. But before I could get more than a couple of answers the lightning broke the trance. The next thing I knew, Jack was coming through the door and, well, here we are."

Jack gave her a speculative look. "You really are a hypnotist?"

She nodded, not speaking. She could not tell if he believed her.

"I knew this was going to get complicated," he said. "Okay, we don't have time to go into details now. Pay attention because the cops will be here any minute. Whatever you do, you will not tell them that you hypnotized Moseley. Do you understand?"

"All right," she said.

She breathed a sigh of relief. Trying to explain her ability never went well.

Arizona looked at Jack. "You're thinking that maybe the guy who stopped in at the real estate office to get a list of vacant rentals was a friend of this man, aren't you?"

"Yes," Jack said. "I think it's a possibility. It would explain a few things."

Winter glanced at Arizona and then back at Jack. "You two are losing me."

"I'll explain later," Jack said. "Here's how we're going to play this. Winter, you tell the straight-up facts but you do not mention that you hypnotized Kendall Moseley or that you gave him any hypnotic commands."

"Fine by me," Winter said. "But why are you so concerned about keeping my hypnosis ability a secret? Don't get me wrong. I appreciate it. But I seriously doubt that the cops would believe I'm much of a hypnotist. In this case they'd be right."

To her surprise, it was Arizona who responded.

"The cops probably wouldn't believe you," she said. "The problem is that they'd put it into their report and once that happens there's a real possibility that it will come back to haunt you."

"How?" Winter said.

"Moseley is headed for a courtroom," Jack said. "That means a jury. A halfway competent lawyer would be able to take your claim about being a good hypnotist and turn it against you."

"But I failed," Winter pointed out.

"Wouldn't matter," Arizona said.

"AZ is right," Jack added. "Moseley's lawyer could convince the jury that you tried to manipulate his client with hypnosis and that Moseley, therefore, was not responsible for his actions."

"Yep," Arizona said, "that's exactly how it would go down."

They might be paranoid but Arizona and Jack were probably right, Winter thought. Besides, it wasn't as if she wanted to blab her secret to the authorities. Furthermore, considering how badly her skills had failed her, there wasn't much point in claiming to be an expert hypnotist.

"Damn," she said.

"All right," Jack said, satisfied. "The three of us are on the same page here. We're not going to mention the words *hypnosis* or *hypnotic commands* to the police."

"Copy that," Arizona said.

Jack looked at Winter.

"What about your family?" he asked. "Can we count on them to keep quiet about your ability?"

"Believe me, they won't say a word about my talent for hypnosis. For years they've advised me to keep quiet about it. They're not even in the country at the moment. They're anthropologists and currently they're in some jungle several thousand miles from here."

Jack nodded, satisfied. "We're good, then."

The first vehicle arrived, lights flashing, sirens screaming. It slammed to a halt in front of the porch.

Jack went to the door to greet the police.

Winter looked at the blood-soaked towel she was holding against Moseley's head.

"I told my boss this guy was going to be a problem," she said with a sigh. "But he refused to believe me."

Arizona peered down at Moseley. "Mind if I ask what you used as the hypnotic command that was supposed to put him into a trance? Professional curiosity."

"The command was 'Winnie-the-Pooh,'" Winter said.

Arizona nodded approvingly. "Always did like those stories."

CHAPTER THIRTEEN

———— ≋ ————

Kendall Moseley came awake to the beep of machines and a ferocious headache. He stirred and managed, barely, to open his eyes. The room was drenched in shadows. Lights blinked in the darkness. There was a needle in his arm. It was attached to an IV bag that hung from a steel pole beside the bed.

A woman dressed in a janitor's uniform stood beside the bed. She was busy working on the IV line. Her gray hair was partially covered by a cap. The lower half of her face was concealed by a disposable mask that was secured with loops around her ears. It was the kind of mask hospital personnel used to protect against infection.

When Kendall looked closely he decided that the janitor's eyes did not go with the gray hair and the stout frame. They were the eyes of a much younger woman.

"Hey," he managed.

The janitor paused and glanced down at him.

"You really fucked up, didn't you?" she said.

Her voice was low and throaty. Sexy. He had to concentrate to focus on what she said because it didn't make any sense.

"Huh?" he said.

"I told the boss that you were damaged goods," the janitor continued. She did not pause in her work on the IV line. "But he was obsessed with what he likes to call the six-degrees-of-separation aspect. He wanted more than just plausible deniability, you see. He wanted to make sure there was no way anyone would have any grounds to suspect that he might have been involved. My partner and I explained that the plan was just too damn complicated. But you know how it is with upper management. The CEO always says he wants your opinion but he doesn't pay attention when you give it to him."

Kendall struggled to clear his head but the pain made it impossible to think.

"Huh?" he said again because he couldn't come up with anything else.

"Have to give the boss credit, though," the janitor continued. "If you had been successful, there would have been no way Salinas and his other two sons could have traced Lancaster's death back to the source. But now, thanks to you, we're going to have to come up with a whole new strategy."

Kendall focused on her hands. They were sheathed in thin medical examination gloves.

"What are you doing?" he said. He could barely get the words out.

"How much do you remember?" the janitor asked.

Kendall tried to think. Blurry memories surfaced. He had flown to Portland, Oregon. A car had been waiting for him. His destination had been programmed into the GPS. There had also been a note on the seat instructing him to check the trunk. Inside he had found a knife and a gun. He had followed the GPS to a small town on the coast.

"I found her," he said, relieved to be able to recall that much. "I found the mind-fucking bitch." He paused. "But something happened."

"You had one job," the janitor said. "You had everything you needed to do that job. You had the map. You had the tools that were required, including a knife and a gun. Meadows was alone in the house. How did you manage to screw up so badly? I know the boss will ask."

"What boss? I don't know what you're talking about. Where am I?"

"You're in a hospital in a town about twenty miles away from the scene. Eclipse Bay is too small to support its own hospital. All they've got is a clinic, so the ambulance brought you here. That worked out well for us, though. No one asked any questions when I decided to play janitor. People never look twice at a janitor, you see."

"You're not really a janitor, are you?"

"No."

Kendall groped for a call button but he couldn't locate it.

"It's just you and me, Moseley," the janitor said. "True, the locals assigned a cop to keep an eye on you, but he's busy drinking coffee and chatting with someone at the nurses' station. We've got a little time here, so talk to me. *What went wrong?*"

Kendall started to get mad. The demanding note in the janitor's voice aroused a frisson of the old, long-simmering anger. All his life women had tried to manipulate and control him. The scariest one of all was the bitch who had looked straight into his head and seen the weakness in him. He wanted to punish her; destroy her.

"I found her," he said. "But she tricked me. And then he showed up."

"Lancaster?"

"I don't know his name. I remember him coming up the porch steps. That's the last thing I can remember. I'm in a hospital?"

"Uh-huh."

"Why? What happened to me?"

"Judging by the conversation I overheard out in the hall, you and Lancaster fought. He won. You lost. You hit your head when you went down. Now you're under arrest for breaking into the cottage and attacking Winter Meadows."

Rage clouded Kendall's brain. "That mind-fucking bitch tricked me."

"How did Meadows trick you?"

"She did something to my brain. She tried to control me. That's why I had to kill her. My friend understands. He explained everything."

"Why would Meadows want to control you?"

"She thinks I'm weak," Kendall said. "Women always make that mistake. I have to teach them a lesson."

"Which you do by beating them so badly that they end up in the emergency room."

"I have to teach them to treat me with respect."

"You were supposed to do more than beat up Winter Meadows tonight. You were supposed to kill her."

"Yes," he said. "Yes, I was going to gut her like a fish. That's exactly what I'll do as soon as I get out of here. She's dangerous. My friend in the chat room told me the truth about her."

The janitor removed the syringe that she had been using to inject something into the IV line. She looked down at Kendall.

"I have a message from your chat room friend," she said.

For the first time since he had awakened in the hospital room, Kendall Moseley experienced a tiny flicker of relief.

"You know my friend?" he said.

"He's my employer."

"I don't understand."

"No surprise," the janitor said. She glanced at her watch. "I'm going to have to run. Got a long drive ahead. I don't have time to explain the full extent of your fuckup."

"Stop talking to me like that. I'm not stupid."

"A highly debatable claim."

The janitor was a mind-fucking bitch, just like all the other women he had known. He tried to stay focused.

"What did my friend tell you?" he said.

The janitor had partially turned away from the bed. She paused.

"Your chat room friend made it clear that after tonight he would no longer require your services," she said.

An icy blast of fear cascaded through Kendall Moseley. He tried to lever himself to an upright position but discovered he could not move. He was shackled to the bed.

"Who are you?" he rasped.

The janitor leaned over the bed. For the first time he saw the hot excitement in her eyes.

"You could say I'm from HR. I'm here to terminate your employment."

He tried to protest but a dark fog was already coalescing in his head. He wanted to shout for help but he did not have enough strength.

"You can't do anything to me," he got out in a hoarse whisper. "My friend will protect me."

"No, your friend will not protect you, because you failed. He doesn't waste time on weak assets like you."

Kendall had one last instant of clarity. His friend had betrayed him and now he was going to die—and all because of the bitch who had fucked with his mind.

CHAPTER FOURTEEN

The bored cop was still lounging against the nurses' station, talking to the attractive, dark-haired woman sitting in front of a computer. He glanced down the hall at the janitor who had just left Moseley's room but he immediately lost interest. He turned back to his cozy conversation and his unfinished coffee.

The janitor got behind her cart and leaned into it with a show of weary effort. She pushed it around a corner into another white-walled corridor. The monitors attached to Moseley would start pinging at the nurses' station any second now.

It was unlikely that the cop and the nurse would remember the janitor who had cleaned Moseley's room shortly before his death, but even if they did, the description would be very misleading. It was amazing what a wig of gray hair, a surgical mask and a heavily padded figure draped in oversized hospital scrubs could conceal.

The janitor trudged down the hall. When she reached the next intersection, she ducked into the women's restroom and removed the janitor's scrubs. She stuffed them into the small daypack she had concealed in the cart but she left the hospital mask in place. No one would question it in a medical setting.

Dressed in the trousers, ancient plaid flannel shirt, baseball cap and sneakers that she had worn earlier when she entered the hospital, she walked out the main entrance. The clerk at the front desk did not look up from his computer.

She cut through the mostly empty parking lot and crossed a quiet street. Devlin was waiting for her in the black SUV parked nearby. He fired up the engine when she emerged from the shadows. She opened the passenger-side door and slipped into the seat.

Devlin put the vehicle in gear and pulled away from the curb.

He had worked under a variety of names but these days he went by Devlin Knight. He thought it had a dashing ring to it. He was good-looking in an open, square-jawed, former-captain-of-the-high-school-football-team sort of way but not so good-looking as to be truly memorable. He kept himself in excellent shape and at thirty-five he still had a body that did justice to the sophisticated Italian designer clothes he favored.

Devlin's physical attributes were not on display tonight. He wore a wig designed to make it appear that he was going bald, heavy glasses and a shirt that had been purchased at a military surplus store. He called it the Pacific Northwest Prepper look.

She had also had a few other names in the past but now all of her very authentic-looking ID's bore the name Victoria Sloan. Classy. Unlike Devlin, her looks were memorable, and she took care to keep them that way because they were part of her tool kit. There had been times in the past when her life had depended on her elegant profile, blond hair, blue eyes, and well-proportioned, very toned body.

It was getting harder and harder to maintain both the face and the body, however, now that she was in her thirties. Just one more reason why the current job was so important. It was a ticket to a new life.

She and Devlin had been a freelance mercenary team for the past few years, having met while working for a certain government agency. They had started out as colleagues but they had become lovers after their first assignment together. The initial attraction had been fueled by adrenaline, shared danger and the thrill of the kill.

At some point it had become clear to both of them that they could do better on their own. A terrorist bombing in a small backwater country had provided them with the opportunity to fake their own deaths. They had reinvented themselves as private contractors who specialized in handling security for an elite clientele. Their customers' business interests usually involved dangerous activities such as gunrunning, drug distribution and conducting small wars.

The sex was no longer the rush that it had been at the start but over time other bonds had taken hold. She and Devlin could finish each other's sentences. When it came to clothes, they shared an appreciation for Italian designers. Their tastes in good food and good wine were aligned.

They diverged in some ways—Devlin had an inexplicable fondness for silly romantic comedies, while she preferred small, intense, slow-moving art films—but for the most part they were more compatible than the vast majority of couples.

Back at the start, she reflected, they had resembled a pair of spontaneous, hot-blooded newlyweds. But now their relationship looked more like a long-term marriage that had fallen into a predictable and familiar, albeit comfortable, pattern. The boredom factor would no doubt have kicked in by now if they had not been intimately bound by their business partnership. The couple that killed together, stayed together—at least until one of them terminated the other.

Their current client had found them on the Darknet. An anonymous broker who made a good living providing introductions between experts with certain lethal skills and customers who were looking to hire individuals with said skills had put them together.

But unlike their previous clients, Lucan Tazewell had made them an offer that no other employer had ever come close to matching. He had dangled the lure of a dazzling new future.

The project was a big one—a business opportunity with a lot of moving pieces—but the payoff promised to be huge. If all went well, she and Devlin would soon become as rich and as powerful as some of their former clients. Even better, they would be legit. No more hiding on the Darknet. They would hang out with celebrities and tech moguls. They would control politicians.

True, there were some challenges, but nothing that could not be handled. When the job was completed she and Devlin would no longer be hired muscle. Lucan Tazewell was going to make them full partners in a billion-dollar hedge fund.

Lucan was different from their previous clients. He showed them respect. He admired and appreciated their talents. But he also had high standards. He expected his orders to be executed with precision. He definitely did not have a high tolerance for failure.

Devlin slowed for a stoplight even though there was no other traffic. When you were leaving the scene of a crime, you never ran. The last thing you wanted to do was draw attention.

"I assume that the Moseley problem has been taken care of," he said.

"Yes, but it's the only thing that went well tonight," Victoria said. She removed the mask. "Tazewell won't be pleased."

The arrangement between the three of them was not yet a full-fledged partnership, she reminded herself. Lucan Tazewell was still the client; still the one who gave the orders.

"It was his plan, not ours," Devlin said. "Tazewell insisted on micromanaging this particular project from start to finish. We warned him that it was risky to use an unstable asset like Kendall Moseley."

"Let's hope Tazewell sees it that way," Victoria said.

Now that she had time to think about all that had gone wrong tonight she was starting to worry. She really did not want to disappoint Lucan Tazewell.

"If he's as smart as he thinks he is, next time he'll listen to us," Devlin said.

"Guess we'll soon find out."

She gripped her heavily encrypted phone and braced herself to deliver the bad news. Lucan insisted on verbal reports when it came to this sort of thing. He did not trust text messaging or email. Both forms of communication left too many tracks.

Lucan answered immediately.

"It's not your fault," he said. "I knew going in that Moseley was a risk."

A thrill of relief swept through her followed by an overwhelming sense of admiration and profound respect. She had worked for people who were unforgiving when it came to failure, even though the failure was their own fault. Few employers had the fortitude to take responsibility for their own mistakes.

Lucan was not like the others. He was strong and smart and infused with the kind of self-confidence it took to shoulder the blame when things went wrong.

She started to breathe a little more easily.

"You heard the news?" she asked.

"I've been monitoring the emergency channels in the vicinity of Eclipse Bay. I picked up enough chatter to figure out that things had gone wrong. I'm assuming the report of an interrupted assault on an unidentified woman is not a coincidence?"

Lucan had a very good voice, she reflected. She liked to listen to it, even on the phone. It was rich and resonant. He could have gone into politics, preached salvation or sung opera with that voice.

"No, it's not a coincidence," Victoria said. She delivered her report as briefly and as clearly as possible. She was a professional, after all. "We're in the clear. There are no links to us or to you. But the bottom line is that Lancaster and the woman are still alive."

"And Kendall Moseley? The initial reports said that he was injured and had been taken to a hospital in a nearby town. I assume he won't be a problem."

Victoria relaxed a little. She was glad to be able to deliver some good news about an otherwise failed operation.

"Sadly, Kendall Moseley died from the traumatic head injury he sustained when he and Lancaster engaged in a struggle in the Meadows cottage," she said.

"Did he die on the way to the hospital?"

"No," she said. "He was in the hospital when he died, but don't worry, he didn't have a chance to talk to anyone, at least not until I got to him."

"You're sure he didn't say anything to the police?"

"Positive, sir," Victoria said. "It's clear from the medical and police reports that Moseley was unconscious at the scene in Eclipse Bay and that he did not wake up at any point during the trip to the hospital. I was actually the one who was with him when he did regain consciousness. Bit of luck there. I tried to question him but he was not very coherent."

"I want to know everything he said."

"Mostly he just babbled on about Winter Meadows. He was delusional. Kept saying that Meadows had fucked with his mind. He seemed to think that she had gotten inside his head and tried to control him."

"He was an obsessed individual. They are, by definition, delusional. I thought I could weaponize Moseley's fantasies but obviously I was wrong."

"He also mentioned his chat room friend but there's no need to be concerned. I can assure you he won't be discussing his buddy or anything else with the authorities."

"Good. What's your status?"

"We're in the vehicle, heading back to Portland. We'll dump the car and catch an early-morning flight to San Francisco. We should be at the Sonoma house before noon." She paused. "Unless you want us to take a more direct approach to the problem while we're here in Oregon?"

"No. Whatever you do, don't make any more moves against the target. I need to do some serious thinking on this end. Can't risk another fuckup."

Victoria clenched the phone a little more tightly. Lucan had indicated that he wasn't going to blame Devlin and her for tonight's debacle, but when it came to clients, you could never really be sure of their reaction to failure.

"There's no need to worry about a police investigation," she said, going for a professional vibe in her tone. "As you're aware, Eclipse Bay is a very small town with limited resources. The police department won't have the kind of budget required to dig deep. And why would they? From their point of view the case is cut-and-dried."

"A stalker with a history of violence against women pursues the latest object of his obsession, his meditation instructor, to a small town and attacks her in the middle of the night," Lucan said. "A neighbor interrupts the assault. There's a fight. The stalker winds up in the hospital and dies from a head wound."

"Exactly," Victoria said. "There won't be a problem, sir."

"The Internet trail is clean, too. Kendall Moseley's chat room friend has disappeared."

"Yes, sir."

"One more thing, Victoria."

A frisson of anxiety rattled her nerves. This job was different. This job promised a future. There was so much at stake.

"Yes, sir?" she said.

"Next time remind me to pay attention to you and Devlin when you two try to tell me that my plan is too damn complicated."

The praise and the promise warmed her.

"Yes, sir," she said. "Thank you, sir."

But Lucan had already ended the connection.

Devlin glanced at her. "I take it the boss isn't blaming us?"

"No." She smiled. "He even went so far as to tell me that next time he'll listen to us when we offer advice."

"We'll see," Devlin said. He drove out onto the main road and turned toward Portland. "You ever wonder why Tazewell is so focused on taking out Lancaster?"

"Obviously he thinks Lancaster is a serious obstacle."

"As far as I can tell, Jack Lancaster is just a guy who used to be a college instructor who couldn't hold a job for very long. He wrote a couple of books. He's got a thing about cold cases. So what? It's not like he's FBI or CIA. He doesn't arrest people. He doesn't have any serious resources he can access."

"If Tazewell thinks that Lancaster is dangerous, we have to assume that is the case."

"Lancaster doesn't seem like much of a problem to me."

"Try looking at this situation from a different angle," Victoria said. "Things went wrong tonight. And what is the result?"

Devlin grunted. "Lancaster and the woman are still alive and Moseley is the one who is dead."

"Yeah. So maybe that means Jack Lancaster is a little more of a problem than you think."

Devlin exhaled slowly and concentrated on his driving for a moment.

"You know what's bothering me about this job?" he said after a while.

"Sure. We've got a lot on the line."

"No, it's not just that we've got a vested interest in the outcome that's making me uneasy. It's the fact that Tazewell and Lancaster obviously have some old history. Whatever is going on here, it isn't just business. It's personal."

"It's definitely personal for us," Victoria said. "This job is going to change our lives. In the future we'll be the clients who go out on the Darknet to hire security. What's more, we'll be making those decisions from the deck of a yacht or while we're drinking good wine on a sunny terrace on the Amalfi Coast."

"I know, but I'm telling you the personal connection between Tazewell and Lancaster makes me nervous. Jobs with that vibe usually turn out to be unpredictable."

CHAPTER FIFTEEN

"I can't believe he's dead," Winter said. "I know Moseley hit his head very hard, but he was alive when they loaded him into the ambulance."

"Head injuries are unpredictable," Jack said. "Evidently he never woke up. There may have been a blood clot or internal bleeding."

They were sitting at the small table in his cottage, drinking coffee. Neither one of them had slept. The first faint glow of dawn was slowly lightening the sky.

The news of Moseley's death had been delivered a short time ago by the Eclipse Bay chief of police. The chief had also supplied the information that in the past three years two women had filed restraining orders against Kendall Moseley.

As far as Jack could tell, Winter was handling the aftermath of the violence with a surprising degree of composure. Probably all that positive thinking and meditation practice. Or maybe she was still in shock.

One thing he knew for sure—he was not thinking positive. What he was thinking was that he needed answers. Information. Data.

After the ambulance had departed, he and Winter and Arizona had given their statements to the police. Their mutual agreement to keep quiet about Winter's claim that she had attempted to hypnotize Moseley had held firm. None of them had mentioned it to the cops.

He could not leave Winter to deal with her blood-splashed cottage, but at that time of year there were not a lot of places she could go. The nearest motel was a few miles outside of town. In any event, he doubted that she wanted to be alone. He was pretty sure that he had seen relief and gratitude in her eyes when she accepted his offer to spend what was left of the night at his place.

Arizona had waved them off and said that she would stay behind to keep a sharp eye on things while the police took photographs and collected evidence.

He watched Winter use both hands to pick up her coffee mug. She looked at him over the rim, her eyes shadowed.

"What do you think will happen next?" she asked.

He gave that some thought. "I think the authorities will wrap things up very quickly. On the surface, it looks straightforward. An obsessive stalker followed you here to Eclipse Bay with the obvious intention of harming you. I interrupted the attack. There was a struggle during which Moseley struck his head and later died of his injuries. Unless Moseley's family decides to file a lawsuit, which, under the circumstances, seems unlikely, tonight will be the end of it, at least as far as the cops are concerned."

Winter stiffened, eyes widening. "A lawsuit? On what grounds?"

"You know what they say, a person can sue for just about anything— but I seriously doubt that we'll have to worry about that possibility. It is, however, one more reason why you are not going to tell anyone that you tried to hypnotize Kendall Moseley."

Winter sipped her tea in silence for a time.

"I'm still surprised," she said after a while.

"That he died?"

"Well, that, too, but mostly I'm surprised that my hypnotic suggestion didn't hold."

He leaned back in his chair and studied her for a moment.

"You're really that good?" he said at last.

"Uh-huh."

She wasn't boasting, he realized. She was simply acknowledging a fact.

"I admit I don't know much about hypnosis," he said, choosing his words with exquisite care, "but I am aware that it is . . . controversial."

She gave him a wry smile. "I know."

"A lot of claims have been made for the powers of hypnosis but very few of those claims have stood up to rigorous scientific testing."

Winter nodded. "In other words, you don't believe that I actually could have hypnotized Kendall Moseley."

"I didn't say that."

She waved that aside with one hand. "Trust me, I'm well aware that most people are skeptical. It's understandable. You're right, it's difficult to run double-blind clinical trials to prove the value of hypnosis. There's another problem, too."

"What's that?"

"There's some research that indicates there's an entire segment of the population—as much as twenty or twenty-five percent—that may be immune to hypnosis, or mostly immune."

"Even if the hypnotist is very good?"

"Evidently, but who can be sure? As you pointed out, there's not a lot of solid research in the field." Winter paused, her eyes narrowing a little. "Still, in my experience, most people can be hypnotized, at least to some extent. And of that group, a sizable percentage can be put into a trance rather easily. I was sure Moseley was one of those people."

"You said that hypnotic suggestions fade over time. Maybe that's what happened in this case."

"Maybe, but I was certain that once I was out of sight, I would be out of Moseley's mind," Winter said. "I thought that by the time the suggestion faded he would have focused on something else."

"Something? Not someone?"

Winter made a face. "The suggestion not to come after me was not the only one that I gave him. I also told him that what he really wanted to do was concentrate on exercise, specifically running, every chance he got."

"You hoped that running would become his next obsession?"

"I couldn't think of anything else that seemed relatively harmless," Winter said. "An obsessive personality is an obsessive personality. Sooner or later it will find something to focus on. I was hoping to protect the next woman who had the bad luck to attract Moseley's attention."

"I doubt if it would have worked. Obsession is not particularly complicated, but it is powerful and very dangerous. I see a lot of it in my work."

"I'm sure you do." Winter drank some coffee and lowered the mug. "Thank goodness the post-hypnotic command that put him straight into a trance was still effective, at least until the lightning strike."

Jack reached for the coffeepot and refilled his mug. "Mind if I ask you what is probably a rather personal question?"

"Of course not. You could have been killed or badly injured tonight and it would have been my fault. You deserve some answers."

"Don't do that," he said, putting some steel into the words.

She paused, the mug halfway to her lips.

"Don't do what?" she asked.

"Don't blame yourself for what happened tonight. It was not your fault."

Her jaw tightened. "Moseley came here because of me."

"He came here because he was a deranged individual. Here's what you need to remember, Winter. We both could have been killed tonight but we survived. What's more, we can both take credit for our survival. You stopped Moseley long enough for me to get a chance to take him down. We did it together."

She took a deep breath and let it out with control. "Okay. Congratulations on putting a positive spin on things, by the way."

"I've been studying with the best."

She managed a smile at that. "What was the personal question you wanted to ask?"

"Don't take this the wrong way," he said. "But if you're such a good hypnotist, why don't you make your living using your ability? Why teach meditation instead?"

"I think of meditation as a form of self-hypnosis."

She sounded defensive, he decided.

"I never looked at it that way," he said.

Her mouth curved a little. "While we're on the subject, how would you describe your lucid dreaming?"

"Huh." He thought about it. "Self-hypnosis?"

"If it isn't a form of self-hypnosis, it's a very similar experience. The line between a hypnotic trance and the dream state is murky. Some researchers think there may not be a hard border; that a trance state is essentially a kind of dream state."

"But you don't advertise yourself as a hypnotist. You don't tell people that you can help them lose weight or stop smoking or get a promotion. You don't promise them that you can cure their pain or anxiety."

Winter set the mug down, folded her arms on the table and contemplated him for a long moment.

"The short answer is that it's darned hard to make a living as a hypnotist," she said. "Trust me, I come from a long line of failed hypnotists who had to find other ways to make a living."

"*Failed* hypnotists?"

"They didn't fail in the technical sense. But they mostly failed in the business sense."

"Why is that?"

"Because a lot of people treat hypnotists the same way they do fortune tellers, psychics, magicians and mentalists," Winter said. "Some genuinely believe that there is such a thing as hypnosis, and it freaks them out. Some desperately want to believe it's for real and that it can cure whatever ails them. Then there are those who want to prove to you that they absolutely cannot be hypnotized. And finally there are the people who are convinced that hypnosis is just a parlor trick and insist that you prove yourself to them. For the record, the last two types are particularly annoying."

"So finding clients who want to use hypnosis for legitimate reasons is something of a crapshoot."

"Yes, it is. Combine that with the disgruntled customers who can't be helped with therapeutic hypnosis but who feel compelled to go online to voice their complaints, and you've got some serious problems with any business model that features hypnosis."

"I see."

"And last but not least, there are those who decide to sue the hypnotist because they think the practitioner took advantage of them while they were in a trance."

"I'm beginning to understand that it might be a tough way to make a living."

"Yep." Winter reached for the coffeepot. "That's why I'm trying to come up with a viable alternative. Meditation instruction."

He watched her refill her mug. "You said you came from a long line of failed hypnotists?"

"The talent seems to run through the female side of my family." Winter set the pot down. "I had a great-grandmother who gave demonstrations of mesmerism on the stage. The audiences loved it, but when she tried to use her abilities to treat people with various neuroses and anxiety issues, she got into trouble."

"What happened?"

"One of her clients claimed that she had used her skills to cheat him out of his life savings. It wasn't true, of course."

"Of course not."

Evidently reassured, Winter plowed on with her story. "The problem was that my great-grandmother had no way to prove her innocence. Then the local newspaper discovered that she had once worked in a carnival. The paper used the front page to label her a fraud and a huckster."

"I know how that feels," Jack said.

Winter's brows shot up. "You do?"

"The media and law enforcement are not always kind to those of us who do cold case work. When I first started out, I was accused of ruining lives and reputations by reopening old wounds. Other people said I was trying to get publicity for my books. The terms *fraud* and *charlatan* and *con man* were thrown around a lot. Then there were the reality TV people who wanted to turn old tragedies into entertainment. And don't get me started on all the fake psychics who followed me around offering their assistance."

"Okay," Winter said. "Now I see why you go out of your way to try to keep a low profile when you take a case."

"Who in your family besides your great-grandmother had problems trying to make a living as a hypnotist?"

"My grandmother tried to market her skills to help people deal with chronic pain."

"How did that work out?"

"Not well," Winter said. "The problem was that the effects of her post-hypnotic suggestions wore off over time."

He frowned. "That's true of any pain therapy. There is no single drug or technique that works for everyone, certainly not indefinitely."

"My grandmother did have some success, but she ran into trouble with the competition."

"Who was the competition?"

"A well-respected doctor who practiced in the same town," Winter said. "Initially he tried to take advantage of Grandma's skills. He offered her a job in his office. She refused because she figured she would do better on her own. She was right—at least until he retaliated by smearing her reputation. He had a lot of friends on the city council. The result was that the chief of police came to her door one day and warned her that if she didn't close down her office, he would arrest her for practicing medicine without a license."

"That's harsh."

"Grandma moved on, married and had a daughter—my mom. Grandpa divorced Grandma and disappeared. Grandma and Mom moved to Los Angeles and set up in business as lifestyle consultants. They did pretty well with that."

Jack smiled. "A very nice bit of repositioning in the marketplace."

"Yes, it was, at least for a while. Grandma did great. She and Mom were successful. Eventually Mom married and had me."

"You never told me what happened to your parents."

"My father died when I was just a baby," Winter said. "I never knew him. Grandma and Mom were both killed in a car accident a few days before my fourteenth birthday."

"So that's how you ended up in the foster care system," he said.

"Yes."

"That reminds me, are you going to try to get a hold of your foster parents and your sister to let them know what happened last night?"

"As I told you, they're in the field doing research on a very important project. I can leave a message for them at the headquarters of the foundation they work for, but it might be weeks before they get it. There's nothing they can do anyway. They would just worry."

"You're probably right. Still—"

"The thing is, it's over," Winter said firmly.

"Over?"

She straightened her shoulders. "Moseley is no longer a problem. I've got to stay focused on saving my business."

"You're worried about your business?"

Winter's jaw tightened. "After what happened tonight, it's going to be a lot harder for me to build a successful career as a meditation instructor."

"Why do you say that?"

"Who in their right mind will want to study meditation with a practitioner who was involved in the death of a former client? That doesn't exactly have a positive vibe, does it?"

He set his mug down hard on the table. "You were not involved in the death of a former client. You were attacked by one and barely escaped with your life. Regardless, Eclipse Bay is a very small town. The news of Kendall Moseley's death won't travel far."

"I wish I could believe that. But if this hits the Internet—which could easily happen—it might destroy me before I can get my business off the ground. Even if it doesn't make a blip online now, there's no telling when it will come back to haunt me in the future. I may need to think about changing my name."

He studied her in silence for a moment while he went deep, trying to come up with a positive spin for her situation. He wanted to reassure her, but the truth was, she might be right.

"Damn," he said instead.

"My sentiments exactly." She surprised him with a faint smile. "Thanks."

"For what?"

"For not trying to sugarcoat the truth. For not saying something cheery and upbeat and totally fake."

"Yeah, well, for now we don't really know how this will play out so don't go full negative on me," he said.

"Wow. Is that your version of thinking positive? 'Don't go full negative'? That's the best you can do?"

"You need to cut me some slack here. I'm still new at the positive-thinking thing, remember?"

"I will admit that sometimes it clashes with reality." Winter picked up the coffeepot again and emptied it into her mug. "You know, I sure wish I'd had a chance to ask Moseley a few more questions. I'd really like to know exactly what overcame that hypnotic suggestion I gave him."

"You said yourself the hypnotic suggestion must have faded."

"Yes, but I'm wondering if it faded so quickly and so completely because someone assisted Moseley's memory and maybe kick-started his old obsession with me."

For a second Jack just stared at her. The ping of awareness going off in his head was more like a code red alarm. He sat forward so quickly and with such force that Winter yelped in surprise and nearly dropped her mug.

"What are you talking about?" he asked very softly.

"It's not the possibility that my hypnotic suggestion might have worn off that worries me," she said earnestly. "I can live with that kind of failure. It's the possibility that someone provoked Moseley and, in the process, encouraged him to remember his obsession with me that's really freaking me out."

"You're freaking me out, too. Damn it, why didn't you tell me about this before, Winter?"

"I needed some time to process something that could well have been a figment of Moseley's imagination. He was delusional, after all. Who knows what the truth is? Besides, I really don't want to believe that my old boss could have sunk so low as to sic a stalker on me in order to get revenge. But the more I think about it, the more I've got to wonder if maybe that's exactly what happened."

Jack felt as if he had just plunged into a sea of ice.

"What makes you believe that someone worked on Moseley and overcame your suggestion?" he asked very softly.

"I had Moseley in a trance for a moment or two before that lightning strike ruined things for me. While he was under I asked him how he found me. He said a friend that he met in a chat room helped him."

"Maybe the man AZ saw picking up a list of empty cottages here in Eclipse Bay. That fits."

"Hang on, let's not jump to conclusions here," Winter said quickly. "What on earth makes you think there could be a connection between Kendall Moseley and a tourist who wanted a list of summer rentals?"

"I don't know," he said. "I need to think about it."

Winter cleared her throat. "They say that you can find anyone these days."

"That's not true," Jack said. "My brothers and I have been looking for someone for a couple of decades and all we've ever found online are the footprints of a ghost. But let's get back to Kendall Moseley. Was he good at navigating things online?"

"I don't think he was particularly tech savvy but it doesn't take a lot of skills to get into a chat room."

"True," Jack said. "And if Moseley was hanging out in certain chat rooms on a regular basis, it wouldn't have been hard for someone to find him and go to work on his old obsession. Tell me about your ex-boss."

Winter shuddered. "Raleigh Forrester. He was really pissed at me when I told him I was going to quit if he didn't stop insisting that I book appointments with Moseley."

"Do you really think this Raleigh Forrester would have wanted revenge just because you quit your job? That seems a little over-the-top."

"I'm afraid the situation was more complicated than it sounds," Winter said. "Forrester was planning to sell the spa to a competitor. I was part of the deal, although I didn't know it at the time."

"What do you mean?"

"I think I mentioned that while I was at the Cassidy Springs Wellness Spa we got a lot of new corporate business," Winter said.

"I remember. Are you saying that new business was because of you?"

"The corporate crowd loved my meditation seminars," Winter said. "I was booked out for six months—really big events. The business was growing rapidly. Forrester's chief competitor made a buyout offer. But the offer was contingent on me signing a three-year contract that included a non-compete clause. Forrester never bothered to tell me about that part until the day I told him I was leaving."

"What happened to the buyout?"

"The deal fell through after I left. Forrester still owes me a month's salary, by the way."

"So this Raleigh Forrester may have had a strong motive for revenge?"

"Well, he had a motive," Winter said. "But I'm not sure it was strong enough to make him send Moseley after me. Still, there was a lot of money involved. Do you think I should tell the police?"

Jack thought about that for a moment. "Probably no point in talking to the cops. There's nothing in the way of proof to give them, just speculation. Forrester will deny everything if he's confronted."

"Why do I have the feeling that you're not buying my theory of the crime?"

"Your old boss may have been the chat room friend who aimed Kendall Moseley at you. It's a logical assumption. But at this moment I am staring down the rabbit hole of a very personal conspiracy theory."

Winter put her mug aside, propped her elbows on the table and rested her chin on her folded hands.

"I'm listening," she said.

"It's a conspiracy theory that my brothers and my dad and I have kept alive for over two decades. We don't talk about it much outside our family because it tends to make people think we're . . . unbalanced."

She did not appear to be nearly as astonished as she should have been. It was as if he had put into words something she had suspected all along; as if she had been waiting for him to drop the full weight of his past on her.

"Go on," she said.

"I was hoping I wouldn't have to tell you, at least not until we knew each other better. I didn't want to scare the daylights out of you."

"What could you tell me that would be more frightening than what I went through last night?"

"I'm starting to wonder if I am the one who is responsible for the fact that you nearly got murdered last night."

She went very still. "Okay, I'll admit that is a little scary."

"Trust me, if I'm right, things are going to get a lot scarier."

Winter watched him with her mysterious eyes. Maybe she was questioning the state of his mental health. That was probably a legitimate concern.

"Who or what is at the other end of this rabbit hole?" she asked.

"Quinton Zane."

CHAPTER SIXTEEN

He needed fire.

The man who had once been Quinton Zane stared at the two-foot-high glass statue of a phoenix displayed on a stone pedestal in the center of the room. He had to exert enormous self-control to overcome the desire to hurl it against the nearest wall.

But the meaningless act of destruction would not be rational. It would not be helpful, and it sure as hell would not be smart. It might even make him look as if he lacked self-control. That was definitely not the image he needed to project. He was, after all, the brilliant Lucan Tazewell, the long-lost heir to the throne of Tazewell Global, and he was here to save the family business.

He was currently starring in a carefully scripted narrative that featured him as the hero. He was the firstborn son of Grayson Fitzgerald Tazewell, founder of a financial empire that was teetering on the brink of bankruptcy. The firm's precarious situation was the result of a series of failed investments and a few sizable loans from some very dubious—and dangerous—people. The money laundering, undertaken in a desperate effort to pull the company out of its death spiral, had not improved the situation.

When Grayson Tazewell had received an offer of financial salvation from the son he had never acknowledged—the son he believed had conveniently vanished into the underworld of off-the-books adoptions—he had seized the lifeline. Under other circumstances he might have been a little more cautious. Then again, maybe not. He had built Tazewell Global by taking big risks.

Regardless, by the time the offer had arrived in his inbox, the circumstances were desperate and he was a desperate man.

Lucan pushed himself to his feet and went to stand at the window of his father's study. He forced himself to review the facts of the situation, but it was difficult to think logically with the acid of fury and frustration burning in his veins.

Knight and Sloan had failed. After all the research, after all the time and energy spent in the chat room manipulating Kendall Moseley, after the painstaking attention to the details of the strategy, the entire plan had collapsed.

He needed a new strategy and he needed it quickly.

But he also needed a little fire. It was the only thing that cleared his head these days.

He tried to focus on the expansive view of the vineyards of the northern California wine country. The neat, orderly rows of vines marching over the rolling hills were illuminated in the early-morning light. It should have been a soothing, calming sight.

The Sonoma house was one of five residences that Grayson Tazewell currently owned. They all had one thing in common: a study from which Grayson could operate the levers of his empire. Each study was identical, right down to the photographs on the wall. Many of the pictures showed Grayson with various politicians, celebrities and spectacularly beautiful women. There were also images of Grayson's first yacht and his first Lamborghini.

In the center was a photograph of the first of the huge houses that Grayson had acquired over the years. It was the house that he had bought to celebrate making his first fortune.

There was a glass case in one corner that contained six bottles of a very expensive, very exotic hundred-and-fifty-proof brandy. Lucan knew that Grayson reserved the stuff for toasting victories and successes.

None of the bottles had been opened recently.

In every study there was a two-foot-high glass sculpture of a phoenix rising from the ashes. All of the pieces had been done by the same artist. In the carefully placed lighting, the figures glowed with the hot reds and golds of fire.

Grayson had failed early on in his career. His first private hedge fund had gone down in flames. The project had been a poorly constructed pyramid scheme and it had collapsed. But he had managed to escape the feds by arranging for his partner to take the fall.

Grayson had survived the disaster and he had learned from his mistakes. He had gone on to reinvent himself.

Just as I did, Lucan thought. Like father, like son.

Grayson bought and sold large houses not because he needed them but because they were testaments to his wealth and power. Sometimes he acquired one merely as a venue to showcase his latest wife. Each of the four Mrs. Grayson Tazewells had been prettier and younger than the last. He had discarded the fourth Mrs. Grayson less than a year ago and had been in the market for a fifth when he had discovered the impending financial disaster.

In addition to the faux Mediterranean château in the northern California wine country, there were the sprawling beachfront estate in the Hamptons, a compound on the island of Lanai in Hawaii, a New York City penthouse with views of Central Park and, the latest acquisition, a dead movie star's mid-century modern classic in Beverly Hills.

Grayson also liked yachts but, unlike his properties, he maintained only one luxury vessel at a time. As was the case with his wives, however, he upgraded regularly, naming each new, larger yacht in honor of the original, *The Phoenix.* The latest Tazewell yacht was *The Phoenix IV.* He had been discussing designs for *The Phoenix V* when he had been blindsided by the realization that his empire was about to disintegrate.

Lucan contemplated the vineyards for a while, trying to calm the rage by focusing on his triumphant future. It was all so clear. When the project was completed he would possess everything that his father had built; everything that should have been his birthright.

He tightened one hand into a fist and gripped the nearest windowsill. After months of careful planning the entire project was now in jeopardy because of the failure of a couple of well-dressed mercenaries.

When he had found them on the Darknet, Devlin Knight and Victoria Sloan had appeared ideal for his purposes—trained, experienced killers with dreams of becoming as wealthy and powerful as their clients. It had been so easy to seduce them. All he had to do was promise them what they wanted most.

He was well aware that Victoria was starting to develop a sexual interest in him. It was not unexpected. Women almost invariably found him attractive. So did a lot of men, for that matter. Genetically he had hit the lottery with his high cheekbones, elegant jaw and brilliant blue eyes. Even now in his midforties he still had what it took to make people of both sexes look twice. But his looks were not his real superpower. It was his ability to convince them that he could make their dreams come true that drew people to him and made it possible for him to use them. He was always the smartest man in the room.

He reminded himself that he needed to tread carefully when it came to Victoria Sloan. Devlin Knight would become considerably less reliable if he thought he was losing his longtime lover and business partner to the client.

So many chain saws to juggle.

He really needed some fire. Just a little, to take the edge off.

He could not fight the urge any longer.

He went back to the desk, opened a drawer and took out a blank sheet of printer paper. He wadded the page into a ball, let himself out the glass door and walked across the stone balcony that overlooked the vineyards.

He was very conscious of the fact that he was not alone in the big house. Grayson had concluded that the emergency situation was so grave that a family war council was called for. To that end he had summoned his other son—his legitimate son—the son he had always acknowledged as his real heir.

Easton Tazewell had dutifully arrived three days ago. He had been accompanied by his wife, Rebecca. The couple had flown down from Seattle.

In his growing paranoia and frantic desire to keep the true status of Tazewell Global a secret from the media, Grayson had let go almost the entire staff of the Sonoma house. Currently there was only a single house-keeper, who came in twice a week and went home early.

It was not just the household staff that had been severely reduced. Lucan had convinced Grayson that he could no longer trust the handful of assistants and financial analysts who had worked for him for years at the headquarters of the firm in San Francisco. They had all been fired. The remaining employees had been given a month's vacation.

Lucan tossed the crumpled paper into the firepit and flicked the switch, igniting the gas. The flames leaped, setting the paper ball ablaze.

He watched the small inferno, smiling a little in anticipation. After all these years he still got the rush of transcendent euphoria that he had experienced the very first time he used the power of fire to destroy the past and light the way to a bright new future. He had been sixteen years old. He could still hear the echo of the screams coming from inside the fully engulfed house.

He had left town with a nice little stake, primarily the money his adoptive parents had obtained from dealing drugs. He had assumed it would be a simple matter to discover the identities of his real parents. He had been wrong. It had, in fact, taken him several decades to learn the truth.

It didn't take long for the crumpled sheet of printer paper to be reduced to ashes, but it was enough. He was no longer feeling agitated and jittery. He was once again calm and clearheaded. Now he could focus.

He switched off the fire. He had work to do.

A new strategy was needed to deal with Jack Lancaster but now there was no longer the luxury of time. Too many moving pieces had been set in motion. Halting any one of them would put the entire project in jeopardy.

Once you had begun the process of destroying your family and taking control of the empire, you could not afford to pause or slow down. You had to keep moving forward.

Jack Lancaster could not be put aside until a more convenient opportunity arose. It was imperative to design a new, more straightforward
strategy. There were risks involved and it was far more likely that, by the
time it was finished, Anson Salinas and his two surviving foster sons
would conclude that Quinton Zane had, indeed, returned from the dead.
So be it.

He turned around, intending to go back into the study, but he paused
when he caught a slight movement in a window in the south wing. He
turned his head and saw Rebecca Tazewell watching him. Her blond hair
was mussed from sleep and she was wearing a bathrobe. Even from where
he stood, positioned above her on the tower balcony, he could feel the
heavy vibe of her suspicion.

Unlike most women, Rebecca did not respond to his charm or his
looks, but that did not really worry him. Grayson Tazewell had never ap-
proved of his daughter-in-law, so he was unlikely to pay attention to any
concerns she might raise. It was amusing to think that Rebecca had guessed
his endgame and knew that there was nothing she could do. She was a
modern-day Cassandra, able to see the future but cursed by the fact that
no one believed her.

Easton Tazewell had a few suspicions, too, but it was doubtful that
Grayson would pay any attention to him, either. The relationship between
the two had been strained almost to the breaking point when Easton had
made it clear that he did not want to take control of Tazewell Global.

Easton had moved to Seattle, married Rebecca, and founded a venture
capital firm that had done very, very well. But in spite of his successful
track record, or maybe because of it, his father had never forgiven him for
walking away from Tazewell Global. Yet, when faced with disaster,
Grayson's first move had been to summon Easton home. And Easton had
answered the call.

Got to love the power of family ties.

So now they were all gathered together in the wine country house.
The drawbridge had been raised and the moat had been filled with alliga-
tors to keep the financial media out. Grayson was not taking any calls or

meetings. He was not inviting friends to join him for drinks. He was not playing golf. He was holed up in the fortress of the Sonoma house with only the people he thought he could trust around him.

The trick was to make certain that Grayson did not realize the enemy was already inside the gates.

CHAPTER SEVENTEEN

———— ≈ ————

"Who is Quinton Zane and how could he be connected to what happened here in Eclipse Bay?" Winter asked.

She had been braced for something out of the blue because she knew Jack well enough now to know that his mind worked in unexpected ways. Nevertheless, he had managed to shake her. It was the dark intensity of his eyes that sent the warning.

For the first time since she had met him she began to wonder if maybe he was in the grip of a true obsession. Maybe he really was lost in a bizarre world defined by a conspiracy.

You know better than that. This is Jack. Give him a chance to explain.

"Wait," she said. "I'm cold. Let's go sit in front of the fire. You can tell me your story there."

Jack nodded once and got to his feet. They moved to the ancient sofa in front of the hearth. She sank down onto the well-worn cushions. He sat beside her, not touching her, and leaned forward, legs braced a little apart. He rested his forearms on his thighs and laced his fingers together.

For a time he gazed quietly into the flames. She waited.

After a while he started his tale.

"When I was twelve my mother got sucked into a cult that was run by a man named Quinton Zane," he said.

Winter was floored. "A cult? Really?"

"Zane referred to his operation as the first in a series of what he labeled Future Communities. There was no religious angle. It was all about money and power. Essentially the community was a pyramid scheme that operated online. Zane promised that everyone who joined—the true believers—would ultimately get very, very rich. Secrecy was imperative, so the members had to cut all ties with family and friends and live in a tightly controlled compound."

Winter shivered. "Naturally. First rule of a cult—isolate the members from all outside influences. Did your mother actually believe Zane?"

"In the beginning he convinced her that she and I were in mortal danger from a mob boss. He claimed to be a government agent who was in deep cover, playing the part of a cult leader, while he investigated the mob guy. By the time Mom realized the truth, it was too late. She and I were trapped in the compound where the members lived and worked. In the end, Zane torched the place. A lot of people died that night."

"Including your mother?"

"Yes, but her body was not found with those of the other women in the community. She was killed in Zane's private quarters, but not by fire. He shot her. No one knows why. All we know is that afterward Zane burned his whole operation to the ground."

"Oh, Jack—"

He ignored the small interruption. She realized that now that he had started, he needed to keep going.

"My foster brothers, Cabot and Max, and I and the rest of the kids in the community almost died that night, too, because we were locked up in a barn on the property. We realized later that we were essentially hostages. Zane had separated us from our parents in an attempt to keep them in line."

Winter took in a sharp, horrified breath. "How did you survive?"

Jack gazed into the flames. "Anson Salinas, the local chief of police, was one of the first responders. He used his vehicle to crash through the locked door of the barn. There were eight of us inside. Somehow Anson got all eight of us into his vehicle and reversed like a hound out of hell. The barn collapsed in flames moments later. Anson saved us, but he and the other first responders could not save everyone that night. My foster brothers, Cabot and Max, lost their mothers, too."

He stopped talking for a while. She did not push him. He had to tell his story in his own way.

After a time Jack resumed his tale.

"In the days that followed, various family members showed up to claim the other kids but no one came for Max and Cabot and me. We were officially orphaned. Anson offered to let us stay with him until the authorities could figure out what to do with us. When it became obvious that we were headed for the foster system and that we would be separated and sent to live with strangers, Anson sat us down and made us an offer we couldn't refuse."

"He offered to be your foster dad," Winter concluded gently.

Jack took his attention off the fire long enough to glance at her. "Anson saved the three of us—not just on the night of the compound fire but in all the other ways that boys need saving when they go through their teens."

"I understand."

"Zane's enterprise was designed to make money online. He got a thrill out of manipulating and controlling people, but at the same time he was trying to build a financial empire. He needed followers with certain business skills: people who knew how to move money around, how to invest it, how to construct shell corporations, how to deposit large sums in offshore accounts—that kind of thing. At the operational level he needed security. There were always armed guards around the compound."

"To keep people from leaving?"

"Yes. He also needed sales reps."

"What, exactly, did they sell?"

"A multistep program that was supposed to lead to enlightenment and financial success. It was the usual old-school mix of mystical psychobabble and positive-thinking shit repackaged into a modern-sounding formula for becoming wealthy. *Envision yourself rich and you will become rich.*"

Winter cleared her throat. "'Positive-thinking shit'?"

He grimaced. "Sorry. Old habits."

She almost smiled. "Baby steps."

"Right."

"At least I understand now why you were so skeptical about my positive-thinking philosophy when you booked that first appointment with me."

"Trust me, your version of positive thinking is a lot different than what Zane promoted," Jack said. He said it with feeling.

"Thanks for that much, at least."

Jack groaned. "Moving right along—at its core, Zane's program was a classic pyramid. The marketing was done online. The clients had to buy their way up through the various steps of the program, and one of the ways they did that was by bringing in new clients."

"Did Zane make a lot of money?"

"Sure. Well-constructed pyramid schemes usually do make money for those at the top, at least for a while. But eventually they collapse under their own weight."

Winter pondered that briefly. "You said Zane needed followers with certain kinds of skills. Did your mother have a particular talent?"

Jack turned his head to look at her again. His eyes were hotter than the flames on the hearth. "You could say that. She was a gambler."

"I don't understand," Winter said. "Why would Zane want a gambler in his cult? That seems . . . counterintuitive. Gamblers are losers."

"My mother was a very, very good gambler," Jack said quietly. "As in the kind of gambler who wins so often and so regularly that she was barred from the big casinos in Vegas."

"I see." Winter tried—and failed—to come up with a diplomatic follow-up question so she went with straight-to-the-point.

"Did your mother, uh, cheat?" she asked, trying not to sound judgmental.

Jack startled her with a short, harsh laugh.

"No," he said. "She didn't have to cheat, but she won on such a regular basis that the casino bosses assumed she was cheating. After she got banned from Vegas and Reno, Mom worked the smaller casinos up and down the West Coast. She was careful to win only small amounts, but people in that world tend to notice players who win consistently, so we moved around a lot."

"You were with your mother while she was working the casino circuit?"

"Sure," Jack said. "Where else would I be?"

"With your father?"

"He died before I was born. I never knew him or any of my relatives on his side of the family. His folks did not approve of my mother. In fairness, not many families would welcome a professional gambler into the clan."

"Sort of like welcoming a hypnotist into the family, I suppose."

"Maybe. My mother had an aunt who looked after me when I was little but after she died, Mom took me with her when she went on the road."

"What about your education?"

Jack's mouth curved faintly. "You could say I was homeschooled. Mom liked to read, so I learned to read, too. And I got a very, very good grounding in mathematics and probability theory."

"From a very successful professional gambler." Winter whistled softly. "Your mother was like you, wasn't she? She had an intuitive grasp of chaos theory. She could calculate probabilities in her head."

"In another life I think she would have ended up in the academic world. Instead, she discovered Internet gambling. Seemed like a good idea at the time because it meant we could finally settle down. All Mom needed was a computer. I was looking forward to attending a real school when Zane showed up looking for my mother."

"How did he find her?"

"Online," Jack said. "He had been exploring online gaming as a potential source of income. It didn't take him long to identify consistent winners and losers. When he stumbled across Mom, he realized that she was not just a lucky gambler. Initially he assumed that she had developed some complex algorithm or maybe figured out how to hack the online games.

Either way, he wanted her for his operation. He tracked her down and then he went into the con."

"He told her that she was in danger?"

"He convinced her that the head of an online gaming mob was convinced that she was cheating. Zane said the mob guy intended to kill my mother and me as a lesson to other gamblers who might try to cheat them."

"He convinced your mother that not only was she in jeopardy, so was her son. No wonder she panicked and agreed to join Zane's cult."

"The next thing we knew we were in the California compound and Mom was bringing in money hand over fist from various Internet gambling sites. Zane showed her how to create new identities at each site so that the Internet casinos could not spot her. And he told her that the whole operation was an elaborate sting set up by the FBI. After a while she realized that it was all a lie but by then it was too late. Looking back it's easy to see that my mother was an ideal match for one of Zane's favorite victim profiles."

"What was the profile?"

"A single woman with no close family, a woman with a specific skill set that he happened to need. He drew in men, too, but they tended to have another profile—the classic cult soldier who is compelled by the charisma of the leader and the promise of status and power."

Winter shuddered. "Such a system could not have endured for long. Sooner or later your mother and the other adults would have realized they had been conned."

"You'd be amazed at how many people will put their faith in a sharp con man and keep the faith for years. But, yes, some of the women did figure out what was going on. They wanted out. The problem for them was how to rescue the hostages."

"Their children."

"My brothers and I recently discovered that a small group of women came up with a plan to hide Zane's profits in an offshore account. The idea was to use the cash to ransom the kids. But before they could carry out the plan, Zane decided to torch the whole compound."

"Why?"

"We don't know what triggered his decision on that particular night," Jack said. "The only thing we know for sure is that Zane never got his hands on the money that the women concealed in the offshore account."

"How did you learn that?"

An ice-cold smile of satisfaction edged Jack's mouth. "Because that money was recently found and distributed among the eight people who were locked up in the barn the night Zane destroyed his operation."

"What happened to Zane?"

"Officially, he died in a fire on a yacht at sea."

"But you and your family don't believe that," Winter said.

"No. We've chased him for years—there have been hints that he's been living and operating in other parts of the world—but we've never found any solid leads."

"Do you really think you've got more to work with because of what happened tonight?"

"I think that there is a high probability that tonight was about me. If I'm right, you were a pawn to be used and then discarded. Collateral damage. It's classic Zane style."

"I feel the need to play devil's advocate here," Winter said. "If you were the intended target, why would Zane go to the effort of whipping Kendall Moseley into a frenzy and sending him after me?"

"I can't be certain of the details of the plan. Maybe I was supposed to die, too. I can envision a double murder–suicide scenario. Moseley kills you and then goes looking for me."

Winter stilled. "Moseley said something about killing me and also the man I was sleeping with. Except he didn't use the word *sleeping*. I thought he was delusional."

Jack nodded, absorbing that information. "So, the plan probably went something like this: After Moseley takes out you and me, Zane, or someone who is working for him, would use Moseley's own gun to kill him.

Very neat. Classic triangle. Obsessed man kills object of his obsession and the man he thinks is having an affair with her and then takes his own life. No loose ends for my brothers to follow. They would have been suspicious but they wouldn't have had any leads. And the cops would not have been interested."

Winter felt as if Jack had dragged her aboard a runaway roller coaster. She caught her breath.

"Isn't there at least a possibility that you're reaching for connections that don't exist?" she asked.

"Sure, there's a possibility that I'm wrong, but I need to find out for certain whether that is the case. Think about it from my perspective. What are the odds that an unknown person would use a chat room to goad a deranged man into trying to murder a woman who just happens to be my new next-door neighbor?"

"It's the coincidence of me being your neighbor that makes you think there's more to this than meets the eye, isn't it?"

"That's one thing, yes. But it's also the fact that Moseley brought two weapons with him last night—the knife and the gun. That doesn't ring true. Why not just one weapon? It's almost as if someone drew up a plan for him to follow."

Winter cleared her throat. "That's a reach, Jack."

"There is another detail that makes me think I'm on the right track."

"What is that?"

"The fact that the man who tried to murder you tonight died before he could talk to the cops. Talk about your amazing coincidences."

Winter took a slow, steadying breath. "At this rate I may have to spring for my very own tinfoil helmet."

"Welcome to the Zane Conspiracy Club. There's more that you don't know. A few months ago there were some incidents in Seattle that convinced me that if Quinton Zane was alive, he would be ready to come out of whatever hole he's been living in abroad and return to the States. But he has to know that he won't ever be safe here unless he gets rid of my brothers and me."

"Because, although everyone else thinks he died in that yacht fire, you and your family believe he's alive. You'll never stop looking for him."

"It's also a good bet that he knows I'm the one who is most likely to spot him coming."

"Because of the way you think."

Jack got to his feet and began to roam the small living room. "If I were in his shoes, I'd want to take me out of the equation first. I'd want to do it in a way that would be guaranteed not to provide Anson, Max and Cabot with solid leads, nothing that would point them or their associates in law enforcement in the right direction. To do that, I'd need camouflage. I'd need a strategy that would throw suspicion in an entirely different direction."

"A known stalker," Winter said. "Kendall Moseley."

"Yes."

"Whew. I'll say one thing for you: When you do conspiracy theories, you do them very impressively."

Jack went very still and watched her intently, not speaking. She knew he was steeling himself in the event that she rejected everything he had just told her.

"For the sake of argument," she continued, "let's go with the worst-case scenario and say you're right. What happens now?"

"We need to talk to the last person to see Kendall Moseley alive," he said.

"That would be someone at the hospital."

"The chief said there was a cop stationed outside Moseley's door. We should be able to find out exactly who came and went from the room."

"You think that the last person to see Moseley alive probably killed him."

"Yes. We need to move fast. We also need to be very careful. If Zane is out there and if I'm reading him accurately, he'll have real trouble processing the failure of his plan. He's not accustomed to screwing up. Failure will rattle him."

"You make that sound like it's a good thing."

Jack glanced at her. "He'll start moving more quickly in an attempt to get out ahead of the situation. That means he'll be motivated to take some risks, which, in turn, raises the probability that he'll make more mistakes."

"How do you know all this, Jack?"

"I've been studying him for years."

"In other words, you've been using your lucid dreaming ability to work out various scenarios."

Once again Jack stopped pacing and met her eyes. "Do you think that sounds a little crazy?"

"No," she said. "'Crazy' is an obsessed individual who tries to murder the object of his obsession. Kendall Moseley was a kind of crazy."

Jack looked satisfied. He went to the window and contemplated the early-morning light on the sea.

"There is one thing I know for certain about Zane," he said. "Whatever form his endgame takes, it will involve fire."

He unclipped his phone.

"Who are you calling?" she asked.

"We need backup," Jack said. "It's time to call home."

CHAPTER EIGHTEEN

———— ≈ ————

"I don't trust him, Easton." Rebecca let the curtain drop and turned away from the window. "He makes me nervous. Do you know what he was doing just now out there on the balcony?"

Easton pushed aside the covers and sat up on the side of the bed. "I assume we're talking about my long-lost older brother?"

Rebecca went to stand in front of the dressing table mirror. She wrapped her arms protectively around her midsection. Her pregnancy wasn't showing yet, but the hormones had certainly kicked in.

"Lucan just burned a wadded-up piece of paper in the firepit," she said. "Why would he do that at this hour of the morning?"

"I don't know," Easton said. "Could be any number of reasons, I suppose. Some information he didn't want anyone else to see, maybe."

She watched in the mirror as he climbed to his feet. He was grim-faced. She knew that he did not like being there under the same roof as his tyrant of a father.

Grayson Tazewell made no secret of the fact that he saw her as a threat and that he hoped there would soon be a divorce. It was the reason she and Easton had not yet told him about the baby. Grayson would be furious. Until the marriage, he had been convinced that he would be able to drag Easton back into Tazewell Global. Instead, the marriage had anchored Easton all the more firmly to Seattle and a future that did not include his father's company.

The news that Tazewell Global was in trouble had come as a shock but it was nothing compared to the jolt that had been delivered by the arrival of Easton's heretofore unknown half brother.

Easton got to his feet and moved to stand behind her. He put his hands on her shoulders and met her eyes in the mirror. She knew that he wanted to offer reassurance but he was not sure how to do it.

"Lucan makes me uneasy, too," he said. "But the Old Man thinks my half brother is the knight in shining armor who will save the company and everything that goes with it."

"I don't care about the business and neither do you."

"True, but the Old Man is obsessed with it. He spent most of his life building it."

"What are we doing here, Easton? Your father thinks Lucan can save the firm. Great. Let them do it together. They don't need us."

"We're here because I don't trust Lucan Tazewell any more than you do."

"Good luck convincing your father that his long-lost son doesn't have the best interests of Tazewell Global at heart. You saw Grayson at dinner last night. He hangs on every pearl that drops from Lucan's mouth."

"Lucan does speak the Old Man's language. Let's face it, Lucan is the son my dad always wanted. And, to be fair, I think it's entirely possible that Lucan does have the company's best interests at heart."

"Really?" Rebecca turned around. "You honestly think that Lucan materialized out of nowhere just to save Tazewell Global?"

"I think it's a strong possibility, yes."

"Do you think he actually feels some loyalty or affection or . . . or a sense of family connection to a father who had completely forgotten about him?"

"I doubt if it was any of those things that brought Lucan back to save the company. But it's entirely possible that his goal is to right the sinking ship."

"Why? He's obviously done very well on his own. He doesn't need a company that is on the brink of bankruptcy."

"I can think of one reason why he's offering to save Tazewell Global," Easton said.

"What?"

"Revenge."

"That doesn't make sense. How would saving the company be an act of revenge?"

Easton cupped her face between his hands. "Think of it this way—it would be a stunning act of payback if, when it's all over, Lucan is the one who ends up as the president and CEO of Tazewell Global."

She caught her breath. "You think he's here to take control of the company? That would absolutely shatter your father. It might even kill him. Tazewell Global is the only thing he cares about."

"Exactly. The company is everything to him. What better revenge than to take it from him and kick Grayson to the curb?"

"That's the real reason we're here, isn't it? You want to try to warn your father."

"It's all I can do." Easton released her. "But it probably won't work. Grayson is dazzled by what Lucan is promising. The Old Man wants to buy what Lucan is selling."

"You've got to admit that your half brother is a very, very good salesman." Rebecca paused. "What if he's a fraud? What if he isn't your father's son?"

Easton gave her a wry glance. "DNA doesn't lie. Dad had that checked out back at the start."

"You think that Lucan may be here because he wants to take control of your father's empire? That is . . . absolutely breathtaking."

"We sound like a couple of conspiracy theorists, don't we?" Easton said.

"Yes, we do. I don't know what is going on here but I do know you can't save someone who doesn't want to be saved. If your father is hell-bent on believing that Lucan is offering salvation, there isn't anything you can do."

"You're right, but I've got to give it one more try." Easton headed for the adjoining bath. "I'm going to take a shower and then I'm going to get on my computer and do some more research."

"Into what?"

"The companies that Tazewell Global invested in during the past year, the ones that suddenly seem to be bleeding cash."

"What are you going to look for?"

"I have no idea. But something doesn't feel right about any of this."

Rebecca gave a soft cry, moved forward and wrapped her arms around him. She pressed her face against his chest.

"Thank you," she said. "Maybe I'm wrong about Lucan. Maybe it's just my imagination. But I can't help it. He scares me."

Easton folded her close. "Regardless of what I find online and regardless of how my conversation with the Old Man goes, we're flying home to Seattle this afternoon."

Rebecca raised her head. "Because your half brother scares me?"

"Yes." Easton smoothed a few strands of hair out of her eyes. "And also because something you said a few minutes ago is starting to worry me."

"What?"

"You said that Lucan is a very good salesman."

"Well, given his business talents, that's not exactly a shock. Your father is an excellent salesman, too. How else do you get investors to put up millions of dollars on speculative purchases?"

"It occurs to me that Lucan might be more than just a great salesman."

"What are you talking about?"

"What if this whole thing is a setup? What if the Old Man is being conned by an expert?"

"That is also a rather breathtaking thought," Rebecca said.

"Whatever you do, don't say another word about it, not in this house.

I'll do my research, lay out whatever I find for the Old Man, and then we're leaving."

"What excuse will you give your father for our sudden departure?"

Easton smiled a little. "I'll tell him the truth. You're pregnant. You need to be protected from stress, and right now the situation in this house is extremely stressful."

CHAPTER NINETEEN

"What's your status there in Eclipse Bay?" Anson roared.

Jack winced and came to an abrupt halt on the bluff path. He held the phone away from his ear. Anson Salinas had an inside voice, but he had been a cop most of his life, which meant that, like an opera star or a drill instructor, he had another voice, as well—the one he had once employed to take charge of barroom brawls, emergency situations and, occasionally, three teenage foster sons.

Anson was no longer a cop. He ran the office of Cutler, Sutter & Salinas, the family's private investigation agency in Seattle. The business was starting to thrive in large part because Anson had turned out to have all the talents of a natural-born CEO, plus he had people skills.

His command post was the reception desk. Anson's was the first face that potential clients saw when they walked through the door. Most were reassured by his air of professional competence and his understanding manner. They sensed that he was a man they could trust with their secrets.

Jack figured the clients picked up on the same vibe that he and Max and Cabot had responded to intuitively on that long-ago night when Anson had driven straight into hell to rescue them and the other kids trapped inside the blazing barn. If Anson gave you his word, you could count on him to always have your back.

"And a bright and cheery good morning to you, too, Anson," he said. "Beautiful day, isn't it?"

"Who are you and what did you do with Jack Lancaster?"

"I'm trying to learn how to project a more positive vibe."

Anson's voice resumed normal volume. "Unless you've got some actual good news I'm going to have to assume you've been spending way too much time with your new meditation instructor."

Jack looked at the cottage at the far end of the beach path. Winter and Arizona had disappeared inside a short time ago armed with buckets, mops, scrub brushes and strong disinfectants. In small towns like Eclipse Bay there were no commercial services offering crime scene cleanup.

"Looks like I'll be spending more time with Winter," he said.

"And that would be because?"

"I just got word from the local chief of police that there appears to be some confusion as to the identity of the last person who saw Kendall Moseley alive. The consensus is that it was a janitor, but no one can locate her."

Anson grunted. "That's not good."

"No, it's not. That means I've got nothing new on this end, and until I figure out what's going on, I don't think it would be a good idea to let Winter wander off on her own."

"Think she's still a target?" Anson sounded thoughtful now.

"She's the only lead I've got so, yes, she may be in danger. It depends."

"On what?" Anson asked.

"On whether Moseley really was murdered last night. The hospital is standing by their verdict. They are convinced that Moseley died due to complications from a traumatic head injury."

"But you're not buying that," Anson said. It was not a question.

"There probably isn't going to be an autopsy," Jack said. "Not in a small town like the one where Moseley died, at least not unless I come up with something more than I've got now. Autopsies are expensive."

"Lot of drugs out there that wouldn't show up in a routine autopsy, anyway," Anson mused.

"Did Xavier come up with anything on Kendall Moseley?"

"Yep, that's why I'm calling. The kid is here in the office with me. He's been working his computer since you called early this morning. He's got some information for you."

The kid's name was Xavier Kennington. He was Cabot's nephew and he wasn't technically a kid. He had just turned eighteen and he was newly enrolled as a freshman in a college in Seattle. Officially he was an intern at the Cutler, Sutter & Salinas agency but in reality Xavier was pretty much the entire IT department. Jack knew that he and Anson, Max and Cabot were all competent when it came to conducting online searches, but none of them could navigate the dark territory of the Internet with the intuitive skill of an eighteen-year-old who had grown up wired into his phone and a computer.

"Let me talk to him," Jack said.

"Hang on," Anson said. "I'm putting you on speaker."

"I'm here," Xavier said.

The eagerness and enthusiasm in his voice made Jack feel old. Xavier was still young enough and fresh enough to get excited about the hunt.

"What have you got for me?" Jack asked.

"I confirmed what the local chief of police told you. Kendall Moseley had a history of violence against women. Sent a couple of girlfriends and an ex-wife to the emergency room. At least two restraining orders were issued. A year ago a judge ordered him to attend anger management classes."

"Obviously that didn't work," Jack said.

"No," Xavier said. "The point is, I didn't have any trouble digging up a lot of information about him online. He wasn't exactly trying to hide."

"In other words, anyone looking for a pawn to weaponize and use against Winter would have had to look no farther than her client list."

"Takes some doing to get a man worked up enough to go out and try to murder a woman," Anson pointed out.

"Especially when you consider that the deranged man in question had been given a post-hypnotic suggestion that should have made him disinclined to follow that particular woman."

"No offense to Ms. Meadows, but if I were you, I wouldn't put too much stock in the power of hypnosis," Anson said.

"I know you're skeptical," Jack said.

"I'm not alone. Hell, if hypnosis really worked, everyone who is trying to lose weight would be thin by now."

"Not everyone can be easily hypnotized," Jack said, going for an academic approach. "Studies show—"

"Forget the studies," Anson said. "Here's what I know—stalkers have a lot of loose screws. The one thing you can be sure of is that a guy like Kendall Moseley isn't going to forget about the object of his obsession just because someone gave him a post-hypnotic suggestion. Not for long, at any rate."

"We also know that Zane was brilliant when it came to manipulating people," Jack said. "He might have encountered a little resistance at first because of the hypnotic suggestion, but in the end, Moseley probably would have been nothing more than a puppet."

"And Zane would have been the puppet master," Anson concluded. He paused. "You really think you were the main target last night?"

"If Zane was involved, yes. If not, well, it's over."

"You know that I'm a founding member of the Zane Conspiracy Club," Anson said. "But I feel it's my job to keep you and Cabot and Max and young Xavier here from shooting at shadows."

"I know," Jack said. "You're the one in charge of common sense. That's why you have the corner office and the big window. Talk to me, Xavier. What else did you come up with?"

"Moseley spent a lot of time in some real sick chat rooms," Xavier said.

"No surprise there," Jack said. "It's his chat room friend I'm after. Did you find him?"

"Not yet, but I'm still looking," Xavier said. "I've got a couple of leads. Moseley was so thrilled with his special chat room friend that he mentioned him in some of the other chat rooms he visited."

Anticipation crackled through Jack. "Any chance you might be able to find the friend?"

"Maybe," Xavier said. "I can't guarantee it, though. Unlike Kendall Moseley, the friend knows how to hide."

"We know Zane has always been good at navigating online, but he's in his late forties now," Jack said. "That means he's not the whiz kid that he was in the past. My money's on you, Xavier."

"Thanks," Xavier said. "But even if Zane isn't as slick as he once was, you should probably consider the possibility that he may have hired himself some cutting-edge talent."

"I doubt it," Jack said. "He won't trust anyone with an online identity that could be traced back to him. He can't afford to take that kind of risk. He would be opening himself up to blackmail, for one thing. No, if he's out there, he will be his own IT department. I'm sure of it. But that doesn't mean he will be working alone. He hides behind people. It's one of the primary aspects of his signature."

"That brings up an interesting question," Anson said. "How did he assemble a new team here in the States without us noticing? We've been watching for him for years. Think he brought people with him from wherever he's been hiding out?"

"Maybe," Jack said. "But that would be tricky. He needs people on the ground here who can blend into the background. Anything else?"

Anson spoke again. "The kid and I saved the best for last. Thought you'd like to know that Xavier had some luck with that old photo of Zane."

"I remember," Jack said. "The one that Cabot found when he investigated the death of that artist a while back."

"There was a name on the back," Xavier said. "Jason Gatley. Couldn't find it in any of the old phone directories but Anson told me that you think Zane probably grew up here in Washington State."

"That's our theory," Jack said. "We're going with it because we know he fired up his first big con—the cult—just outside of Seattle. That was when he was in his early twenties. Makes sense that he would have started out on his home turf, a place where he knew the territory."

"I decided to do a search of Washington State high school yearbooks," Xavier said. "The good news is that a lot of yearbooks have been digitized."

"People who research their ancestry love them," Anson said.

"Anson and I went through every single yearbook that we could find for Washington high schools that date from around the time that we figured Zane would have been a student," Xavier continued. "We didn't find any matches. We were starting to think that Zane hadn't grown up in Washington after all. And then Anson had a really cool idea. He suggested we look at high schools that had a history of having lost their student records in a fire, schools that had not gotten around to digitizing their old yearbooks."

"Brilliant idea, Anson," Jack said.

"Should have thought of it earlier," Anson said. "We found a handful of schools that had some fire damage. Finally came up with a solid hit. Tell him, Xavier."

"Gatley attended a small, rural school in Eastern Washington," Xavier said. "The school was closed years ago. Luckily I was able to track down a former teacher. Anson talked to her."

"She remembered Gatley," Anson said. "She says she was sure that there was something wrong with the boy but it was nothing she could put her finger on. She just figured he would end up either very, very rich or in prison."

"The problem," Xavier continued, "is that the trail ends there in that small town. Anson and I couldn't find any leads. Gatley or Zane just disappeared at some point in his senior year in high school."

"People can still vanish if they know what they're doing," Jack said.

"And if they know how to rewrite their own personal history," Anson added. "Looks like that's what Jason Gatley, aka Quinton Zane, did. There is no record of him ever getting a driver's license. No college records. No property tax records."

"But you did find something, didn't you?" Jack asked.

"How did you know?" Xavier asked.

"Call me psychic. Probably a side effect of all that meditation I've been doing lately."

"Whatever. Get this," Xavier said. He was trying to sound as cool and professional as Anson but excitement crackled in his voice. "It looks like Jason Gatley was adopted at birth in a private, off-the-books transaction."

Jack registered another ping somewhere on his private mental Internet.

"Now that," he said, "is very interesting. How did you come up with that information?"

Anson chuckled. "No records doesn't mean there are no memories and it doesn't mean that people won't talk. I had a chat with the chief of police of the town where Gatley grew up. He's retired now and living in Arizona. But when I got a hold of him, he was more than willing to talk. He said a couple named Gatley who had never had children showed up one day with an infant boy. They claimed the baby was a nephew and that the mother had died but the gossip in town was that they bought the kid on the black market."

Jack tightened his grip on the phone. "Did you find any family connection?"

"No," Xavier said. "The baby just appeared out of nowhere."

Anson cut in with the rest of the story. "The cop I spoke with said pretty much the same thing the teacher said—that it was obvious as the kid got older that he was going to be trouble. The chief figured the boy would end up dead or in jail. Then he realized just how smart Gatley was and he revised his assessment. Decided the kid might become a killer. He said everyone in town breathed a sigh of relief when Gatley vanished."

"Did the chief have any idea of where Gatley was headed when he left town?" Jack asked.

"No," Xavier said, barely able to contain his adrenaline high, "but get this: Gatley disappeared shortly after the couple that adopted him died in a house fire."

Another ping. Jack got a cold rush of certainty.

"People don't change their personal currents," he said softly.

"The chief told me that he always suspected that Gatley was responsible for the fire that killed his adoptive parents," Anson concluded. "But there was zero evidence."

"We need to know more about that adoption," Jack said.

"We're still looking," Anson said. "But we don't have any leads at the moment, and I've gotta tell you, I doubt we'll find any."

"What about the Gatley couple?" Jack said.

"Nothing," Xavier said. "I couldn't even find tax records. If that's Zane's work, the guy is good."

Anson snorted softly. "I might be able to turn up a few more people who remember Zane as a kid but I don't think it would add much to our profile."

"I agree," Jack said. "Keep your heads down, both of you. We have to assume that Zane is watching."

"Pretty sure the phones are safe," Xavier said. "I've got the latest encryption on all of them."

"Are Cabot and Max working cases at the moment?" Jack asked.

"Yep," Anson said. "Corporate business has been brisk ever since the Night Watch case. Cabot's on a missing person job for a very wealthy entrepreneur. The family doesn't want any publicity."

"Max is trying to find a pair of swindlers who scammed a group of senior citizens out of their life savings," Xavier said. "The seniors don't want their relatives to know what happened. You know how it is."

"The victims don't want to be humiliated in front of their families," Jack said. "They're afraid they'll be declared incompetent."

"Right," Anson said. "But Max and Cabot will drop everything to head to Eclipse Bay if you need them."

"Keep them in the loop but tell them I think it's crucial that they don't react at this point," Jack said. "If Zane is watching and concludes that we suspect he was behind the attack on Winter, there's a forty or fifty percent probability that he'll leave the country. If he does, we'll lose him again."

"Only forty or fifty percent?" Xavier asked. "Why isn't it ninety or a hundred percent probability that he'll run?"

"Because I think he's committed now," Jack said. "He'll have a hard time turning back."

"You got a plan?" Anson asked.

"Working on one," Jack said. "I'll call you back when I have a better idea of what I'm doing."

Silence hummed for a moment.

"Call soon," Anson said.

He ended the connection.

CHAPTER TWENTY

Jack clipped the phone to his belt and stood looking down at the thrashing surf. The wild waves appeared chaotic; all the more so today in the wake of the storm. But the reality was that they were the end result of the spectacularly complex network of currents generated by the unfathomable power of the world's oceans.

There were fierce forces at work but there was also a rhythm, a pattern. If you had enough data you could unravel the deepest mysteries of the sea. Theoretically, if you had enough data you could predict a rogue wave.

Sometimes he wondered if he had followed the wrong career path. He could have lost himself in the study of fluid dynamics. Instead, he had immersed himself in the deep, dark undercurrents of the criminal mind.

Then again, maybe he had never really had a choice. Winter claimed that in order to do his best, most satisfying work, he had to heed the call of the inner voice that urged him to explore certain kinds of crimes. He had to work the cold cases, the cases that kept people awake at night.

He understood the dark lure of what Winter labeled his "mission." But he had studied enough bad guys to know that there were serious risks involved. He wondered if Winter realized that his *mission* was damn close to what could be described as a compulsion. And compulsions were driven by very deep, very dark currents.

He told himself that he could always swim back to the surface. But what if he got caught in a riptide and became disoriented, like a diver hit with the unpredictable effects of nitrogen at depth? The poetical term for it was *rapture of the deep*. The slang was *narced*. It could thrill you or terrify you. It could also kill you.

"Jack?"

Winter's voice yanked him out of the dark thoughts. *Back to the surface.*

He turned away from the crashing waves with a sense of relief and watched her come toward him. The dark fire of her hair was tightly bound up under a scarf to protect it from the cleaning operation. The old-fashioned apron that Arizona had provided covered her from throat to knee. For once she was not wearing all black. She had on an old, faded pair of jeans and a plaid flannel shirt. Her hands were sheathed in oversized cleaning gloves.

Beautiful, he thought.

At the sight of her the ominous darkness that hovered at the edge of his own personal Darknet receded. The crisp, blustery day got a little brighter. And suddenly the currents of his investigation began to come into sharper focus.

"How's the cleanup going?" he asked.

"It's not as bad as I thought it would be." Winter came to a halt in front of him. "Most of the blood was soaked up by the rug under the coffee table. We wrapped it in the sheet of plastic that AZ brought with her. She's going to discard it in the town dump. I'll never be able to look at the coffee table the same way again but AZ understands. She promised to replace it. Aside from that, it's mostly a matter of sweeping and straightening."

"Good." He glanced at the cabin and then looked back at her. "Did you come out here to take a break?"

"No." She searched his face. "I came out here to see how the conversation with your foster dad went."

And maybe because she had seen him standing on the edge of the bluff, looking down at the surf, Jack thought. The possibility that she might suspect he was a little unstable was starting to really piss him off.

He reminded himself that at the moment he had other priorities.

"Here's what I've got, based on what I know about Zane," he said. "If he's back and making big moves like the one last night, it's because he feels safe, in control of the ground. And because he thinks he's well hidden."

"But you think the screwup last night will agitate him, maybe cause him to take some risks."

"Right."

"I keep wondering why he would try to come back in the first place. You said he's an expert on running cons and pyramid schemes. Do you think maybe there's a lot of money at stake?"

"No—or, at least, it's not just about the money."

"You seem very certain of that," Winter said. "But con men are all about the money, aren't they?"

"No, that's a secondary objective. The real rush for a con artist is the thrill of manipulating the mark. Trust me, if making another fortune was Zane's goal, it would be easier and much safer for him to continue operating abroad. He knows that."

"What else would draw him back?" Winter asked.

"If Zane is back, it's because there is something he wants very badly, something he can't get living on another continent. Sooner or later I'll figure out what that is. In the meantime, I don't think he'll pull the plug and walk away because of what happened last night, not unless he feels he has no choice."

"Are your brothers going to start investigating, too?"

"I told Anson to keep them in the loop but I don't want to pull Max and Cabot in on this just yet. We need to verify that Zane really is behind Moseley's attack on you."

Winter gave him a knowing smile. "This time Zane is the mark. You're going to try to draw him out into the open, aren't you?"

"Thus far no one seems to have a better idea."

"I admit I'm not an expert on this kind of thing but it looks like Kendall Moseley is your only good lead."

"Right."

"You're going to go down to California to start digging into his life, aren't you?"

"Yes," Jack said. "I want you to go to Seattle and stay with Anson for a few days."

"No," she said.

"Winter—"

"You need me," she said. "You're going to be interviewing the people at the spa where I used to work, including Raleigh Forrester. I can tell you right now he's not going to be cooperative. But I can lean on him for you."

"You're going to *lean* on your former boss?"

"Yep."

"How, exactly, do you propose to lean on him?"

"It's complicated," Winter said smoothly. "But here's my logic. If I go with you, anyone who happens to be watching us—Zane, for instance— will most likely assume that we have concluded that the attack last night was, indeed, aimed just at me. If you send me to Seattle and then travel down to California by yourself, Quinton Zane will have every reason to wonder if you're looking for him."

"Your logic leaves a little something to be desired."

"Keep listening. If we do it my way, Zane can still tell himself that we aren't looking for him, not yet, at any rate."

"What makes you so sure of that?"

"Because, unlike you, I've got a really good reason to go back to California."

"What's that?"

"Now that I'm no longer hiding from Moseley, I'm free to collect my last paycheck from Forrester and pick up the things I had to leave in a self-storage locker. I want my red sofa. I think it will look great in my cottage."

"Don't you think the fact that I'm traveling with you will make Zane wonder about what is going on?" Jack asked.

"Maybe," Winter said. "But it's also possible he'll believe what everyone else in Eclipse Bay believes."

"What?"

"That you and I are involved in a torrid affair."

"As cover stories go, it's damned weak."

"Face it, Jack. This is your only real shot at keeping Zane in the dark. If you ship me off to Seattle, he will know for sure that you suspect him. There is no other reason why you would send me to stay with your family—not now that the guy who attacked me is dead."

"Damn."

"Got a better idea?"

"Well, no."

She smiled. "Don't worry, I can take care of myself. We'll make a great team. You'll see."

"Uh-huh."

"Good. It's settled, then. When do we leave?"

"We both need sleep. Neither of us got any last night. We'll drive to Portland this afternoon. Spend the night at an airport hotel. Fly down to the San Francisco Bay Area first thing in the morning. Rent a car—"

"Van."

He paused. "Van? Why the hell do we need a van?"

"I'm going to pick up my things at the storage locker, remember? It's part of our cover story."

"You've got enough stuff to fill up a van?"

"We'll need the van for my sofa."

"That means we'll have to drive back here to Eclipse Bay."

"I can drive the van if you'd rather fly."

He groaned. "Never mind, we'll figure it out. Right now all I care about is that we're at the front door of the Cassidy Springs Wellness Spa sometime tomorrow."

Enthusiasm glinted in Winter's eyes. "Raleigh Forrester will be there and he won't be expecting us. We can take him by surprise. That's settled, then. I'd better go help AZ. I have to tell you, she tackled the cleanup job like a pro."

"A pro?"

"Between you and me, I don't think this is her first experience with cleaning up a crime scene. She knew just what to do with the blood spatters."

Jack glanced past Winter. He watched Arizona haul a black plastic trash bag out onto the front porch.

"Obviously a woman with a lot of hidden talents," he said.

Arizona noticed him and raised a gloved hand in greeting before disappearing back into the cottage.

Winter followed his gaze. "If I didn't know better, I'd think she was enjoying herself."

CHAPTER TWENTY-ONE

———— ≈ ————

Winter had held her breath when they checked into the airport hotel in Portland. She and Jack had talked about a lot of things during the nearly two-hour drive from the coast but whether they would share a hotel room was not one of them. She had sensed that Jack did not like the idea of letting her too far out of his sight but she had no idea if that translated into rooming together.

She should have known better than to waste time obsessing over how he would handle the delicate situation. At the front desk Jack did not request one room or two separate rooms. He asked for—and got—connecting rooms.

Sometimes you overthink things, Winter told herself.

But even the thought of sleeping in a room that was connected to the room in which Jack was sleeping would probably be enough to keep her awake half the night.

From her perspective, that single hot kiss on her front porch had changed a lot of things. Nearly getting murdered, however, and teaming up with Jack to find Quinton Zane had absolutely upended her world. She was flying.

She decided she should probably meditate before she tried to sleep.

They ate an early dinner in the hotel restaurant and went upstairs. Without comment Jack unlocked the door between the rooms and then he paused. He took off his glasses, yanked a handkerchief out of a pocket and proceeded to polish the lenses.

"I don't plan to do any lucid dreaming tonight, but sometimes, when I'm a little sleep deprived, for example—"

"Like tonight?"

He jaw tightened. "Like tonight. Sometimes when I'm a little sleep deprived or when I'm really involved in a case—"

"Which you are at the moment."

"Yes." He exhaled slowly, slipped on his glasses with exquisite care and fixed her with a steady, determined look. "Sometimes under those circumstances I sleepwalk. In the past when I've done that I've always been inside the fire maze."

"Interesting."

"Actually, it's a pain in the ass because people who are unlucky enough to catch me in the act always freak. I guess I'm a scary sight."

"I understand," she said. "If you start to sleepwalk, I'll wake you up."

"No." He looked alarmed.

"What if you leave your room and go out into the hall? We don't want hotel security wondering what the heck is going on," she said.

"That's unlikely."

"Why?"

"I've never actually gone through a closed door while I was sleepwalking. I have enough awareness of my surroundings to prevent myself from doing that. But I have walked through open doors so I'm telling you to keep your door closed. If you do hear me moving around and if it makes you feel uncomfortable, you can always lock your door."

She understood that he didn't want her to see him in a sleepwalking state. It would embarrass him.

"I'm sure it won't be necessary to lock my door," she said gently. "Good night, Jack."

He nodded once, very brusque, and started to retreat into his own room, pulling the door closed behind him.

"Good night," he said.

"Oh, Jack?"

He paused. "What?"

"Don't forget your escape word. Repeat it to yourself just before you go to sleep. Meditate on it for a moment. With your lucid dreaming ability you should be able to call it up if you need it."

He frowned. "The escape word is for my intentional dreams in Ice Town. My problem is with the old fire maze dream."

"Your special word will work there as well. If you get lost in that maze dream, just look for the word. It will be there. You will find it."

"Huh," he said.

"What?"

He smiled a little. "Did you just try to hypnotize me to reinforce my escape word?"

She was shocked. "No. I would never do that, not without your permission."

"Whatever. But just so you know, I've got my escape word down. I'm not going to forget it. Ever."

He closed the door.

She got undressed and went through the getting-ready-for-bed ritual. By the time she emerged from the bathroom, face scrubbed, teeth brushed and wearing her nightgown, the adjoining room was very quiet. Jack was probably already in bed and, no doubt, asleep.

She turned out the light in her own room, opened the curtains and sat down on the edge of the bed.

For her, meditation was not about trying to empty the mind. She had long ago decided that was not only impossible, it made no sense. The brain could not be turned off except by death. Awake or asleep or meditating, it hummed along, working 24/7. Sensory input was received, processed and analyzed. Logical connections and intuitive leaps were made. Information was organized. The vital functions of the body were serviced and maintained. Above all, it did its most important job—it maintained a coherent vision of reality, and it somehow did that in both the dream state and the waking state. The two realities were experienced very differently but, astonishingly, each worked. Mostly.

She focused on her breath and slipped into the light, self-induced trance with the ease of long habit, practice and natural talent.

Memories surfaced. She let them come . . .

. . . *The two women looked as if they had just walked out of a jungle, boarded a couple of long-haul flights and caught an airport cab that had driven them straight to the social worker's office. They wore jungle trek gear—utility trousers and shirts studded with zippered pockets, scuffed boots and floppy, wide-brimmed hats. They each gripped a canvas duffel bag.*

Both were in their midthirties. One was tall with light brown hair and a sharply etched profile. The other was shorter and built along compact, wiry lines. Her hair and eyes were very dark.

The light of the overhead fixtures gleamed on the matching gold wedding rings on their hands.

"Aunt Helen." Alice leaped out of her chair. "Aunt Sue. I told them you would come and get us. They didn't believe me."

"Hello, sweetie." The tall woman opened her arms. "I am so sorry it took us so long to get here."

Alice flew across the room and flung herself into the arms of the tall woman first, and then she hugged the shorter one.

The tall woman looked at the social worker. "I'm Helen Riding. This is my wife, Susan. We were working in a village upriver at the time of the plane crash. We didn't find out what had happened until we took a canoe back down the river to the town to pick up supplies. There was a message from the foundation. That's when we learned that my sister and her husband had both died and that Alice had been taken into foster care. But when we got in touch with the foundation people, no one seemed to know where she was."

"That's because Alice and her friend, Winter, got lost in the system," the social worker said. "Rather deliberately, I think." She got to her feet to shake hands. "I'm Brittany Nettleton, the caseworker for the girls. I can't tell you how happy I am to see you."

Winter didn't know which of them—Brittany or her—was the most astonished to meet Helen and Susan Riding. Winter was pretty sure the social worker had shared her own doubts about the existence of Alice's aunts. The only reason she and Alice were in Brittany's office now was because a volunteer at a shelter had said they could trust her.

Alice had been determined to keep checking in with the system because she was convinced that it was the only way her aunts would be able to find her. She had been right.

"Alice said you would come," Brittany said.

"Of course." Susan put a comforting hand on Alice's small shoulder. "We would have been here long before now if we had known what happened."

"This is a somewhat complicated situation." Brittany glanced uneasily at Winter and then turned back to Susan and Helen. "I would like to explain things to you privately. Alice and Winter, why don't you two go down the hall to the lunchroom and get a soda?"

"Yeah, sure," Winter said.

She knew what was coming. By the time she and Alice returned, the situation would have been explained to the aunts. Brittany would take Winter aside and inform her that only Alice would be leaving with Helen and Susan Riding. Winter would be going to a different home.

Except that she wouldn't be going to a new foster home, Winter thought. She could take care of herself on the streets. In fact, she would leave right now while everyone figured she was getting a soda. That way she would not have to say good-bye to Alice. Wouldn't have to watch Alice cry. Wouldn't cry herself.

"I don't want a soda," Alice announced in a loud, ringing voice. "I want to go with Aunt Helen and Aunt Sue right now. Winter is coming with me, aren't you, Winter?"

Winter shrugged. "The system doesn't work that way, kid. Don't worry about me. I can take care of myself, remember?"

Alice ignored her. She faced Helen and Susan.

"Winter is my sister," she explained.

Brittany sighed. "Alice, you know that Winter isn't your sister."

"Foster sister," Alice clarified quickly.

"Not anymore," Winter said. She went to the door of the office and wrapped one hand around the knob. "You're out of the system now. You're going home."

Helen and Susan exchanged unreadable looks.

Brittany cleared her throat. "As far as I've been able to tell, the girls have been together for nearly two months now."

"In a foster home?" Susan asked.

"Not exactly," Brittany said. "They've got a history of running away. I think mostly they've been living on the streets. They're here now only because I promised them I would do my best to find the two of you for Alice."

Helen and Susan looked stunned.

Helen turned to Alice.

"You've been living on the streets all this time?"

"It wasn't so bad," Alice said with a touch of pride. "Winter and I took care of each other. I told you, we're sisters."

Brittany looked at Helen and Susan. "Two months on the streets is a very long time for a couple of girls their age. There may be some separation anxiety issues when Alice leaves with you. I'll make sure that Winter gets counseling."

Helen and Susan exchanged glances again. A silent message was sent and received. Susan smiled at Brittany.

"There's no need to send Alice and Winter down the hall for a soda," she said. "Winter will be coming with us—assuming that's what she wants, of course."

Alice gave Winter a triumphant grin. "Told you that my aunts would take both of us."

Winter had been about to open the door. She froze, a disorienting sense of unreality sweeping through her. It wasn't that simple. It was never that simple—not in the world she had entered when she had been orphaned.

Brittany fixed Helen and Susan with a considering look. "Are you sure you know what you're doing?"

Helen and Susan looked at Winter.

"Positive," Helen said.

Susan turned back to Brittany. "About that paperwork you mentioned—"

Brittany got a very serious, very determined expression and went back around behind her desk. She slipped on a pair of glasses, cranked up her computer and started tapping keys.

"I'll close out Alice's file today," she said. "That will be a straightforward matter. Family members took her into their care."

"What about Winter?" Alice asked.

Brittany paused long enough to peer over the rims of her glasses. "Under most circumstances that would be much more complicated. However, it turns out that Winter disappeared several times in the past year. I haven't had time to open a new file on her. Terrible backlog here in the office, you know. I don't see why she can't disappear again. If she wants to come back into the system, she knows where to find me."

Alice glowed and turned to Winter. "See? You're coming with us."

Helen smiled at Winter. "It's your choice, but why not give us a chance? We'll find a hotel. Susan and I need to get cleaned up and then we'll get some dinner and talk about what we're going to do next. If you don't like what you hear, you can always go back to the streets."

Winter braced herself. "There's something you should know about me."

"Okay," Susan said. "You can tell us over dinner."

Sometime later, halfway through an extra-large, family-size pizza, Winter told Helen and Susan about her talent for hypnosis. She was pretty sure it would be the end of the whole we're-all-gonna-be-a-new-family thing. They would assume she either had serious psychological problems or she was flat-out lying. At least she had gotten some pizza out of the deal.

"We think Winter might be a real witch," Alice concluded proudly.

"Not a witch," Helen said. She studied Winter with a thoughtful expression. "Everyone has a talent, but some talents are more complicated than others. We'll figure out what to do with your skill set, Winter. But with an ability that powerful you're going to need to establish rules for using it."

"Rules?" Winter said.

Susan smiled. "A code, one you can use to determine when and how to use your talent."

"Everyone needs a code to live by," Helen said.

"How do I figure out my code?" Winter asked.

"Don't worry," Susan said. "You will. That's part of what being a family is all about. Now, then, brace yourself, ladies. You're going to be homeschooled. Except you won't be at home, at least not very much of the time. You'll be with us in the field."

Alice's eyes lit up with excitement. "You're going to take us with you when you do your research?"

"We'll need to get passports for both of you," Helen said. "And some trek gear. There will also be a few shots involved. Oh, and Winter?"

"Yes?"

"Until you know what you're going to do with your talent and decide on your personal code, it would probably be a good idea not to mention the hypnosis thing to anyone outside the family."

"Okay," Winter said.

CHAPTER TWENTY-TWO

---≈---

Jack turned off the lights, got into bed and spent some time alternating between listening to the silence in the adjoining room and running scenarios for Quinton Zane's endgame. *Always assuming that my suspicions are correct.* At this point he did not have enough information to know if he really was chasing Zane or just another ghost.

When he was weary of telling himself he had to get more data before he concluded that Zane was behind the attack on Winter, he stopped and thought about Winter instead.

Eventually he fell asleep.

And plunged into the fire maze dream . . .

. . . The dreamer walked through endless hallways of molten lava, searching for the burning footprints that would tell him he was on the right path. From time to time he glimpsed a figure in the dark shadows of the flames but whenever he tried to pursue it, the ghostly silhouette vanished down yet another fiery hallway.

He stopped at the intersection of two corridors and listened carefully. Faint laughter echoed from somewhere deep in the maze. Zane.

The dreamer moved more quickly, following the sound. He told himself that he was closing in on his quarry but a part of him knew that he was rushing forward into a trap. Still, he went deeper into the maze because he was close . . . so close . . .

He turned a corner and found himself in the seething, flaming heart of the maze. Zane was there, waiting for him; smiling in triumph.

"Welcome to my world," Zane said. "I control everything here. You are on my ground because you walked straight into the trap I set for you."

"I don't belong here," the dreamer said.

"I'm afraid it's much too late for you to leave," Zane said. "This is like the Hotel California. You can check in but you can't check out."

The dreamer looked around, searching for the corridor that would take him back to the entrance of the maze. But everywhere he turned he saw only hallways of fire that dead-ended in walls of scorching flames.

He could not afford to panic. There was a way out. All he had to do was find the escape word.

A figure appeared at the end of a fiery hallway, beckoning to him. He recognized her instantly.

"Winter," he said.

And just like that he was out of the dream. Relief threatened to overwhelm him. He drew a deep, steadying breath.

"What's wrong?" Winter asked.

He looked around and saw her in the opening between the two bedrooms. The perspective was wrong, he thought. He was in bed. He should be viewing Winter from a different angle.

But he was not in bed. He was standing at the window. Winter was watching him anxiously. He looked down. At least he was not in a hospital gown and festooned with electrical leads this time, but all he had on was a pair of white briefs and a white undershirt.

"Shit," he said.

Well, at least she wasn't screaming. But, then, he had a feeling it would take a lot to make Winter scream.

"You were dreaming, weren't you?" Winter said.

"Yeah." He groaned. "Sorry I woke you up. I thought I told you not to come in here."

She was dressed in a long nightgown. Her hair was loose around her shoulders and her feet were bare. She looked way too soft and inviting.

He wished he had a robe to put on but there wasn't one.

"I heard you say my name," Winter said. "I thought you might need help."

"It was the damned fire maze dream. I didn't dream it on purpose. It was just waiting for me after I fell asleep."

"I was afraid it wouldn't go away quietly," Winter said. "You reran that dream many times. You spent time and energy constructing the maze. I'm sure the imagery is still very vivid for you. But it will fade as you become more familiar with your new dreamscape."

"Good to know." He paused. "The dream was different tonight."

"In what way?"

"For the first time I got to the heart of the maze. Zane was there, waiting for me. Laughing at me. He said I had walked into the trap he had set. He told me that this time I wouldn't be able to get out of the maze."

"Well, obviously you did."

He nodded slowly, unable to take his eyes off her. "I used the escape word."

"I'm glad it worked." Winter hesitated on the threshold. "Well, if everything is okay, I'll go back to bed."

"Winter."

She had started to retreat back into her own room but she stopped.

"What?" she said.

"That's my escape word. *Winter*. I used it tonight to end the dream. That's why you heard me calling your name."

"You used my name," she repeated softly.

He wondered if he had somehow managed to offend her. "Is it okay with you?"

She looked as if she had to give her answer some deep thought.

"Yes," she said finally. "Yes, it's okay to use my name. I mean, whatever works for you."

"It works for me."

"Good. That's good, then."

She started to retreat into her own room.

"Tell me the truth," he said. "Do you think that the dreaming thing means I might be borderline unstable?"

She turned back. "I've told you, I'm sure that what you do is a form of meditation or self-hypnosis."

"You're sure? Because I have to tell you, sometimes I wonder if I'm sunk so deep in the currents of my conspiracy theory that I can't see the true patterns."

She strode briskly across the room and stopped in front of him, inches away.

"Here's what I know," she said. "You were born to do what you do."

"Weave conspiracy theories?"

"No. One of my foster mothers once told me that everyone has a talent. Yours is hunting bad guys."

"I don't have any choice when it comes to this particular bad guy."

"Maybe it was Zane, the demon from your childhood, who ignited your passion for what is now your life's work. But a talent for hunting bad guys must have been there from the start. Sooner or later it would have manifested itself. It was just a matter of time. You not only found your mission, you have a code, and you live by that code. You are a decent man, a man of honor, Jack Lancaster. Do you realize how rare that is in today's world?"

He smiled. He did not know if it was the result of the incredible relief he felt because she hadn't screamed when she saw him surfacing from the maze dream or because she didn't think he was crazy. Maybe it was a combination of the two. Whatever the case, he felt good. Better than good.

He raised his hands to capture her face.

"I love it when you talk dirty," he said.

This time she was the one who smiled.

"In that case I must remember to do it more often."

"Winter."

She put her arms around him and raised her lips to his.

"Yes," she said. "Absolutely yes."

He covered her mouth with his own.

CHAPTER TWENTY-THREE

―――――≈―――――

The kiss was inferno-hot and soul-deep. It swept over her and through her, a storm of energy that intoxicated her senses.

She had been in a self-imposed trance for most of her adult life, afraid to trust a lover with her deepest secrets. But Jack's kiss shattered the invisible barrier that she had erected to protect her heart. The past and the future did not magically disappear but for now they could be set aside. Jack knew the truth about her talent and he was okay with it. He did not think that she was weird or delusional. He not only believed her; he was not afraid of her.

She was free to hurl herself headlong into the exhilarating torrent of desire. She returned his kiss with all the fierce, hot energy of a woman who had suddenly decided to take risks. She needed this kiss. She deserved it. She had waited long enough to find out what it was like to be caught up in the raw energy of passion.

Jack groaned and tore his mouth from hers. His glasses were still on the nightstand so there was nothing to mask the heat in his eyes.

" 'Tyger Tyger, burning bright,' " she quoted softly.

"What?"

"Not what, *who*. William Blake."

"You're thinking about poetry?" He sounded incredulous.

"Forget it." She slid her thigh up the side of his leg, tango-dancer style. Her nightgown rode high above her knee. "Kiss me."

"No problem."

He kissed her again, hard and deep. She tightened her arms around him. His heavily aroused body thrilled her. *She* had summoned this response from him, she thought. He wanted her. She was dazzled, euphoric; a little giddy at the knowledge that she had the power to command so much intense passion from a man who wielded so much self-control. It was even more exciting to know that she was capable of responding with equal heat.

With an obvious effort Jack took a step back and caught her chin with his thumb and forefinger.

"You look . . . fierce," he said.

It wasn't quite what she had expected him to say. He hadn't used words like *beautiful*, *gorgeous* or *lovely*. That was the thing about Jack. A man who was driven to find predictable patterns in others was himself unpredictable in some unexpected ways. He was right about one thing, though—she was feeling very fierce. Sultry. Intense. Hot.

She traced the unyielding line of his jaw with her fingertips. He did not blink—just continued to fix her with his relentless gaze—but she could feel the sensual tension that tightened every muscle in his body.

"Are you good with fierce?" she asked.

He bound one of his hands in a fistful of her hair.

"Fierce definitely works for me," he said. "Just like your name works for me. *Winter*."

The way he said her name—low and rough with desire—thrilled her.

He cradled her head in his palm, drew her closer and kissed her again. By the time he finished she could hardly catch her breath.

"What about you?" he said. "Are you good with fierce?"

"I think so, yes."

"You *think* so?"

"Never actually been there," she admitted. "Just sort of skirted the edges of it a few times."

He surprised her with a husky sound that was half exultant laugh and half sexy growl.

He caught her wrist, drew her to the side of the bed and hauled her nightgown off over her head. She thought that his hands trembled a little. The garment pooled at her feet.

He gripped her waist, the edge of his palms resting on the curve of her hips. For a moment he just looked at her.

"I knew you would be perfect," he said. "And you are. Perfect. I've been looking for you for a very long time, Winter. My whole life."

"I'm right here," she said.

She knew that his judgment was probably clouded by desire but in that moment she did not give a damn. Her judgment was most likely clouded, too. It seemed like a win-win, at least for tonight. Tomorrow could take care of itself.

She got him out of his white T-shirt and flung the garment across the room. His shoulders were sleek and powerful. His skin radiated a vital, elemental heat that made her want to wrap herself around him.

He drew his hands up her rib cage until his thumbs rested just beneath her breasts. Then, very deliberately, he caught her earlobe lightly between his teeth, sending the message that he could match her when it came to fierce. A shiver of excitement sparked through her.

Before she realized his intent he scooped her up in his arms and let her fall lightly onto the tumbled white sheets. He did not take his eyes off her as he got out of his briefs and cast them aside.

She was taken aback by the size of his erection but in the next instant fascination set in. She took him in her hand and stroked him.

He groaned and came down on top of her, bracing himself on his elbows. He began to kiss her thoroughly and completely. When he worked one hand down her body to the hot, wet place between her thighs, she shuddered. The little eddies of excitement deep inside her became a riptide, pulling everything tighter and tighter until she could hardly bear the tension.

She shifted beneath him and sank her fingers into the taut muscles of his perspiration-slick back. He wedged a leg between her thighs, opening her up to his ever more intimate touch. She raised one knee, issuing a silent invitation.

"You first," he whispered.

It was both a command and a promise. She was about to warn him that if they waited for her to climax first, they might be there indefinitely. But before she could get the words out of her mouth he did something amazing with his fingers.

And she was lost.

She was not prepared for her release. It came out of nowhere, splashing through her, flooding her senses, stopping her very breath.

She was still dealing with the cascade of sensations when he thrust into her, going deep. She did not know if the shock of his entry triggered a second climax or simply extended the one that she was riding. All she could do was hang on tight.

Jack surged into her again and again before he sank into her fully, filling her completely. In that moment his body was so hard and taut he could have been channeling lightning.

She opened her eyes and watched him with a sense of wonder. A hunger for which there were no words sharpened the planes and angles of his face.

When the storm had passed, Jack collapsed on top of her, rolled onto his side and looked at her. There was still some fire in his eyes.

"Told you I was good with fierce," he said.

CHAPTER TWENTY-FOUR

———— ≈ ————

Winter raised her arms up over her head in a luxurious stretch that reached all the way to her toes.

"That was . . . amazing," she said.

Jack smiled. He looked very pleased with himself. "Yes, it was. Did you mean what you said earlier? That sex had never been fierce for you until now?"

"Yep. You?"

"The word *fierce* was not in my sexual vocabulary until tonight. What do you think that says about us?"

She levered herself up, pushed him onto his back and then leaned over him, folding her arms on his chest.

"I don't know what it says about you," she said. "But I do know what it says about me."

"I'm listening."

"It means that until tonight I've spent most of my life worrying that I could never trust any man with the truth about myself."

"The hypnosis thing? It got in the way of relationships?"

"Are you kidding?" she said. "Every damn time."

"Hard to believe."

"I've told you that I'm a very good hypnotist, but even you don't know the whole truth about me."

"Is that right?" Jack tangled his fingers in her hair. "So what is the whole truth?"

"When I was fourteen years old I almost killed a man."

"With hypnosis?" Jack sounded intrigued but not alarmed. "How does that work?"

"My subject, if you want to call him that, was a foster parent in one of the homes where I was staying for a while. He tried to assault another girl who was sleeping in the same room with me. I frightened him. In hindsight, I think I must have caused him to suffer a panic attack. I made him believe that his heart was failing. He lost consciousness. I thought he might be dead. He wasn't but I didn't find out for several days that he had lived, because Alice and I took off that night."

"Impressive. Who is Alice?"

"My foster sister." She waited. When he didn't offer anything more she felt compelled to push a little harder.

"Is that all you can say?" she said.

"Is there anything else I should say?"

"My talent doesn't make you nervous, does it?"

"Should I be nervous?"

"No. But on a couple of other occasions I've made the mistake of telling a man what I could do with my ability. I felt I had an obligation to be up-front and honest, you see."

"Not always a wise policy."

"No, it isn't," she said. "The first time was with my first serious boyfriend. I was in college. We were talking about getting married after we graduated. My family had strongly advised me to keep my talent a secret but I didn't want to keep that kind of secret from the man I thought I was going to marry."

"I take it he did not react positively?"

"At first he thought I was joking. He insisted that I prove I could do what I claimed."

Jack groaned. "I'll bet he wanted you to run an experiment on him."

"Yep."

"He either wanted to prove that you were a fraud or that he couldn't be hypnotized."

"You guessed it."

"He was an idiot."

"I didn't put him into a deep trance," she said quickly. "I just made him a little . . . anxious. But when he realized what was happening, he went straight into a full-blown panic attack. It was horrible. I didn't know what to do. I managed to get him calmed down but when it was all over he dumped me."

Jack settled more comfortably into the pillows and folded one arm behind his head. "Was that all he did?"

"Well, he also said I should be locked up in a psychiatric hospital. Did I mention that he was majoring in psychology?"

Jack yawned. "Some people have no sense of adventure."

"There was also Dr. Edward Cresswell. He's a researcher who studies hypnosis. He has his own lab. I thought maybe he could help me figure out how to use my talent in a medical setting. He wanted me to give him a demonstration, too, but he wanted to observe. One of his research assistants volunteered to let me put him into a trance. I did."

"How did that go?"

"Pretty well. I told you I'm good. Cresswell was very enthusiastic about me and my ability. He gave me a job in his lab. I was thrilled. I thought I was going to be on the cutting edge of research into hypnosis. I thought I would be helping people. I thought that I had finally found my calling."

"Obviously the good times did not last," Jack said.

"It didn't take me long to find out that, until I joined her team, Cresswell had been falsifying his research. He had been making a good income off the grants he was receiving from private donors and foundations, but it was all a fraud, at least until I came along. People were starting to question some of his findings."

Jack raised his brows. "Because they couldn't replicate them?"

"Exactly. Cresswell hoped I could save his ass. My job was to convince the people handing out the grant money that his studies were accurate. I was supposed to give demonstrations to prove that the fake research was the real deal. I refused to cooperate in perpetuating the fraud. I handed in my resignation. Cresswell was furious. He managed to convince his colleagues I was a fraud. He smeared my reputation. I realized afterward that I would probably never be able to work in the field of hypnosis research again."

"Another career path down the tubes," Jack said.

"Yes."

"Was that when you decided to become a meditation instructor?"

"It was the only thing left that held any appeal. And now that may turn out to be a dead end, too."

Jack whistled softly. "You did tell me it was hard to make a living with your talent."

Something in his voice snagged her attention. She glared at him.

"You knew about my experience at Cresswell's lab, didn't you?" she said.

"They say you can find almost anyone online these days."

"But you booked a session with me anyway."

"I prefer to form my own conclusions," Jack said.

"Well, now you can understand why I'm anxious to get my own business up and running, not just because I want to find a good use for my talent, but also because I really don't want to work for someone else. I want to be my own boss."

"Right." Jack eyed her thoughtfully. "Do you mind if I ask you a personal question?"

She hesitated. "No, I guess not."

"Are you always this chatty after sex?"

"No," she said. "I just get up and go home."

"Same with me. Staying until morning changes the dynamic, doesn't it?"

"Makes it feel like it isn't just another date," she said. "Feels more like the start of a relationship, which is awkward because you're pretty sure it won't turn out to be the start of a relationship."

"Whoa." Jack held up a hand, palm out. "What happened to the positive thinking?"

"I hate to admit it, but that doesn't always work when it comes to dating."

"Well, one thing we know for sure tonight."

"What's that?"

"Neither of us is going to get up and go home," Jack said. "We'll both be staying until morning."

"Not much choice when you think about it," she said. She was aware of feeling rather wistful. "Extenuating circumstances and all that."

"That's one way to put it. Would you mind if I went to sleep now?"

She realized he sounded a little irritated. She wondered what she had said that annoyed him.

"No," she said. "I think maybe I can sleep now, too."

CHAPTER TWENTY-FIVE

---≈---

The receptionist behind the sleek front desk of the Cassidy Springs Wellness Spa was tailor-made to complement the lobby décor—trendy and stylish in a fashionable, minimalist way. Her blond hair was caught up in an elegant bun. Her flowy gray pants were topped by a kimono-like jacket belted at the waist with a white sash.

She looked up from her computer and fixed Jack with a polite, polished smile. Her teeth were so white and so bright he was pretty sure he could have used them to read a newspaper.

"May I help you?" she said. Then she noticed Winter. Her eyes widened and she jumped to her feet and gave a little squeal of delight.

"*Winter*. You're back. About time. It's so good to see you. Why didn't you text or call? It was like you just dropped off the face of the earth. I've been worried about you."

"Hi, Gail," Winter said. "I just came back to pick up my last paycheck."

Gail rounded the end of the white stone counter and hugged Winter. "I've missed you."

"I've missed you, too," Winter said.

Gail wrinkled her nose. "But you probably haven't missed working here, have you?"

"Well, no."

As far as Jack could tell, Winter had returned the hug with genuine warmth. He waited quietly.

Gail finally released Winter, took a step back and surveyed him with polite curiosity. He thought she looked a little wary now.

"Who is this?" she asked.

"Jack Lancaster," Winter said, "a friend of mine. Jack, this is Gail Bloom."

Gail smiled but Jack got the impression she had to work at it.

"A friend, hmm?" she said.

"A very *close* friend," Jack said.

"Uh-huh," Gail said. She turned back to Winter. "Good to know you haven't been spending all your time meditating on some remote mountaintop since you've been gone."

"It was a seaside, not a mountaintop," Winter said.

Gail glanced at the entrance to a hallway and lowered her voice to a conspiratorial whisper. "Are you coming back to this place? Because if that's your plan, I strongly advise against it. Just between you and me and your good friend Mr. Lancaster, I've got my résumé out."

"Why?" Winter asked.

"Forrester is still trying to sell the spa and that means he's not putting any money into it. Things are going downhill fast. You haven't been replaced. The acupuncturist quit a few weeks ago and most of the aestheticians are looking for other positions."

A woman emerged from the hallway. Unlike Gail, she did not rush forward to greet Winter with a warm hug. Something hard glittered briefly in her eyes.

"Winter," she said. "What are you doing here?"

"Long story, Nina," Winter said. "Jack, this is Nina Voyle. She handles the nutritional supplements and teas here. Nina, Jack Lancaster."

Nina was dressed in the spa's gray uniform. She was in her early forties but she had the smooth, sculpted features of a woman who spent a sizable portion of her salary on Botox, dermal fillers and maybe some other, more invasive procedures.

She nodded at Jack. "Nice to meet you."

"And you," he said.

Nina turned back to Winter. "You're wasting your time coming back here. Forrester is still pissed at you. And even if you offer to return to your old job I don't think you can save this place. It's fading fast."

"I'm not here to ask for my old job," Winter said. "As I was telling Gail, I just dropped by to pick up my last paycheck. After we leave we're going to get some lunch. Jack and I have a couple of errands to run and I'm hoping the manager of my apartment complex collected my mail while I was away. Then I'm going to get my stuff out of the Cassidy Springs Self-Storage. After that I'll be leaving town for good."

Gail's eyes widened. "Did you get a job in another spa?"

"No, I've decided to go into business for myself," Winter said.

"No kidding?" Nina looked skeptical. "How's that working out for you?"

Before Winter could respond, a man appeared from the hallway. His light brown hair was expensively cut. So were his trousers. His black crewneck pullover was formfitting. The sleeves were cut short to emphasize the muscles of his upper arms. His watch was gold and there was a large ring on his left hand. It was too flashy to be a wedding band.

"Winter," he said. He looked stunned at first. In the next second, relief appeared in his eyes. "You're back."

"Just dropped in to pick up that paycheck you owe me," Winter said. "Oh, and I also want to ask you a couple of questions. But first, meet my friend, Jack Lancaster. Jack, this is my ex-employer, Raleigh Forrester."

Raleigh acknowledged the introduction with a brusque, impatient inclination of his head and then turned back to Winter.

"What's going on here?" he asked.

"I thought you'd like to know that my life has gotten very exciting lately," Winter said. "I'm sure you'll hear the news eventually, but I wanted you to be among the first to know."

"Know what?" Raleigh asked, cautious now.

"Night before last, Kendall Moseley tried to murder me."

Raleigh stared at her. Gail's mouth fell open in shock.

"What?" Nina managed.

"The good news is that I'm alive," Winter said, widening her hands in a ta-da gesture.

"Did the police catch Kendall Moseley?" Gail asked, her eyes huge.

"Yes," Winter said. "Luckily, Jack, who happens to be my neighbor, realized something was wrong and came to my rescue. There was a struggle. Moseley was injured and taken to a hospital, where he died."

"You were almost *murdered*?" Gail whispered. "By Moseley? That's hard to believe."

Raleigh snorted. "Yeah, really hard to believe."

Winter gave him a cold smile. "I guess you had to be there."

"Hey." Raleigh took a step back. "What's that supposed to mean? You can't blame me for whatever Moseley did the other night."

"I told you he was dangerous," Winter said.

"Exactly," Raleigh said. "Obviously he was crazy. There was nothing I could have done to stop him."

"You insisted that I book a whole series of meditation sessions with him," Winter said. "*Private* sessions."

"He was a good client. I had no way of knowing that he was a whack-job."

"I told you that he was a whack-job."

"It's not like you're a trained psychiatrist."

"I've got news for you, Raleigh. You don't have to be a psychiatrist to diagnose crazy. You just have to be willing to look past the money."

"What do you expect me to do about it now? You said Moseley was dead."

"You owe me," Winter said. "I suggest that you and I and my friend Jack have a private chat."

"If you're talking about suing me—"

"Your office," Winter said.

There was a lot of steel in her siren-like voice but she wasn't trying to hypnotize Forrester, Jack decided. She was just making it clear that she was really pissed off.

"Fine," Raleigh growled. "I'll talk to you. But there's no reason to include your friend."

"Actually, there is a reason," Winter said. "Jack is looking into this situation for me."

"What's to look into?" Raleigh said. He shot Jack a suspicious look. "Whatever happened, it's finished, right? You said Moseley is dead."

"I'm just here to clean up a few details," Jack said.

Raleigh narrowed his eyes. "Are you a cop?"

"No," Jack said. "I'm a consultant."

Raleigh glared. "What kind of consultant?"

"It's complicated," Jack said.

He reached inside his jacket and took out three of the all-purpose business cards that he kept handy. For reasons that eluded him, people always seemed to take him more seriously if he presented a card. His read simply, *Jack Lancaster, Consultant,* followed by his phone number. He gave one of the cards to Raleigh and then offered the remaining two cards to Nina and Gail. Nina glanced at them but she didn't take one. Gail frowned and snapped one out of his fingers.

Raleigh scowled at the card in his hand. It was clear he wanted to refuse a private meeting but it was also obvious that he did not want to continue the confrontation in front of Nina and Gail, who were watching the scene, fascinated.

"All right," he snarled. "We'll talk. But if you think you're getting some kind of settlement from me, you're the one who's crazy."

He swung around and stalked down the hall. Jack and Winter followed Raleigh into an expensively appointed office. Raleigh stationed himself behind a steel-and-glass desk and fixed Winter with a grim look.

"What do you want?" he said.

"Two things," Winter said. "My last paycheck and the key to Kendall Moseley's locker."

Raleigh acted as if he hadn't heard the first demand. He focused on the second.

"I can't give you the key to Moseley's locker," he said with a righteous air. "Lockers are private. You know that. They are for the personal use of our clients."

Jack decided it was time for him to say something meaningful beyond *Hello, my name is Jack. I'm with her.*

"The client in question is dead," he said.

Raleigh gave him a dismissive glare. "I only have your word on that."

"Google it," Jack suggested.

"It doesn't matter if he's dead or not," Winter said to Raleigh. "As the owner of the spa you have the right to open a client's locker at any time. It's in the fine print on every contract that people sign when they take out a membership here."

Raleigh's jaw flexed. "What do you expect to find in Moseley's locker?"

"Gee, I don't know," Winter said. "Maybe some proof that Kendall Moseley really was an obsessive stalker."

"You think he'd keep that kind of evidence in his spa locker?" Raleigh asked.

"He was a crazy, obsessive stalker," Jack said. "There's no telling what he might have stashed in his locker."

Raleigh glowered at Winter. "Moseley's locker is in the men's dressing room. You can't go in there. We're busy this morning. Guys will be in there."

"No problem," Winter said. "Jack will go with you."

Raleigh leveled his gaze at Jack.

"You're not a member of the spa," he said.

"Don't worry about me," Jack said. "I think I can fake it."

"Members only in the locker rooms."

"Pretend I'm a prospective member and you're giving me a tour," Jack said.

Raleigh gave up.

"Follow me," he said.

Approximately two minutes later Jack stood beside Raleigh in the men's locker room. Together they examined the narrow metal cabinet that Raleigh had just opened.

"Shit," Raleigh said. He sounded genuinely shaken. "Winter was right. Moseley really was crazy."

In addition to the usual paraphernalia associated with a man's locker— deodorant, a shaver, a pair of shower flip-flops—there were photos. Dozens of them. Almost all of them were of Winter. They had clearly been taken from a distance and without her knowledge.

There were enlarged photos of her walking into an apartment building. Photos of her getting into her car. Photos of her coming out of a grocery store. Photos of her in the spa's parking lot.

There was also a single photo of Winter walking alone on the beach at Eclipse Bay. Jack saw one photo of himself, too. It showed him leaving Winter's cottage one afternoon.

"What the fuck?" Raleigh said. "Looks like there are little rips in all those pictures."

"Yes," Jack said. "It does look like that."

In every picture of Winter a sharp blade had been used to make a small, precision cut—right across her throat.

Jack pulled on a pair of plastic gloves and reached into the locker to pick up the two Eclipse Bay photos. Neither picture had been taken with the same camera that had been used for the photos of Winter in Cassidy Springs. The Eclipse Bay images had been captured by a high-powered telephoto lens.

Raleigh was clearly panic-stricken. "If word gets out that there was a crazy killer using my spa, it will be the last straw for this place. I'll be ruined."

"Yeah, could be a real promotion nightmare, all right," Jack said.

He shuffled through the photos but there was nothing else of interest. No helpful notes scrawled on the back. No names. No references to a mysterious friend.

He slipped the two photos that had been taken with a long-range lens inside his jacket and turned to leave.

"Hey, what do you think you're doing?" Raleigh called after him.

"Salvaging some evidence. Call me psychic but I'm getting a vibe that tells me that as soon as Winter and I leave the building today, you're going to clean out this locker and make all this evidence disappear."

Raleigh hurried after him. "I've got every right to empty this locker."

"Yes, you do," Jack said. "Good luck trying to keep this quiet."

CHAPTER TWENTY-SIX

Gail Bloom waited until Winter and Jack Lancaster left and got into a van parked in front of the lobby entrance. Then she looked at Nina.

"I'm amazed that Winter got that paycheck out of Raleigh," she said.

"So am I," Nina said. "It probably helped that she had Lancaster for backup."

"Yes. Lancaster was very helpful, wasn't he? I'm going to get some coffee. I'll be back in a few."

"No rush," Nina said. "I'll watch the front desk until you get back. Not like we're swamped with business."

"No."

Gail walked outside into the warm California sun but she did not go into the café next door. Instead, she kept walking until she reached the corner. She stepped into the shady side street. When she was sure she could not be overheard, she took out her phone and called the number the good-looking undercover detective had given her. He answered immediately.

"This is Knight. What do you have for me?"

"Winter showed up here today, just as you predicted," Gail said. "And she wasn't alone. A man named Jack Lancaster was with her. They got the boss to open Moseley's locker. I think they found some photos."

"Did Lancaster and the woman give any indication of where they were headed?"

"Winter said they were going to have some lunch and run some errands. After that, they are going to Cassidy Springs Self-Storage to get the stuff Winter left in a locker there."

"What are they driving?"

"A rental van. Guess they need it for Winter's things. Look, are you really sure she's in trouble?"

"Yes," Knight said. "Your friend is in a lot of trouble. But we'll take care of her. Don't worry, we're good at this kind of thing."

CHAPTER TWENTY-SEVEN

An hour and a half later Winter stood in the center of Kendall Moseley's apartment and watched Jack conclude his search. He had gone through each room of the place in typical Jack style—methodically and with attention to detail.

The good news was that, after Jack slipped the manager a crisp hundred-dollar bill, the manager had not objected to letting them look around. He had warned them that they probably wouldn't find much because the local police had paid a visit earlier that morning. He had only seen one evidence bag.

Jack emerged from the kitchen.

"Nothing," he said.

"If there was anything interesting in here the cops probably bagged it this morning," Winter said.

"No. They wouldn't have found anything, either, except what whoever cleaned up the place wanted them to find. Probably more photos and maybe the camera Moseley used to take them."

A chill raised the small hairs on the back of Winter's neck.

"You think someone got in here last night to make sure there was no evidence of the chat room buddy?"

"I think it's more likely that this place was staged shortly after Moseley left town to head to Eclipse Bay. Whoever was running him knew he wasn't going to come back alive."

"Where does that leave us?"

"It leaves us hoping that Xavier can pull up some online leads to Moseley's chat room buddy," Jack said. "Let's grab a bite to eat, pick up your mail and then get your stuff out of the self-storage facility."

"We're going back to Eclipse Bay?"

"I doubt it," Jack said. "But if Zane is watching, I want him to continue to believe that we are focused on Moseley and your sofa."

She cleared her throat. "Just so you know, I am focused on that sofa."

CHAPTER TWENTY-EIGHT

———— ≈ ————

"I really appreciate this," Winter said. "I hated leaving so much of my stuff behind. I had to put a lot of things into storage because I couldn't fit all of them in my car."

Jack glanced back into the shadowed interior of the van. It was, he reflected, a small space.

"You're sure everything in your locker will fit into the back of this vehicle?" he asked.

"Yes," she said. She unclipped her seat belt. "When you move around as much as I do, you don't accumulate a lot of things."

He thought about his own history of moving around. Currently he only traveled with what he could carry in his SUV.

"I know what you mean," he said.

"I'll get out and open the gate." Winter took a slip of paper out of the pocket of her jacket. "I've got the code."

She opened her door, jumped down to the ground and went quickly to the security box beside the big gate.

Jack waited, one hand resting on the wheel, and studied the sign that advertised safe, secure, climate-controlled storage lockers. There was an impressive-looking chain-link fence crowned with some coiled barbed wire around the facility but aside from that, the rest of the security appeared somewhat iffy. But he had been raised by a cop and his family was in the security business. He was inclined to be picky when it came to such matters.

The storage locker facility was located on the outskirts of town in a largely rural area. There were only two other vehicles in the parking lot. Both were parked close to the small office.

Winter got the gate open. She hurried back to the van and climbed inside.

"Looks like a prison, doesn't it?" she said.

"No," Jack said. "Prisons have better security."

He got the feeling Winter might have rolled her eyes at that remark but he couldn't be sure. He suspected she was focused on her precious sofa.

He glanced at the small office as he drove through the gate and into the yard. On the other side of the window he could see a woman sitting at a battered desk. She had her back to the view of the front gate, so he could not see her face, but something about her posture told him that she was probably in her early thirties, trim and athletic.

She wore a gray hoodie. Her dark hair was anchored in a ponytail. She appeared to be engrossed in whatever was on her phone. She was not paying any attention to the two security camera monitors mounted on the wall beside the desk.

"Don't you need to check in at the office?" he asked.

"No," Winter said. "When I rented the place they gave me the code. That's all I need to come and go. The place is open twenty-four-seven but the office is only staffed during the day."

Jack brought the van to a halt and waited until the automatic gate closed behind him.

He studied the large lockers that lined the exterior of the main building. They were designed for vehicles and boats.

"I assume your locker is inside?" he asked.

"Yes, it's in the climate-controlled part of the building," Winter said. "It can get cold here during the winter and hot in the summers. I didn't want to take any chances with my sofa. You have to be careful with upholstery."

"I'm looking forward to seeing this sofa."

"It's beautiful. I fell in love with it the first time I saw it. Had to max out my credit card to get it. I'm still making payments."

He wondered if she had ever fallen in love at first sight with a man but then he decided he probably did not want to know the answer.

"You do realize that credit card debt is the worst kind of debt because the interest rates are so high?" he said instead. "You could probably have gotten a better deal from the mob."

"Trust me, this sofa was worth it," Winter said. "Besides, it will be paid off next month."

So much for the financial lecture, he thought.

"The loading dock entrance is on the left side," Winter continued. "I've got the code for it, too. There will be some equipment inside that we can use to load my stuff into the van. It won't take more than a couple of trips to empty the locker."

"Does it occur to you that by this time in our lives we should probably have more stuff?" he said.

"They say a lot of stuff just weighs you down," Winter said.

But he thought she sounded wistful.

"Maybe that depends," he said.

"On what?"

"On whether you want to move on or put down roots."

"I'd like to put down roots, but things keep happening, so I keep moving on."

"I know the feeling," he said.

He drove around to the side of the building and stopped in front of the loading dock entrance. It was sealed by a wide metal garage door that could be rolled up when needed. A regular-sized door was located to the left of the dock.

He shut down the van's engine and climbed out of the vehicle. Winter was already at the regular-sized door, punching in another security code.

She got the door open, went up three concrete steps and disappeared inside. He followed her. A row of motion-activated fluorescent fixtures winked on, illuminating the interior space immediately around the loading dock in a cold, bluish light. The rest of the cavernous two-story facility was steeped in a gray gloom that filtered in through small, grimy windows set high up on the walls.

As was the case with the overhead fixtures, the service door at the top of the steps was on an automatic timer. Jack heard it close behind him. The muffled clang reverberated through the space, echoing off the concrete floor and the metal doors of the lockers.

There were two floors of storage lockers arranged in orderly rows of intersecting aisles. Signs marked the route to an elevator and a flight of stairs at the rear of the building that could be used to access the upper floor.

A couple of sturdy-looking motorized pallet jacks resembling small forklifts and an array of hand trucks stood near the loading dock.

"It's a real maze in here," Winter said. "The lights come on whenever you enter a new section. They shut off as soon as you move on. The place is sort of creepy when you're here on your own. At least it creeps me out."

I don't like it, either, Jack thought. But he did not voice his visceral response. His intuitive dislike of enclosed, tightly packed spaces with limited exits was one of his many quirks. He knew Max and Cabot shared that particular quirk. A history of having been trapped in a locked barn that was burning down around you left an impression on a person.

Winter glanced at the nearest pallet. "We'll need one of those for my sofa. Do you want to drive or shall I?"

He looked at the pallet. For the first time he started to take some real interest in the project.

"I'll handle the pallet," he said.

He stepped up onto the rear of the forklift-like device, where the accelerator and steering bars were located. Experimentally he squeezed the trigger accelerator. The hefty battery-powered motor hummed and whined. The pallet started to roll forward. He released the accelerator. The pallet stopped.

"This thing could carry a refrigerator," he said.

Belatedly he noticed that Winter was smiling.

"If you're going to make a joke about men and their toys, I should warn you that I will be hurt," he said.

"I won't say anything about men and their toys if you promise not to lecture me about the perils of credit card debt."

"I guess I had that coming."

Winter beckoned with one finger. "Follow me. My locker is at the back. The rent is cheaper there because it's an inconvenient location."

She set off down one of the aisles formed by two rows of storage lockers. Another bank of overhead lights came on, illuminating the path that led to the next intersection.

Jack revved the motor a little. The pallet rolled forward at a sedate pace.

Winter glanced at one side of the aisle. "Evidently not everyone gets the hang of driving that thing. Look at all the black marks on the bumpers."

Jack glanced at the bumpers that lined both sides of the locker canyon beneath the metal doors. A number of black smudge marks had been left by the pallet's thick tires. The bumpers were designed to deflect the wheels and keep the vehicle going in a relatively straight line so that it didn't crash into a locker. The pallet, with its heavy motor and steel carrying arms, was large enough to be a serious hazard. Given a little momentum it could easily punch a good-sized hole through the metal siding of a storage locker door.

"Don't worry," he said. He gunned the engine a little. "I'm a professional."

Winter glanced back over her shoulder. "But I probably shouldn't try driving that thing at home, right?"

"Right."

Winter laughed. Inexplicably, the atmosphere seemed a little brighter. Her voice and her laughter had the power to charm him. He could have sworn she had cast a sparkling little spell on him just now.

He should probably be very worried, he thought, but somehow he couldn't work up the energy. Too many other things going on, more dangerous things. A man had to have priorities.

"How did you get your sofa into the locker all by yourself?" he asked.

"The gardener at my apartment complex offered to bring it here on the back of his truck," Winter said.

At the next intersection she vanished around a corner. Jack followed on the pallet. The lights in the canyon behind him winked off.

They made their way to the back of the big building. Winter finally came to a halt in front of one of the smaller lockers, number C-115.

He coasted to a stop and watched her work the combination on the padlock. When she got it open he helped her roll the door up into the top of the locker. Metal squeaked and clanked.

He surveyed the contents of the locker. There were a handful of packing boxes, a small desk, a lamp and one bulky object heavily swathed in sturdy plastic. There was enough light to make out the crimson upholstery under the layers of protective covering. The sofa.

It was not a very big sofa.

As if she knew what he was thinking Winter touched the outer wrapping with a protective hand and looked at him.

"It was designed for an apartment or a small condo," she said. "Technically, I suppose you could call it a love seat."

Love seat. That brought up some interesting mental visuals.

"Right," he said, keeping his tone very neutral. "It should fit into your cottage in Eclipse Bay."

"Yes." She looked pleased. "It will be perfect there."

In addition to the boxes and the furniture, there were a roll of heavy-duty sealing tape, a pair of scissors and what was left of the thick plastic that had been used to protect the sofa. Mute evidence of a hasty packing job and a quick departure.

"I've got to hand it to you," he said. "Looks like you've got this whole minimalist-lifestyle thing nailed."

Her mouth tightened. "I've had a lot of practice."

"Will you be moving back to California when this is over?"

"To be honest, I haven't given it much thought," she said. "But I like Eclipse Bay. If I can figure out how to make a living there, I may stay." She paused. "You?"

"Eclipse Bay works for me," Jack said. "For now. But I'm mobile."

"Same with me."

There was a short silence. They both contemplated the plastic-covered sofa. Jack moved toward it and tested the weight by hoisting one end. It was surprisingly light. He wondered if that was indicative of cheap construction but he was wise enough to keep his mouth shut.

"I can handle the other end," Winter said quickly.

She hurried forward to assist him. Together they got the sofa as far as the open door of the storage locker. Jack was preparing to angle his end onto the long carrying arms of the pallet when he heard a door open somewhere in the dimly lit building. Not the loading dock door, he decided. Someone had entered the building using the main entrance, the one nearest the office.

A bank of fluorescents came on in the far corner of the big building.

"Sounds like we have company," Winter said.

Jack paused. "Yes."

He listened for footsteps. Voices. The clatter of a hand truck or the hum of a motorized pallet.

Silence.

That bothered him. Sound carried and echoed in the big space. A new arrival intent on accessing one of the lockers should have been making some noise.

He got a cold, prickly feeling on the back of his neck. He looked at Winter and discovered she was watching him. Everything about her had gone still.

"What?" she whispered.

He motioned for her to set down her end of the sofa.

Together they lowered the love seat to the floor. It came to rest half in and half out of the locker, angled across the threshold.

A loud clang reverberated throughout the facility. The overhead fixtures illuminating the aisle in front of Winter's locker went dark, plunging the entire section into deep shadow.

A woman called from a distant corner of the building.

"There's been a power failure. We apologize for the inconvenience. Please make your way toward the main exit."

"What in the world—?" Winter said.

"We may have a problem," Jack said quietly.

He unclipped his phone and tapped the flashlight app. Moving quickly, he went to the box of packing materials and grabbed the roll of heavy sealing tape and the scissors.

CHAPTER TWENTY-NINE

———— ≋ ————

Winter's first instinct was to take out her own phone and fire up the flashlight, but before she could do that, Jack handed his phone to her. She realized he wanted to have both hands free.

She trained the narrow beam of the light on his fingers and watched, bewildered, as he cut a couple of foot-long lengths of the heavy packing tape.

She started to ask him what he was doing but as if he knew exactly what she was about to say, he shook his head. She got the message.

The unseen woman spoke again, her voice echoing in the stillness.

"There's nothing to worry about," she called. "If you can't see well enough to get to the loading dock, stay where you are. I have your locker number. I'll come and get you."

Footsteps sounded in the distance. Winter realized that the woman was making her way toward locker C-115. She wondered how the clerk knew exactly which customer was inside the huge building. Then she remembered the security cameras. No need to be alarmed.

Except that Jack was clearly alarmed and that meant she should be, too. Damn. The deep, slow breathing thing wasn't a lot of help at a time like this.

Jack was standing on the platform at the back of the motorized pallet, working on the handlebars. She watched him depress the trigger accelerator and secure it in the On position with one length of the tape. The pallet began to move forward, slowly at first, heading straight down the center of the aisle toward the wall at the far end.

Jack wrapped the second strip of tape tightly around the accelerator and then jumped off. The heavy pallet rumbled forward, gaining momentum.

"What are you doing?" the woman called. She sounded closer now. There was an icy note of command in the words. "Answer me."

The pallet was moving faster. The motor developed a loud whine. As the device picked up speed, the steering became less stable. The pallet veered to the left. The wheels struck a bumper. The impact jolted the miniature forklift back into the center of the aisle. It continued on its way for a short distance before once again ricocheting off another bumper.

The pallet had become a semi-guided missile.

"What the fuck is going on?"

A man's voice this time.

"Shit," the woman said. "They're heading for the loading dock. They're going to get away."

Two sets of running footsteps sounded in the shadows. They pounded away in the opposite direction, toward the wall where the loading dock was located.

Jack took the phone out of Winter's hand and killed the flashlight.

"Follow me," he said, speaking directly into her ear. "Try not to make any noise."

He started toward the stairwell that led to the upper floor of the warehouse. Winter hurried after him. With luck the loud whine of the speeding pallet combined with the running footsteps of the two people chasing it would camouflage any sound that she and Jack might make.

A few seconds later the pallet crashed into the loading dock door with a shrill screech of metal on metal. A burglar alarm shrieked.

"They're going to get away," the woman shouted to her companion.

"No, it's a diversion," the man said. "They're hiding in the locker."

"The cops will be here soon."

"It will take them a while to respond," the man assured her. "We've got time to finish this."

Jack reached the stairwell. Winter was so close behind that she bumped into him. He paused long enough to break the glass in a small box and pull the red lever.

The shrill screech of the fire alarm combined with the clang of the burglar alarm was incredibly disorienting. Winter put her fingers in her ears and followed Jack into the stairwell.

Shots roared in the shadows. The noise boomed and echoed throughout the space.

Winter made it to the second floor, right behind Jack. He closed the door behind them, grabbed the nearest large object—a sturdy hand truck—and wedged the carrying edge under the doorjamb. It wouldn't be impossible to open the door, Winter thought, but it would take some effort and some time.

When he was finished with the door, Jack stepped into the open elevator and pushed the lock button so that it would not descend.

"They can't get to us up here," he said, raising his voice to be heard above the level of the alarms.

He, too, shoved his fingers in his ears.

It seemed like forever before the first faint wails of the responding emergency vehicles sounded in the distance.

The sudden silence when the alarms were shut off felt odd. Winter shook her head in an effort to clear the ringing in her ears.

"The shooters got away, didn't they?" she said.

"Assuming they have some sense of self-preservation, yes," Jack said. "Probably better if you let me talk to the cops. I've talked to a lot of them in my time. I know cop speak."

"Fine by me," she said.

She realized she was shivering. She wondered if she was going to have a panic attack. She had every right.

But when she tried to analyze her reaction, she realized that what she was feeling wasn't panic. It was fury.

CHAPTER THIRTY

———— ≈ ————

The Cassidy Springs police detective introduced himself as Nichols. He was middle-aged with a stocky build and thinning hair.

"There were two of them," he said. "Miller, the real clerk, heard them talking. Looks like you and Ms. Meadows had the very bad luck to interrupt a drug heist gone bad. The pair that tried to take you out came here to find a stash of heroin that they assumed was hidden in one of the lockers. The clerk said it sounded like they thought you and Ms. Meadows were the competition."

"We just happened to be in the wrong place at the wrong time, is that it?" Jack asked.

"That's what it looks like. I'll talk to the clerk again when he calms down but the bottom line is that, aside from a brief look at the man with the gun, who was evidently wearing a wig and a pair of large sunglasses, he didn't see much."

The responding officers had discovered the badly shaken but otherwise unharmed clerk bound and blindfolded in the small employee bathroom.

"I heard what he told you," Jack said.

"You've got to admit, it's a reasonable explanation for what happened here." Nichols glanced at his notes. "The man in the wig and glasses entered the office first, pulled a gun and ordered Miller to get down on the floor. Then the woman entered, wrapped some duct tape around the clerk's wrists, blindfolded him and marched him into the bathroom. They locked the door."

"Interesting that they didn't kill him," Jack said, thinking about it.

"Back at the start of the robbery they probably saw no reason to risk a murder charge," Nichols said. "Why add that complication to their plans if it wasn't necessary? They knew the clerk could not identify them. A simple robbery at a storage locker would not generate an extensive investigation. Homicide is a whole other matter."

"They didn't have any problem with the idea of killing Ms. Meadows and me," Jack pointed out.

"Like I said, they figured you two were after the same stash."

Jack glanced out the window of the office. A short time ago Winter had given her statement to Nichols in short, terse sentences. As soon as she was finished, she had hurried away and disappeared inside the locker building.

He was starting to get more than a little worried about her. He reminded himself that she was probably in shock. People who had been through a violent event did not always act in a predictable fashion and Winter had survived two potentially lethal situations in a little less than forty-eight hours.

"It was an ambush, Nichols," he said quietly.

Nichols' jaw hardened. "I need a motive."

The Quinton Zane conspiracy theory was not going to fly in this situation, Jack thought.

"The fact that an obsessed stalker tried to murder Ms. Meadows the night before last doesn't make you curious?" he said. "Or are you a fan of amazing coincidences?"

Nichols exhaled heavily. "I'm listening."

Jack did a fast calculation. He needed the police to keep looking into both attacks, because they had resources that he and the small investigation firm of Cutler, Sutter & Salinas lacked. There was always the possibility that the authorities might turn up a lead to Zane without realizing what they had. He had to keep the lines of communication open.

"The only solid connection between the attack on Ms. Meadows in Oregon and what happened here today is the Cassidy Springs Wellness Spa," he said. "Winter and I paid a visit there earlier today. While we were at the spa, Winter mentioned to a couple of her former colleagues that we would be coming here this afternoon to empty her storage locker."

"Go on."

"The man who attacked Winter in Eclipse Bay was a client at the spa."

"But he's dead," Nichols pointed out. "That doesn't leave me much to work with."

"It's all I've got at the moment." Which was pretty damn close to the truth, Jack thought. "How long was the clerk locked up in the bathroom?"

Nichols consulted his notes. "About an hour."

"And during that time he overheard them talking about stealing a cache of drugs but he never got a good description of either the man or the woman."

"That's right." Nichols looked at his notes again. "They discussed disabling the security cameras. They talked about how they would search for the drugs."

"They didn't have a locker number?"

"No. The clerk said he heard them talking about some of the customer files. He said it sounded like they weren't sure what name they were searching for. At one point the gunman spoke to the clerk through the door. He wanted to know the location of the master light switch box inside the locker facility and then he demanded to know how to lock the front gates." Nichols paused. "At no time did the clerk hear the robbers talk about setting up an ambush. When you arrived, they were alarmed. He said they were sure you were after the drugs."

"It was all about stealing drugs."

"Right."

Jack thought about dumping the Quinton Zane conspiracy theory on Nichols after all but decided against it. Nichols's first move would be to research the old cult fire case. What followed would be all too predictable. Nichols would learn that Zane had been declared dead a couple of decades earlier. At that point the detective would start to question Jack's mental stability. He would conclude that Jack was an obsessed conspiracy buff or that he was suffering from some form of PTSD dating back to the cult fire.

No good ever came of talking about Quinton Zane to law enforcement. Doing so was, in fact, a surefire way to destroy a career that depended, in part, on professional relationships with cops. Cutler, Sutter & Salinas needed to cultivate those connections.

But the more he thought about it, the more it seemed like a good idea to have someone start poking around the Cassidy Springs Wellness Spa. At the very least it might convince whoever was watching that at this point they still believed the threat was coming from that direction.

"Maybe I'm overreacting," he said finally.

Nichols cocked a brow. "Don't worry about it. Tends to happen when someone tries to kill you. Tell you what, I'll talk to some folks at the spa and see if anything pings."

"Do me a favor," Jack said. "Keep me in the loop if you find anything interesting."

"I'll do that." Nichols closed his notebook. He was clearly intent on heading for the door but he stopped and took out a business card. "If you think of something else I should know, give me a call, all right?"

"Sure."

Jack took the card and waited for Nichols to walk out the door. But Nichols was not quite finished. He stopped again, this time with his hand on the door handle.

"My boss called me a while ago," he said. "He told me that you have something of a reputation for digging into cold cases. He also said you've had no law enforcement training and that from time to time you've managed to piss off a few people. You were a professor or something."

"You're going to warn me not to try to run my own amateur investigation," Jack said.

"My advice is to stay out of this, Lancaster. I still think this is a drug case. People who deal drugs are dangerous."

"I've heard that," Jack said.

Nichols went out the door and walked toward a small cluster of uniformed officers.

Jack left the office and went through the open gate. He crossed the yard that surrounded the locker building and walked into the cavernous space.

He found Winter in the aisle in front of her locker. Her back was toward him. Her arms were folded very tightly beneath her breasts.

He knew she had heard him coming up behind her but she did not turn around. He halted and looked past her. She had removed several layers of plastic to reveal a number of bullet holes in the red sofa.

He wasn't sure of her mood and he had no idea what to say so he put his hand on her shoulder. She gave a soft, anguished cry and spun around. She buried her face against his shoulder and sobbed.

He put both arms around her and held her while she cried. She was soft and delicate and surprisingly vulnerable. He wanted to kill the two people who had reduced her to tears.

She did not cry for very long. When she regained her composure she stepped back, sniffling a little, and wiped her eyes with the sleeve of her jacket.

"Sorry," she mumbled.

"It's okay," he said.

She grimaced and went to where her tote bag sat on the floor of the locker. He watched her unzip the bag and retrieve some tissues. She blotted up the last of the tears, took a deep breath and straightened her shoulders.

"I was doing all right until I saw the bullet holes in my sofa," she said.

"I understand."

"Thank you," she said. She gave him a watery smile.

"For what?"

"For not reminding me that it's just a sofa and that it can be replaced and that I should be grateful we're still alive. Blah, blah, blah. It's all true but thanks for not saying it anyway."

"No problem," he said.

"They thought we were hiding inside the locker, didn't they?" she said.

"That's what it looks like," Jack said. "They sprayed the interior, hoping to take us out before they ran."

"They came here to kill us."

"Well, that's definitely my theory but it's only fair to tell you that the cops have a slightly different take."

She spread her hands. "What other take is there?"

"The clerk overheard some conversation between the two shooters that led him and the police to believe this was intended to be a burglary. The shooters said something about finding a locker with a cache of drugs. They gave the clerk the impression that we were from a rival gang."

Winter frowned. "The clerk heard them say that?"

"Evidently."

"Think he was in on it?"

"I considered that but I'm inclined to doubt it. He looked too shaken. I think there's a ninety-three percent probability the shooters intended him to overhear the conversation that led him to think it was a drug-related burglary."

Winter blinked. "Ninety-three percent?"

"I never go with a hundred percent until all possibilities have been ruled out."

"I see. Well, your theory would explain why they didn't kill him, wouldn't it? They wanted to be sure the cops wrote off the murders as drug-related. They set up the clerk so he would point the police in the wrong direction."

Jack smiled a little. "Careful. That's exactly the kind of thinking that can make people believe you're a conspiracy theorist."

"Sometimes even conspiracy theorists are right. So the cops are going to waste a lot of time chasing phantom drug dealers."

"These days, drugs are the easy explanation for a lot of law enforcement problems," Jack said. "And most of the time it's the right explanation."

"I suppose so." Winter straightened her shoulders. "But we've got another theory of the crime."

"Yes, we do. However, for now we are going to act like we're good with the version of events that the cops and the clerk bought."

"We can't just stand around and wait for Zane to send his killers after us again."

"I agree," Jack said.

"So? What's our next step?"

"We find a secure place to spend the night."

"Define *secure*. Will we have to camp out in the woods in order to avoid detection?"

"I think we can do a little better than that."

"That's good," Winter said. "I really hate camping." She looked at the remains of the red sofa. "There was only one more payment left on it."

CHAPTER THIRTY-ONE

―――≈―――

"He's back, isn't he?" Octavia Ferguson said.

Anson Salinas dropped his phone into the pocket of his shirt and looked at the woman he loved.

"Looks like it," he said. "At this point we have no choice but to go with Jack's conclusion. He's convinced Zane was behind the attack in the self-storage facility this afternoon. Unless we can find hard proof that this is not the case, we have to assume Zane has returned."

Octavia nodded and rose from her chair. She walked across the living room of her home and looked out at her spectacular garden. Anson was pretty sure he knew exactly what she was thinking. A few months earlier the garden had served as the setting for the wedding of her granddaughter, Virginia, and Anson's son Cabot. It had been a day of joy for all of them, a day when they could forget about the past for a while. A day to look toward the future.

But now that future was on hold for everyone who was haunted by Quinton Zane.

Anson's heart ached because he could not shield Octavia from the truth. Not that she wanted to be protected, he thought. Octavia was a strong woman. She would not thank him for trying to pretend there was no danger.

After he had lost Madeline decades earlier he had never expected to love deeply again. He figured a man was unlikely to experience that kind of joy twice in a lifetime. But recently Octavia had entered his life and he had discovered that he had been wrong.

Not that Octavia was anything like Madeline, he reflected. Maybe that was why he felt free to love her. They shared a unique bond because they had both suffered from the nightmare that Quinton Zane had ignited some twenty-two years before. Octavia had been among the anguished relatives who had arrived on the scene the day after the compound fire to claim their surviving family members. Octavia had been one of those who had assumed the task of picking up the pieces of a life shattered by violence.

She had lost her adult daughter on that terrible night, but her granddaughter, Virginia, had been one of the kids trapped in the barn. Anson had managed to save the children. Virginia had gone home with Octavia. They had moved on with their lives just as Anson and his three foster sons had done. But the specter of Quinton Zane had hovered around all of them.

"I had hoped that the bastard who murdered my daughter and all those other people was dead," Octavia said.

Anson got up and went to stand beside her at the window. He put his arm around her shoulders and pulled her close against his side, trying to lend her strength even as he absorbed some from her.

"My sons and I always knew there was a strong possibility Zane did not die in that yacht fire at sea," he said.

"What made you so sure?" Octavia asked.

"Zane was smart and he was a survivor. He was also a complete sociopath. It seemed likely that when he torched his California operation, he had an escape plan in place."

"Why has he come back now?" Octavia said.

"I don't know," Anson said. "But if he is back, it's because he's got his endgame figured out."

"You make it sound as if he's already light-years ahead of us."

"He'll certainly think so," Anson said. "But that kind of self-confidence carries its own risks. And we've got our own ace in the hole."

"Jack?"

"He's our first line of defense. Of all of us, he's the one who has the best chance of anticipating Zane's endgame. Once Jack gets a handle on that, we can come up with our own ending."

"Zane knows that, doesn't he? That's why he went after Jack first."

"Yes," Anson said. "This won't be over for any of us until Quinton Zane is dead or in prison for the rest of his life."

"I would prefer dead," Octavia said.

"So would I."

CHAPTER THIRTY-TWO

———— ≈ ————

"As promised, we are not camping out," Winter said. "Heck, this place even has indoor plumbing." She looked around the hotel room. "Do you think we're safe here?"

"*Safe* is always a relative term," Jack said.

"Thanks for that upbeat observation."

"There's a high probability that we're safe here, because when I checked in, I used another set of ID's and I paid cash. As far as the front desk and the hotel computer are concerned, we're just a couple from Arizona."

He had taken other precautions as well. After the interview with the police they had left her belongings, including the ruined sofa and her cell phone, in the locker at Cassidy Springs Self-Storage. Jack had kept his phone because, as he had explained, Xavier was sure its encryption was good enough to protect them.

After dumping the van at the rental agency they had caught a taxi, paying with cash, and used the new ID's at a different agency to pick up another vehicle.

Winter managed a wan smile. "Don't sugarcoat it for me. I can handle the truth."

"I know," Jack said. "That's why I gave it to you."

He was, she concluded, dead serious. On second thought, make that *very* serious. Under the circumstances, *dead* seemed like a poor word choice.

They were spending the night in another chain hotel. It was located near a freeway interchange on the outskirts of one of the cascade of suburban towns that flowed down the San Francisco peninsula. The place was as anonymous as such an establishment could get. Everything, from the carpet to the bathroom vanity, was done in various shades of boring.

Jack had requested connecting rooms again. She was not sure how to take that. It was possible he was being a gentleman. It was also possible that he was not interested in spending another night in the same bed with her. And it was probable that she was overthinking the entire matter.

They were currently in her room, seated at the small table in front of the window. A short time ago room service had removed the dinner they had ordered. In spite of the harrowing afternoon, or maybe because of it, they had succeeded in downing two large Caesar salads, a couple of grilled salmon entrées and the large basket of sourdough bread that had accompanied the meal. They were in the process of finishing the last of the wine.

After checking in they had each retreated to their respective bathrooms to clean up and change clothes. There was nothing like almost getting killed to make a woman want to take a shower, Winter decided. The hot water had rinsed away the sweat of stress and fear but it had done nothing for her nerves. Neither had the wine. She was in the grip of a strange restlessness.

That was certainly not the case as far as Jack was concerned. After his shower he had changed into a fresh pair of khaki trousers and a fresh white shirt—he evidently had an unlimited supply of both—and now he was clearly in his element. She envied him. His conviction that they were chasing Quinton Zane—or being chased by Quinton Zane—had infused him with energy and purpose. He was fully engaged in his mission.

"Do you always travel with a lot of cash and fake ID's?" she asked. She held up one hand, palm out. "Not judging. Just asking for a friend."

Jack's mouth curved in a very brief, very grim smile. "Tell your friend the answer is yes. My brothers do, too. What can I say? It's sort of a family tradition."

"Inspired by Quinton Zane."

Jack stopped smiling. His eyes were icy-hot. "We've always packed a couple of sets of fake ID's because we knew that if Zane ever did show up, one of us or all of us might have to go off the grid with little or no warning. After what happened a few months ago in the Night Watch case in Seattle, Max and Cabot and I got a few new sets of ID's. When you go down a conspiracy theory rabbit hole, you prep for the worst-case scenario."

"I get it, believe me."

"We've all kept go-bags and cash on hand for years. Recently Max and Cabot both got married. They've made similar provisions for their wives. After Xavier began interning at Cutler, Sutter and Salinas, Anson made sure he got whatever he might need to disappear for a while, too."

"Wow. I'm impressed. You all have multiple fake identities? How in the world did you manage that?"

Jack gave her a pitying look. "Haven't you heard? You can buy any-thing online."

She widened her eyes. "Really? You just went online and ordered up a lot of fake identities?"

Jack lounged back in his chair and stretched out his legs. "All right, it's not quite that simple. Until recently we relied on my brother Max's connec-tions. He used to be a profiler for a government agency. He knows people."

"But now?"

"Now," Jack said, "we've got our own in-house IT department."

"Xavier."

"He's much better at going into the dark corners of the Internet than the old-school government intel crowd."

"I see," she said.

The restlessness was getting worse, she thought. The hotel room felt small; like a trap that was slowly closing on her. She set down the empty glass, got to her feet and began to prowl the room.

Jack watched her, his eyes tightening at the corners. "Are you okay?"

"I need to meditate," she said. "I need to breathe. But I'm too wired."

"I'm wired, too. No surprise. We've both taken a couple of heavy adrenaline jolts in the past few days."

A tiny ping of awareness sparked across her senses. She paused in mid-stride and turned to look at Jack. The cold fire in his eyes told her that he was doing one of his quiet, intense burns. She was pretty sure it wasn't the same nervy sensation that was agitating her, though. Jack was in hunting mode.

"What's wrong?" she asked. She folded her arms. "I mean besides the obvious?"

"I need to think," Jack said. He tapped one finger on the table in a slow, controlled pattern. "I've missed something important. I need to figure out what it is. We've been moving so fast since the night Moseley attacked you that I haven't had time to process the new data that has come in."

"We've got new data?"

He looked surprised by the question. "I've got a lot more to work with now than I had forty-eight hours ago."

"Because of what happened at the self-storage place today?"

"Among other things. For example, I'm sure the clerk survived because he had a role to play, although he didn't know it. He heard what the shooters wanted him to hear. He believed that it was a for-real drug heist, and now the cops believe that, too."

Winter gave that some thought. "If you're right, the pair who shot at us must have been very good actors."

"Not good actors," Jack said softly. "Pros."

A chill iced her nerves.

"As in, professional killers?" she asked.

"I'm thinking professional mercenaries."

"Let me guess, you can find talent like that on the Internet, right?"

"If you know where to look," Jack said.

She shuddered. "I suppose it makes sense that Zane might have hired a couple of mercenaries to do his dirty work. Judging by what you've told me, he can afford the best."

"Huh."

"Now what? Another ping?"

"Maybe." Jack tapped the tabletop again. One time. "Zane never just hires talent. You can't get real loyalty simply by paying a good salary and offering benefits. And Zane always demands loyalty. He only uses people he can trust. People who are bound to him by fear or some equally powerful emotion. People he thinks he can control. He *seduces* the people who possess the skills he needs by promising them what they want most in the world."

Winter considered that for a few seconds.

"But doing it for the money is sort of the basic job description of a mercenary, isn't it?" she said finally. "What could Zane promise a couple of professional killers except a lot of cash?"

"That," Jack said, "is a very good question. It may even be the second most important question I need to ask tonight."

"What is the most important question?"

"Who is Zane hiding behind? He always uses human shields. It's one of his signatures. Once I get the answer to that question it should be easy to figure out what he promised his two mercenaries."

Jack gripped the arms of his chair and pushed himself to his feet. He started toward the connecting door.

"Where are you going?" Winter asked.

He paused in the doorway and looked back at her. "I need to take another look at my Recent Suspicious Fires file. Each of the cases in it has some element that makes me think Zane could have been involved but until now I haven't been able to isolate whatever it was that didn't look right. Now that I've got more data I can try to eliminate a few."

"Go," she said. She waved him away into the other room. "I need to meditate."

He nodded once and disappeared into the other room. He left the door partway open.

She sat down on the side of her bed and composed herself.

CHAPTER THIRTY-THREE

"Winter?"

Jack's voice brought her out of the light self-induced trance. She opened her eyes and saw him looming in the doorway between the two rooms. There was a new intensity in his eyes. She could have sworn that the energy in the atmosphere was charged lightning-hot.

She got to her feet. "You found something?"

"Not yet, but I'm close," he said. "Very, very close. I've narrowed the list of possible cases down to a handful. One of them is important. I'd stake my life on it. But I'm losing my focus. The problem is that I've studied these cases from too many different angles. They're just a jumble of facts now. Chaos. I need to find the butterfly that flapped its wings. I think you can help me do that."

"How?"

"I want you to look at the data in my files with me."

"Okay, but I'm not exactly a trained forensics investigator."

"I just want you to review the details with me and ask questions. Lots and lots of questions. Anything. Everything. You'll bring a new perspective to the information because you'll be seeing the data for the first time. I'm hoping you'll ask the question that I haven't asked. The right question."

"How do you want to do this?"

"I want you to put me into a trance and walk through the cases in my hot file one by one. Interview me."

"You want me to *hypnotize* you?"

"Promise me you won't make me squawk like a chicken."

CHAPTER THIRTY-FOUR

———— ≋ ————

She sat down at the small table. Jack took the opposite chair. She was surprised when, without a word, he put the small chunk of black obsidian on the table. She had not known that he had brought it with him.

All the lights were off. The room was lit only by the otherworldly glow of the screen of Jack's computer. She was shivering a little.

"Feels like we're going to hold a séance," Jack said.

"Ignore the theatrics," she said. "I turned the lights off for my sake, not yours. The darkness will help me to concentrate on asking the right questions."

She knew she was not the only one who was affected by the edgy vibe in the room. Everything about Jack was sharp and focused. *Like a soldier preparing to go into combat,* she thought.

"Before we do this you need to focus on your escape word for a moment." He smiled. "Don't worry, I'm not going to forget it."

"I'm serious," she said. "Pay attention. When I do this with other people, I control the trance. I tell them what to look for. I ask the questions. When the session is over, I pull them out of the trance. But you're different."

"Because of the lucid dreaming thing?"

"And because you're not even a typical lucid dreamer. You're unique. I'm not sure how you'll respond in a true hypnotic trance."

He looked amused. "What could possibly go wrong?"

She glared at him. "I think there's a very real possibility that you'll take control of the trance, just as you do when you go into a lucid dream."

"Will that be a problem?"

"To be honest, I don't know," she said. "If I sense that the situation is going sideways, I'll try to bring you out of the trance."

"You'll *try* to bring me out of it?"

"I might not be able to do that if you take control and convert the trance into a lucid dream," she explained. "And you might be in too deep to realize what is going on."

"What's the worst-case scenario here?"

"I don't know," she admitted. "I'm sure that eventually you would wake up or something would shatter the trance."

"Good to know," he said.

She realized he was not taking the danger seriously.

"I think it's also possible that you might be stuck in it for a while," she said.

"Stuck?"

"Maybe in a form of sleep paralysis. That's the sensation some people get when they wake up but discover they can't move or speak. The condition doesn't last more than a minute or two but it can be terrifying."

"I've heard of that but I don't have any history of suffering from it, just the sleepwalking."

"And that's another possibility," she said. "You might start sleepwalking again. What I'm trying to say is that you are not a normal subject. We need to be prepared for the unexpected. I want you to be sure you have your escape word with you when you go into the trance in case I can't bring you out of it."

He folded his arms on the table and fixed her with eyes that burned.

"I promise you that I will never forget my escape word, Winter," he said.

It was a vow.

She swallowed hard. "Okay. Good. That's great."

"Let's get started. I need answers and I need them as fast as possible."

She took a slow, centering breath. *Here we go.*

"Focus on the obsidian key," she said, automatically slipping into the voice she used for inducing a trance.

Jack looked down at the stone.

"Unlock the gates and walk into Ice Town. This is your world. You have created it. You know it well. You can go down any street or alley. Nothing can stop you. Nothing can hide from you in this place. All is calm, cold and still. Your destination is the ice garden in the center of town. From there you can observe what is going on around you."

Jack did not move. He kept his attention on the obsidian. He was not making any attempt to fight the trance.

"You have reached the garden," she continued. "I will ask you questions. You will answer them. Do you understand?"

"Yes."

Jack's voice was entirely neutral.

She reached out to his computer and tapped a few keys to open his notes and observations on the first case in the Recent Suspicious Fires file. She wasn't sure where to start, but he had instructed her to ask her own questions, so she decided to go for it.

"We are looking at the file you created for the Talcott case," she said. "There is a list of items that were found at the scene. The first thing is the victim's wallet. Why did you put it on the list?"

"Because there was a piece of paper with a series of numbers on it."

"What did the numbers mean?"

"They were the combination to the victim's floor safe."

"What was inside the safe?" she asked.

"The safe was empty. Ninety-eight percent probability that the killer took the contents."

"The next item on the list is a metal bracelet. Why is that on the list?"

"It was an emblem of membership in a BDSM club."

"Oh." She wasn't sure where to go with that. "Did you, uh, visit the club?"

"I interviewed the dominatrix."

"What did she tell you?"

"She told me that the victim had been engaged in an affair with one of the other club members."

"Did you pursue that aspect of the investigation?"

"Yes."

"Did you learn anything useful?"

"No."

She worked her way through the remaining items on the list. When she got to the end she started to open another file. But something made her hesitate.

"You kept this case in your hot file," she said. "Why?"

Jack touched the obsidian stone and looked at the computer screen.

"There is something missing from the list," he said.

"What is missing?"

"The key."

Winter took a closer look at the file notes. "The victim's keys were found near the body."

"One was missing when the body was recovered. It turned up later in a drawer in the victim's desk at his office."

"Which key was missing?" she asked.

"A safe-deposit box key."

"Who took it?"

"The killer."

"Why did the killer put it into the drawer of the victim's desk?"

"She had no way to return the key to the dead man's house. She left it in his desk drawer instead."

"You're sure?"

"Ninety-seven percent," Jack repeated in the same eerily uninflected voice.

"Do you know the identity of the killer?"

"Yes."

"Who murdered Talcott?"

"His administrative assistant."

"Was she arrested?"

"No. Eighty-five percent probability that she won't be arrested."

"Why not?"

"No evidence."

"But you're sure she did it?"

"Yes," Jack said.

"Shall I leave this case in your hot file?"

"No. It doesn't belong in the file. The probability of a connection to Zane is very low."

"Why are you certain of that?"

"Because the administrative assistant is still alive," Jack said in a flat tone of voice.

"Why does that fact make you sure this case is not linked to Zane?"

"If Zane had used the assistant to get the key, he would have gotten rid of her as well as Talcott."

"Why?"

"She would have been a loose end. Zane does not leave loose ends. Next case."

Startled by what amounted to a command, Winter shot Jack a quick, searching look. She wondered uneasily if he was starting to take over the trance and convert it into a lucid dream. And what should she do if that was, indeed, what was happening? They were both in uncharted territory.

She turned back to the computer, tapped a couple of keys and opened the next case file. "The Barnsville fire. Took place in a warehouse. An employee died. It was ruled arson but no one was ever arrested. Why is it in your hot file?"

"I left it open because there was no clear motive. No one tried to collect on the insurance. It was the work of a pyro but now I'm ninety percent sure it wasn't Zane."

"Why not?"

"Too sloppy."

They worked their way quickly through three more cases of suspicious fires involving a death. One by one Jack instructed her to remove each from the hot file.

In the end there was only one case left.

"The car fire on the empty desert road outside of Las Vegas," Jack said finally. "A woman named Jessica Pitt was killed. Investigators believed that she may have been smoking and fallen asleep at the wheel. Eighty-six percent probability that's the one."

"Why?"

"It's too clean," he said. "No loose ends. *Winter.*"

And just like that he was out of the trance. It was as if he had flipped a switch. His voice was once again normal. His eyes lost the otherworldly look. A new intensity charged the atmosphere around him.

"You're awake," she said.

"Yeah. Thanks. You helped me clarify my thoughts."

"You're sure that car fire was caused by Zane?"

"Eighty-six percent sure," Jack said. "I need a little more data."

"If there are no loose ends in the car fire case, how will you pursue the investigation?"

"I said it was too clean and that there are no obvious loose ends but there are two very big unanswered questions."

"What are they?"

"What was Jessica Pitt, a woman who had been married and divorced three times, doing on that empty road outside of Vegas at two in the morning?"

Winter raised her brows. "Driving to or from Las Vegas?"

"Obviously, but that leads me to the second question: why was she alone?"

"There are probably a lot of reasons why a woman would find herself alone in a car late at night. I've driven alone at night countless times."

"Not out there on that road in the desert, though," Jack said.

"Well, no, but—"

"It feels like Pitt was either on her way to meet a man or else returning after having met him."

"What makes you say that?"

"Because Jessica Pitt always had a man in her life," Jack said. "She was beautiful, glamorous and financially ambitious. She married for money and when she was between marriages she was actively hunting for another rich husband. She was between men at the time of her death. It had been several months since she and her last husband had separated. I researched her life when the case first landed in my hot file. I found no indication that there was another man in the picture. There should have been someone."

Winter gestured toward the glowing computer screen. "It says that the car fire was ruled accidental. Why did you put this case in your file?"

"In addition to a rather spectacular fire in a deserted location, Jessica Pitt is a partial match to the standard profile of Zane's favorite target," Jack said. "She's a single woman with no close family. In addition, she lived on the West Coast, in an expensive little boutique town about a hundred miles north of Los Angeles. Burning Cove."

"You said she's a partial match to a Zane victim profile. What's missing?"

"Desperation. Desire. Fear. A need so powerful that when Zane offered to give it to her, she fell for the con. Once we know what's missing from Jessica Pitt's profile, all the answers will fall into place."

"Assuming she really was one of his victims."

"Assuming that," Jack agreed.

"But you really think there's a connection between them, don't you?"

"I told you, there's an eighty-six percent probability that there is a link. With a little more data I should be able to increase that probability or rule her out altogether."

Winter sighed. "Okay, you said she had a pattern of marrying for money. Did she have a lot of it at the time of her death?"

"Yes, but not enough to tempt Zane." Jack got to his feet and began to pace the room. "I told you, if he's back, it's not because he needs money. And if he murdered Jessica Pitt, it's because he got what he needed from her and no longer had any use for her."

"I don't know, Jack. Seems like a stretch. There must be some other reason why you're so sure Pitt was connected to Zane."

Jack stopped at the far end of the room. "The location of the fire."

"You mean the desert road? Why is that important?"

"That fire occurred in a place that would have made it easy for Zane to watch."

Winter shivered. "He likes to watch his fires?"

"Make no mistake. Zane is smart and sophisticated, but at his core he's still a classic pyro. Pyros always like to watch their work. Out there, alone in the desert, he could have watched for as long as he wanted."

It seemed to Winter that there was a new chill in the atmosphere.

"You're really in his head, aren't you?" she asked quietly.

"It's what I do, Winter."

She got the feeling that he was waiting for her to render judgment on him.

"I understand," she said gently. "It's why you're good at what you do. It's your gift."

Jack watched her in silence for a long moment.

"Are you okay with that?" he asked.

"Yep."

"That's all you can say?"

She smiled. "Yep."

He nodded once, evidently satisfied, and resumed prowling the room.

"That car fire occurred a couple of months after Cutler, Sutter and Salinas closed the Night Watch case in Seattle," he said. "So the timing works. I had a feeling that the fallout from what happened in that case would eat at Zane; maybe enrage him. Rage leads to obsession. That's the point of no return."

"Do you think he would let rage and obsession push him into taking risks?"

"Yes." Jack looked as if he were gazing into another dimension. "Damn it, I need to know more about Jessica Pitt."

He returned to the table, sat down and pulled his laptop close. His fingers began to move over the keys as if he were playing music. The blue-green radiance of the computer screen sparked on the lenses of his glasses.

"Looks like we're going to be up for a while," Winter said. She got to her feet. "I'll make some coffee."

"Good idea."

She went to the console that held the in-room coffeemaker and picked up the small pot. She started to move into the bathroom to fill the pot with water from the sink but she paused and looked at Jack.

"I do have one question before you start digging into Jessica Pitt's past," she said.

Jack did not look up from the screen. "What?"

"When you interviewed the professional dominatrix in the Talcott case, did she, by any chance, try to convince you to become a client?"

"She's a businesswoman." Jack did not take his gaze off the computer screen. "She offered me a fifty percent discount on a starter package of six sessions."

"Please tell me you declined."

"I declined. Not my style."

"How would you describe your style?"

Jack stopped playing the laptop keys long enough to turn his head and fix her with a look that made her catch her breath.

"Anything involving you would definitely qualify as my style," he said.

She suddenly got a little light-headed.

"Good to know," she said. "I'll get the coffee going." She hesitated on the threshold. "But if you ever decide you want to experiment with little whips and fuzzy handcuffs, be sure to let me know. They say you can buy anything online these days."

"I'll remember that."

CHAPTER THIRTY-FIVE

———— ≈ ————

An hour later Jack sat back from the computer, took off his glasses, massaged his eyes and stretched. Winter looked up from the notes she had been making for him and took a beat to admire the view. Jack reminded her of a large hunting cat when he stretched.

Evidently unaware of her interest, Jack put on his glasses and got to his feet. He headed toward the in-room coffeemaker.

"The question I keep coming back to," he said, "is where was the man in Jessica Pitt's life following her third divorce? He ought to be there."

Winter glanced at her notes. "Because according to your theory she always had a man around."

"Not just any man—a wealthy man." Jack disappeared into the bath to fill the coffeepot. "She had a long, unblemished record of successful marriages followed by even more successful divorces that left her in what people used to call very comfortable financial circumstances. If she had followed her pattern, she should have been well on her way to marriage number four."

Winter tapped her pen against the sheet of hotel room paper. "Yet there was no husband in sight after marriage number three ended."

Jack reappeared from the bath and dumped the water into the top of the coffeemaker, added a pod of coffee and hit the On switch.

"People don't change their patterns," he said.

Winter tapped the pen against the paper. "One thing to keep in mind here is that the career path Jessica Pitt followed probably gets more complicated as a woman ages."

Jack lounged against the console and folded his arms, waiting for the coffee to brew.

"She still had her looks," he said. "She spent a fortune keeping herself in marketable shape."

"You think there *was* a man in the picture, don't you?"

"Yes."

"Well, if she was seeing someone in secret, she must have had a really good reason for keeping the relationship under wraps. Maybe the guy was married."

"Or maybe Zane insisted on her silence," Jack said.

"What would make her agree to keep the affair secret?"

"That's easy," Jack said. "Zane promised her something she wanted very, very badly."

"So the real question here is, what did Jessica Pitt want that she didn't get from her three ex-husbands?" Winter said.

"Exactly." Jack glanced at the laptop. "I've hit a wall with the online research. I couldn't find much beyond her three marriages. And that, by the way, is another indicator that Zane was involved. Jessica Pitt's past is very neat and tidy. You'd think she had never heard of social media."

"What does that tell you?"

"It tells me Zane may have scrubbed Pitt's online life. I'll call Xavier first thing in the morning. He may be able to pull up something more about Jessica Pitt."

"I'm sure Xavier is good," Winter said, "but there may be a more efficient way to find out if Jessica Pitt was seeing someone in secret at the time of her death."

"How?"

"Ask someone who knew her."

"One of her friends?" Jack nodded. "Good idea. You can clean up social media to some extent but it's a lot harder to erase people's memories."

"I doubt if she had a lot of close friends," Winter said, "at least not the kind she would have confided in. She sounds like the type of woman who would have viewed other women as competition. But one thing I think you can be sure of—she would have been a regular at her spa."

"Oh, yeah," Jack said. "Charges for various services at a place called Timeless show up every week on her credit card statements."

Winter put down the pen. "In my experience, everyone talks to their spa therapists."

Jack's eyes heated. "Huh."

"Just so you know, the spa business runs on tips."

"Oddly, I am not surprised. Burning Cove is about a four-hour drive from here. If we get started early in the morning we can be there by noon."

"We're not going to fly?"

"No. I don't have any ID's for you to use. Besides, given the security at airports these days, it will be just as fast to drive."

"You should get some sleep," she said.

"Me? What about you?"

"I assume that since we are on the run we are going to sleep in shifts," she said. "Neither one of us will be comfortable if the other one isn't keeping watch."

Jack gave her a speculative look. "Sounds like you've done this kind of thing before."

"I know how to stay awake at night when necessary. I taught myself the trick a long time ago. It's just a matter of focus."

"I assume you learned the skill while you were in the foster care system?"

"Yes," she said, "I did. Don't worry. I won't fall asleep."

"What, exactly, do you plan to do if there's a mysterious knock on the door?"

"I've got a flashlight in my carry-on. I can put someone in a trance fairly quickly with light. Hmm. Maybe we should buy a gun tomorrow."

Jack shook his head.

"Easier said than done in California," he said. "There's a waiting period and other restrictions. My brothers know people. I'm sure one of them could arrange for someone to loan me a gun but between you and me, it's not a practical idea. I'm not a very good shot."

"Hmm," she said.

He eyed her warily. "What?"

"I just figured, given your mission and all, that you would know how to use a gun."

"My mission?"

"Your work," she clarified. "Solving cold cases."

"One of the things I like about cold cases is that they are *cold*. People are a lot less likely to shoot me when the crime I'm investigating happened twenty or thirty years ago. I leave the hot cases to my brothers."

"Oh. I guess that makes sense. Well, anyway, about tonight. We'll be sleeping in shifts, right?"

"Right."

"Why don't you sleep first?" she said. "You're the one who has been doing most of the work tonight."

He gave that some thought and then he nodded once, silently acknowledging that she could do the job.

"Wake me in four hours," he said.

"All right."

He went into the other room. She heard the bed squeak a little beneath his weight. And then there was nothing but silence.

She sat in a chair, composed herself and found a focus.

CHAPTER THIRTY-SIX

—≈—

"I can't talk about one of my clients."

The aesthetician's name was Melanie Long. She was a walking advertisement for the industry in which she labored. At fortysomething her skin had been rendered porcelain-smooth by the assiduous application of exfoliating products and peels. The natural contours of her face had been artistically enhanced with injections of various chemicals.

Winter was sure Melanie had also had some surgical work done, but it was very good work.

The Timeless spa was an exclusive establishment in the heart of the exclusive town of Burning Cove. The entire town, spa included, had obviously been constructed according to some very rigid architectural rules. Virtually all of the buildings—gas stations, shops, private homes and hotels—looked as if they had been designed as a Hollywood version of the Spanish Colonial style.

Red tiles gleamed on the rooftops. Whitewashed stucco walls reflected the dazzling California sun. There were swimming pools, gardens and shady courtyards everywhere. And the whole lot was perched on rolling hills that overlooked the sparkling Pacific Ocean.

It was, Winter reflected, the same ocean that Eclipse Bay overlooked, but Southern California was a very different world and there was a very different lifestyle to go with it.

It had not been difficult to discover the name of Jessica Pitt's regular aesthetician. Winter had walked up to the front desk and pretended to be an acquaintance of Jessica Pitt. She had requested an appointment with Pitt's aesthetician. *Sorry, can't remember the name.* She and the receptionist had commiserated briefly and solemnly about Pitt's terrible accident and then Winter had learned that Melanie Long was very popular and booked out for the next two months. The receptionist had offered the name of another therapist.

"No, I'll wait for an appointment with Melanie Long," Winter had said. "I know that Jessica would have selected the best when it came to aestheticians."

When she was finished she had walked out of the spa and joined Jack, who had waited in the rental car. He had pulled up the spa's website, which featured pictures of each of the masseuses, aestheticians, acupuncturists, brow designers and nail technicians. When Melanie Long had emerged from the spa's lobby around one o'clock in search of lunch, it had been easy to recognize her.

They had waited until she was seated beneath an umbrella on a restaurant patio, a very small salad and a glass of sparkling water in front of her, before they approached. Initially she had been startled and wary. But after Jack had explained that they were investigating the death of Jessica Pitt, she had been clearly intrigued. *Thank goodness for all the CSI and cop dramas on television,* Winter thought.

"We're not asking you to gossip about a client," she said smoothly. "We're just trying to clear up some loose ends for the insurance company."

Melanie gave her a steely smile. "You mean, you're trying to find something that would give the insurance company a reason not to pay off."

"I'm shocked, *shocked* by your cynicism," Jack said. "Yes, we are working for a corporate entity, but here's the good news for you—we are in a position to compensate you for any useful information."

"You mean you're going to bribe me?"

"Think of it as a gratuity," Winter said.

"How much gratuity are we talking about?" Melanie asked.

Jack took out his wallet and put two crisp bills on the table.

Melanie eyed the money. "Thought it was just drug dealers who carried nice, fresh hundred-dollar bills."

"Drug dealers and insurance company investigators," Jack said.

"Interesting." Melanie studied him intently. "Add another bill and we'll talk."

"I'll do that if your information is good," Jack said.

Melanie considered briefly and then scooped up the two bills. "Okay, not bad for five minutes' work. What do you want to know?"

Winter leaned forward a little. "We're trying to find out if Jessica Pitt was seeing anyone at the time of her death."

"If she was, she didn't mention it to me," Melanie said. "That's it? That's all you want to know?"

"She seems to have been a woman who always had a man in her life," Jack said. "Are you sure there wasn't one?"

"I didn't say she wasn't seeing someone. I'm just telling you that if there was a potential new husband in the picture, she didn't talk about it during our skin therapy sessions."

"What did she talk about?" Winter said.

Melanie shrugged. "Mostly how she was going to screw her ex."

Winter did not risk a glance at Jack but she could tell that he had gone very still.

"Just to clarify," he said carefully, "are you telling us that Jessica Pitt was sleeping with her most recent ex-husband?"

"I didn't say she planned to sleep with him," Melanie said. "She wanted to screw him, as in she wanted revenge."

"Did she want revenge because he divorced her?" Winter asked.

"She wanted revenge because he tricked her into signing a complicated prenup that left her with a lot less than she thought she was going to get out of the marriage."

"What did she think she was going to get?" Jack asked.

"Half ownership in the ex's business." Melanie shook her head. "I'm no financial genius but I could have told her that wasn't ever going to happen. But evidently she believed that the guy was her ticket to the big time.

Then he dumped her and she found out about all the fine print in the prenup. She was pissed."

"Any reason why she thought she would end up with a piece of his company?" Jack asked.

Melanie grimaced. "Jessica was really smart when it came to financial stuff. She had an MBA. She was working for the West Coast office of a big Wall Street firm when she met husband number three."

"That's very interesting," Jack said. "I didn't find anything online that indicated Pitt had an MBA or a career in the financial sector."

Winter caught his eye and knew immediately that he was adding another layer to his rapidly evolving conspiracy theory. It was easy to see that he was already convinced Zane had gone online and scrubbed away a few key details about Jessica Pitt—details that might cause a committed investigator to keep digging into Jessica Pitt's life.

Melanie was still talking. It was as if, now that the floodgates had opened, she didn't see any reason to turn off the torrent of information.

"Jessica told me over and over again that she was the one who had taken her husband's firm to the next level in the financial world," Melanie said. "I think he owns some kind of investment company."

"Yes," Jack said. "Tazewell Global. It's a hedge fund."

Melanie nodded. "She said Tazewell owed her. All she could talk about in the weeks before her death was how she was going to make him pay."

"Did she happen to mention that she might be getting a little help with her revenge project?" Winter asked. "Maybe from a friend?"

Melanie looked like she was trying to frown in deep thought. Her eyes narrowed a little but the skin on her forehead did not move.

"At her last appointment Jessica said something about meeting a friend in Las Vegas. She wanted to look good. I asked her if she was going to fly. She said, no, she was going to drive. I was surprised because it's a good four-and-a-half- or five-hour drive from here, depending on traffic. But she said she was looking forward to a road trip."

"One more question," Jack said. "Did Jessica Pitt smoke?"

Melanie looked horrified. "Of course not. She cared way too much about her skin to take up smoking. What made you ask that?"

"According to the first reports of the accident, the investigators concluded that Jessica Pitt was smoking and fell asleep at the wheel," Jack said.

"She may have fallen asleep but she would not have been smoking," Melanie said.

CHAPTER THIRTY-SEVEN

―――― ≈ ――――

"An obsession with revenge is exactly the kind of thing that Quinton Zane could work with," Jack said.

"As your faithful sidekick, I feel it's my job to remind you that you're making a big leap here," Winter said. "There are a lot of questions that we haven't answered, as in, why would Zane want to manipulate a woman who harbored a grudge against her ex? And why use Jessica Pitt in the first place?"

They were sitting in a shady sidewalk café drinking cappuccinos. Well, *she* was drinking a foamy cappuccino. Jack was drinking an Americano, straight up. No milk, no sugar.

Twenty minutes ago they had both concluded a precision strike on a couple of clothing boutiques. The result was that they each had a few shopping bags filled with some new, grossly overpriced stuff. All the purchases had been made with cash, specifically Jack's cash, because she'd had exactly forty-seven dollars and change in her wallet when they had left Eclipse Bay and Jack was adamant that they not use credit cards.

Life on the run certainly complicated the simple things, like doing laundry, she reflected.

"Good question." Jack swallowed some of his Americano and lowered the cup. "If Zane targeted Jessica Pitt, he had a reason, and that reason most likely involved her ex-husband and the ex-husband's hedge fund."

"We still don't know if Zane was behind what happened to Jessica Pitt."

"It was Zane, I'm sure of it now."

"Because Jessica Pitt is dead?"

"Because Jessica Pitt died in a fiery crash on a lonely desert road and because all traces of her business background were scrubbed from social media and the Internet." Jack paused to finish his coffee. He set the cup down and opened his laptop. "And it's that last bit that interests me the most at the moment."

"If someone wanted to alter Jessica Pitt's life story, why not erase that third marriage?"

"Because it would be next to impossible, not to mention extremely time-consuming, to try to erase all public records of a marriage. Too many people would know about it, for one thing. You can change your identity online, but erasing a life is a lot harder. Zane would have been working quickly. He probably figured that getting rid of Jessica Pitt's obvious connections to the financial world would be enough."

"Enough to do what?"

"Stop someone like me from looking any deeper into Pitt's past."

Jack went to work on his laptop. Winter drank the rest of her coffee and thought about powerful obsessions. They probably didn't get any stronger than a lust for revenge.

After a while, Jack tapped one final key and looked up. His eyes had the cold, intense glitter that she had learned to recognize. It was the look she had seen so often in Eclipse Bay when he was deep in the research of a cold case.

"Husband number three was Grayson Fitzgerald Tazewell," Jack said. "He's the founder and CEO of Tazewell Global. The headquarters is in San Francisco. Tazewell has been married four times. Jessica was number four. He has one son by his first wife, who died several years ago. The son is now married and lives in Seattle. He started his own venture capital firm there. A successful business as far as I can tell."

"Got a photo?"

"Yeah, there's one of the son, Easton Tazewell, and one of the father, Grayson."

Winter leaned forward to get a better look. Easton and Grayson bore a striking resemblance to each other. Both were handsome, broad-shouldered men. Easton's hair was still blond but his father's had gone almost white. The picture of Easton had been taken at what looked like a black-tie charity event. His wife, Rebecca, was also in the photo. The picture of Grayson showed him on a golf course.

She lounged back against her chair. "Are you thinking that if Zane is involved in this, his goal was the hedge fund?"

"Maybe, but not because he needed the money. A hedge fund would be an ideal front for him, though. Private hedge funds are notoriously opaque. If you aren't very close to the seat of power, you have no idea of what is happening at the top. Some of the big funds have operated billion-dollar pyramid schemes for years. They get away with it because the financial records and transactions are anything but transparent."

"I see where you're going with this. Who would know more about the workings of a secretive hedge fund than an ex-wife who understood the financial world?"

"And who would have more reason to want revenge against the owner of the fund than an ex-wife who believed that she would become an equal partner in the firm?" Jack said. "Jessica Pitt gave Zane the inside information he needed to move in on Tazewell Global. When he was in position, he got rid of her."

"When he was in a position to do what?" Winter said. "And why that particular hedge fund?"

"We need to know more about the fund," Jack said. He unclipped his phone. "One of Cutler, Sutter and Salinas's clients is a lawyer who is well connected. If he doesn't know anything about Tazewell Global personally, he'll know who to ask. I'll have Anson give him a call."

"And then you and I need food and sleep. Also, I want to take a shower and change clothes."

"Good plan. We'll find a hotel."

"I saw a beautiful one on the way into town. The Burning Cove Hotel."

"Not that one," Jack said. "Way too many cameras in a place like that."

CHAPTER THIRTY-EIGHT

———≈———

"You must think that I'm a complete fool, just another easy mark." Grayson Tazewell flattened both hands on the top of his desk and shoved himself to his feet. His voice was a low, harsh rasp. His face was red with fury. "Easton was right about you all along. What made you believe that you could walk into my company and take control? Tazewell Global is *mine*. I built it from nothing. I would rather see it destroyed than hand it over to a fast-talking con man like you."

Lucan closed the door of the study with great care and walked a few steps into the room, giving himself a couple of beats to come up with a response. He had anticipated this scene for months, ever since he had discovered that Tazewell was his biological father. But it was happening too soon. And the dynamic was all wrong.

In his fevered imagination he had been the one in control of the scene. He had played it out a million times in his head. He would summon Grayson Tazewell into the richly paneled study of the wine country estate. He had hungered—lusted—for the moment when he would inform his father that the Tazewell Fund belonged not to the son who physically resembled him but to the one who had inherited Grayson's ruthless streak; the son who was his true heir.

The timing for this scene was unfortunate, Lucan thought, but now that the initial shock was over he could feel his blood heating. He was going to savor the hot rush of victory.

"Looks like my brother got to you," he said. "You do realize that Easton is jealous of me, don't you? He knows that I'm the only one who can save Tazewell. You know it, too."

"You're the one who pushed my company to the brink of bankruptcy, you fucking son of a bitch. You packaged those offerings in start-ups that didn't even exist except on the Internet." Grayson seized a file of papers and hurled it across the desk. "Nothing but steaming piles of shit. All of them."

Lucan watched the computer printouts fly from the folder and scatter across the carpet. He smiled.

"You fell for it, didn't you?" he asked. "The dazzling Grayson Fitzgerald Tazewell, the hedge fund magician of the West Coast financial world, fell for the same kind of con that he has run dozens of times."

"That's not true."

"We both know it's true," Lucan said. "Like father, like son. Like me."

Grayson swept out a hand to include the study, the wine country view; his whole world. "I didn't build all of this with fake investments, you lying bastard."

"Sure you did. It's true that you were damned good, I'll give you credit for that much. You had a knack for dumping the losers when it looked like they were going to be a problem. But right from the start you've been running a series of giant pyramid schemes. You created your own artificial bubbles in various tech areas. Just high-stakes versions of the old-fashioned pump-and-dump routine. What's more, you got away with it for decades. Right up until I came along."

"I've been able to read the market like no one else, you stupid SOB."

"No, your real talent was the ability to manipulate markets like no one else, at least in the short term. But because you were so good and it was all so easy, you got lazy. After I found out who you were, I watched you for months. I studied you. I dug into your past maneuvers. And when I was ready, I dangled the bait. You didn't just reach for it, you lunged for it with both hands."

"You're destroying my company."

"I told you at the start that I'm here to save Tazewell Global. That was the truth."

"Bullshit." Grayson slammed one fist against the desktop. "This is about revenge, isn't it?"

"I don't need your money. I have plenty of my own. My only goal is to save Tazewell."

"Why? If you hate me so much, why first destroy and then try to save my company?"

Quinton smiled slowly. "Because when this project is finished, it's going to be my company."

"You're crazy. Fucking crazy."

"It's my price for rescuing Tazewell Global. I was going to wait awhile before I had you sign the papers and transfer the assets, but under the circumstances, there's no reason not to do it now. Everything is ready to go. I'll have Victoria print out copies of the contract. We'll sign them today. You will make a formal announcement to the financial media this afternoon. Day One of your retirement starts tomorrow."

"You can't possibly believe I'll sign your fucking papers."

"The alternative is that the news of the sudden bankruptcy of Tazewell Global goes out today. It will contain enough information to ensure that the feds and a team of FBI agents will be at your door very early tomorrow morning. Not only will Tazewell go down in flames, but you'll go to prison. Everything you've built is on the line. You've got two sons but we both know that I'm the only one who can save your company and your precious reputation."

"No," Grayson roared. "I won't let you do this to me. You think I can't protect what's mine?"

He wrenched open the center drawer of the desk and reached inside.

A gun, Quinton thought. He was stunned. Grayson was reaching for a gun to kill the one person who could save the empire. Tazewell would rather go down with his company than let his rightful heir have it.

The realization came as a blinding flash of the obvious. *Well, shit. We really are alike.*

Enraged, Lucan grabbed the glass phoenix off the pedestal and hurled it at Grayson, who instinctively lurched to the side. The heavy statue slammed into his shoulder and then crashed to the floor, shattering.

Grayson grunted in pain but he managed to retain his grip on the pistol.

But Lucan was already rounding the corner of the desk. He grabbed Tazewell's gun arm. Grayson fought back with the rage of a man who has nothing left to lose. Off balance now, he went down hard on one knee. He made another desperate attempt to aim the pistol but Lucan clung to his gun arm.

And then they were both on the floor, struggling wildly. Their movements were hampered by the desk and the wall. Lucan was on top, both hands wrapped around Grayson's forearm in a desperate effort to get control of the gun.

The pistol roared. The boom exploded through the room and reverberated off the walls.

Grayson stiffened violently.

And then he went utterly limp.

It took Lucan a few seconds to realize that he had been partially deafened. The gun had gone off very close to his ear. He was vaguely aware of the muffled sound of the door slamming open. He looked up in time to see Victoria coming in low, pistol in hand. Devlin was braced above her. He swept the room with his weapon.

They took in the situation in a heartbeat.

"Are you hurt, sir?" Victoria demanded.

"No." Lucan finally remembered to breathe. He rolled off the dead man and sat up slowly. He was shaking. He could not bring himself to look at the body. "No, I don't think so. He . . . he went for a gun. He was going to kill me."

"Understood, sir," Devlin said. "Move away from the body."

Lucan got to his feet, feeling uncharacteristically clumsy and awkward. He took a few steps back and forced himself to look at Grayson. The bullet had entered through the jaw and exited out the side of the head.

There was a lot of blood and other matter on the windows and the floor of the study.

Victoria went forward to check for a pulse.

"Dead," she announced. She rose quickly. "You're sure you're all right, sir?"

"Y-yes," he said. "Yes, I'm okay."

He was shocked at the slight tremor in his voice. He had trouble keeping his balance. Devlin reached out to assist him.

"I said I'm all right," Lucan snapped.

"Yes, sir." Devlin's hard eyes got a little harder. He stepped back.

"He was going to kill me," Lucan whispered.

"Yes, sir," Devlin said. "How do you want to handle this? We can call the cops and go with self-defense—"

"*No.*" Jolted by the possibility of having to deal with the police, Lucan concentrated and managed to pull himself together. "Are you out of your fucking mind? We can't get the police involved in this. It would ruin everything."

"Understood, sir," Devlin said. "Just laying out options. This is going to get complicated."

"No, it's not," Victoria said. "There's no one on the grounds or in the house. The housekeeper went home two hours ago. It's highly unlikely that anyone heard the shots. We can make this go away, sir."

"How?" Lucan asked. He was unable to take his eyes off Grayson.

"We'll clean up the scene," Victoria said matter-of-factly. "Take the body into the hills. Bury it. There's a good chance it will be found eventually but if it is, it will look like Tazewell was killed because he wandered into a drug operation while out hiking."

"Owners of powerful hedge funds don't just vanish while out hiking, you idiot," Lucan said. "When Easton Tazewell finds out his father has gone missing, he'll launch a search."

Devlin studied the body. "You know, this could pass as a suicide."

Frantic now, Lucan seized on the option. "Suicide. Yes, that might work. Tazewell found out he was facing bankruptcy. He couldn't stand the humiliation of failure."

"I don't think your half brother is going to buy that story," Victoria warned. "He'll want a full-scale investigation. If that happens, it will come out that you and Devlin and I were all in the house on the day of the shooting. The housekeeper was here earlier. She saw us. We can probably finesse it but there will be a lot of questions and there's a real risk that your identity will be exposed."

"Let me think, damn it," Lucan said. "We need to get this right. We've got time."

"No, we don't, sir," Devlin said. "We have no idea where Lancaster and Meadows are. All we know for certain is that they are on the move. It appears that the Cutler, Sutter and Salinas people are all still in Seattle but it's hard to tell what that means."

"Because you can't get past their damned encryption," Lucan hissed.

And neither can I, he admitted to himself.

"Their tech security is very good, sir," Victoria said.

"They've upgraded in the past few months," Lucan muttered. "All right, we know that Anson Salinas, Max Cutler and Cabot Sutter are still in Seattle. That's a good sign. It means they don't have any leads. They may be spending a lot of time online looking for us, but our security is good, too. Just to be on the safe side, from now on we use burner phones. Understood?"

"Understood," Devlin said.

Lucan tried to think. "The good news is that Lancaster has no way of knowing about the Tazewell connection and he can't possibly know the endgame. But things are becoming unstable. We are going to have to bring this project to a close on a much faster timeline than I had intended."

"It isn't just Lancaster and his brothers we have to worry about," Devlin said. "There's also the problem of your half brother."

"Easton and his wife are in Seattle," Lucan said. "We don't have to worry about them, at least not now."

"The *problem* is that there's no way to know when Easton might decide to contact his father to check on the status of the situation here," Devlin said.

"Sir, don't forget that we have a contingency plan for an emergency such as this," Victoria said quietly. "We can close up the house. Instruct the housekeeper and gardener not to come in until they receive instructions to do so. Drive to San Francisco and catch a plane out of the country this evening. By the time someone finds the body, we will have disappeared."

Lucan wanted to howl with fury. It wasn't supposed to end like this.

He got the rage under control with a monumental effort and took another look at his father's body. The shock had subsided but a strange excitement was flooding his veins. It took a moment to identify the sensation, and then it hit him—he was thrilled. Elated. Triumphant.

He was now in full control of his father's empire. All he had to do was finish what he had started. And then his new life could begin.

"We don't know where Lancaster is," he said. "But we do know where Easton and Rebecca are. We will deal with them first." He glanced at his watch. "Book flights for Seattle. We can be there in a few hours. We'll take care of that end of things tonight. Tomorrow we move on to the next step."

"What is the next step?" Devlin asked.

He sounded skeptical.

Lucan described the plan he had conceived.

"Got it," Victoria said.

"Risky," Devlin said. "Lot of moving parts. You sure you don't want to go with something simpler and more straightforward?"

"If you don't think you can handle the job, you're free to resign now," Lucan said.

Devlin glanced at Victoria. "I can handle it. I'm just saying it's complicated, that's all."

"The boss is right," Victoria said. "Anything less complicated would be even riskier. You know as well as I do that it's not easy to just grab people off the street these days. Too many cell phones and security cameras around. This is a situation that requires distraction."

Devlin's jaw hardened. "I'll book the flights to Seattle."

"Too bad we can't use the Tazewell Global jet," Victoria said.

"Talk about a red flag," Lucan said, irritated. "A private jet can't fly in and out of major airports without leaving a trail."

Victoria flushed. "But Lancaster can't possibly know about the Tazewell connection."

"I'm not taking any chances," Lucan said. "We need to set the stage here because eventually the body will be found. When that happens, I don't want anything left behind here that could possibly link to me."

Devlin didn't say anything but his eyes narrowed a little.

"I don't want anything left that links to you or Victoria or me," Lucan amended smoothly. "I'm trying to protect all three of us. Now, move, people. I want to be out of here and on our way to Seattle within the hour."

Devlin swung around and strode out of the room. Victoria followed quickly.

Lucan waited until they were gone and then he took one last look at the body.

"I've got it all, you son of a bitch," he said softly.

Riding the hot rush of triumph, he crossed the room to the glass case that held the outrageously expensive hundred-and-fifty-proof brandy. He grabbed two bottles and headed for the door.

The only thing that had changed was the timing. It was still going to end the way it was supposed to end—with fire.

CHAPTER THIRTY-NINE

———≈———

There was nothing like a shower and fresh underwear to reinvigorate a woman, Winter decided. The combination did as much good as a session of meditation. Life got simpler when you were on the run. The essentials took on a whole new level of importance.

She pulled on the new pair of black panties and the new black jeans. Then she fastened the new black bra and slipped the new black T-shirt over her head.

She emerged from the steamy bath to find Jack standing in the doorway of the connecting rooms. He was wearing his new khaki trousers and—surprise!—a long-sleeved white shirt.

The energy in the atmosphere around him was so intense she was pretty sure she could have used it to charge a computer. Behind the lenses of his glasses his eyes had the icy-hot look she had come to recognize. Hunting mode.

"Why do I get the feeling you've had another insight?" she said.

"I just reviewed some information from that lawyer I told you about."

"The one who is a client of Cutler, Sutter and Salinas?"

"Right. He made some calls to people he knows in San Francisco. Evidently a couple of months ago there were rumors circulating that suggested Tazewell Global might be having financial problems. The situation was bad enough that a handful of the biggest clients pulled their accounts.

Grayson Tazewell managed to smooth things over, but he hasn't been seen in public since that time."

"I can tell you think that fits in with the latest version of your conspiracy theory," Winter said.

"Yes, it does. Running a con on a hedge fund would be right up Zane's alley. Tomorrow we're going back to San Francisco. I want to check out the headquarters of Tazewell Global."

Winter was startled by the little rush of excitement that ruffled her senses. She smiled.

Jack's eyes tightened at the corners. "What?"

"This business of hunting bad guys is sort of cool," she said.

Jack used both hands to carefully remove his glasses. He took out a handkerchief and polished the lenses with a thoughtful air.

"You think I'm fortunate because I've found my passion, as you put it?" he said.

"Yes. I think that is a rare and valuable gift."

"It may have its uses but I wouldn't call it a gift." He stowed the handkerchief in his pocket and put on his glasses. "At times it feels a lot like a curse."

"Every talent has a downside. The trick is learning how to manage both aspects—the light and the dark."

He was silent for a moment. He did not take his eyes off her.

"Now what?" she asked.

He walked slowly, deliberately across the small space that separated them and came to a halt in front of her.

"You may be right about me," he said. "I think I have found my passion."

"Right. Solving cold cases and finding answers for people."

"No," he said. "That's the work I do." He cradled her face between his hands. "At the moment my passion is standing right in front of me."

Heat lightning crackled in the room. A sensual thrill shivered through her. She put her hands on his shoulders.

"Jack," she whispered.

It was all she could say. It was enough.

With a husky groan of raw hunger, Jack covered her mouth with his own. The kiss crashed through both of them, fueled by the adrenaline that was flooding Jack's veins. Winter clenched her fingers into his shoulders to steady herself.

He broke the kiss long enough to pull off her new T-shirt and toss it onto the foot of the bed. The new bra followed a short time later.

And then the new jeans.

Last, but not least, the new panties landed on top of the heap of clothing.

The kiss got deeper. Hungrier. She freed her mouth and, feeling very daring, she reached up and slipped off Jack's glasses. There was something wildly intimate about the small act; something very personal.

Without the lenses, Jack's eyes were even more fierce. Fire and ice.

She unfastened the waistband of his trousers and lowered the zipper. Everything about him, including his erection, was fierce. And exciting. Very, very exciting. She wrapped her fingers around him.

He uttered a low, rumbling growl, fit his hands to her waist and lifted her up off her feet. He carried her across the room with quick, urgent strides. She closed her eyes, sure that she was going to land on the bed.

She was shocked when she felt the unyielding wall against her back. Her eyes snapped open.

"What on earth?" she said, disoriented.

"Wrap your legs around me," he ordered in a husky whisper.

Bewildered but too dazzled to ask any questions, she obeyed.

He braced her against the wall.

"Hang on," he said.

Anchoring her with one arm, he used his free hand to stroke her until she was melting; until she dug her nails into his shoulders. He guided himself partway into her.

She gasped and closed her eyes against the tight, full sensation. Slowly he eased in and out, each time going a little deeper. It was maddening. Desperate, she tried to take control of the rhythm and ride him. But he was the one in command of the situation. Everything inside her was squeezed to the breaking point.

Her release struck, shattering her senses. She gave a soft, astonished cry. He surged into her one last time, finally filling her completely.

He put his mouth against the curve of her shoulder to muffle his roar of satisfaction.

CHAPTER FORTY

"I'll take the first shift," Winter said.

Jack was on his back, propped up against a couple of pillows. He had one arm folded behind his head.

"You took the first shift last night," he said.

"You should sleep first because you are relaxed and ready to get some rest."

"What makes you think that?"

"Everyone knows that men find sex very relaxing. You are living proof."

"I am?"

"Just look at yourself." She sat up amid the tumbled bedding and held one sheet over her breasts. "A short time ago you were all wired and ready to go back to work. Then we had wild sex and now you look ready to fall asleep."

He eyed her through half-closed eyes. "Are you saying that you're not sleepy?"

"I'm feeling energized at the moment."

"I can see that."

She thought he would refuse. Instead, he inclined his head once.

"All right," he said. "Give me three hours and then wake me."

"You need more than three hours of rest."

"So do you. Wake me in three hours and we'll discuss the matter further."

She had pushed him far enough, she decided. The man could be stubborn.

"Okay," she said. She got up and stood beside the bed. "Go to sleep. I'll wake you in three hours."

He did not argue any more. Instead, he turned onto his side and closed his eyes. She gathered up her clothes, switched off the bedside lamp and went to the connecting door. There she paused.

"It isn't because you're grateful to me, is it?" she asked softly.

"What are you talking about?" he mumbled into the pillow.

"You said that I was your passion. I just wanted to be sure that it's not just because you're grateful to me. Because I helped you get control of the lucid dreaming and the sleepwalking."

"For the record, I don't sleep with people just because I happen to feel grateful to them," he said. He was still talking into the pillow.

"What do you do when you feel grateful to someone?"

"I write a nice thank-you note and I email it. Can I go to sleep now?"

"Yes," she said.

She went on into the other room. She had not received a thank-you note by email, she reminded herself. That was a good sign. She would think positive.

The following day, Jack was in the passenger seat of the rental car when his phone rang. He glanced at it and saw an unfamiliar number.

"It's a Cassidy Springs number," he said.

"Someone from the spa?" Winter suggested.

She was driving so that he could review his notes before the visit to Tazewell Global. They were on Interstate 5, heading north to San Francisco.

"Maybe," he said.

He took the call.

"This is Gail Bloom," Gail said, her voice quivering. "I need to talk to Winter. Please. It's really important. I tried her number but it threw me straight into voice mail. You gave me your card, so I decided to try the number on it."

Jack thought about Winter's phone, which he had insisted she ditch in the storage locker on the grounds that it might have been hacked. There was no need to explain that to Gail.

"Winter is driving, Gail," he said. "I'll put you on speaker."

"No," Gail yelped. "Don't do that. I need to talk to her privately."

"In that case, you'll have to wait until we can find a place to pull off the interstate."

"Hurry," Gail said.

Jack signaled to Winter. There was an off-ramp coming up fast. She took it and found a place to pull over. Jack changed places with her, got behind the wheel and headed back toward the interstate. Winter buckled herself into the passenger seat and picked up the phone.

"What's going on, Gail?" she asked. She listened intently for a moment. "All right, slow down. Tell me exactly what happened. Yes, I heard you. Yes, I can be in Cassidy Springs tonight, but let's talk about this. No, wait, don't hang up—"

Winter sighed and ended the connection. "Gail sounded scared. She says she wants to meet me tonight at the Cassidy Springs Wellness Spa at nine. She has something important to tell me about Raleigh Forrester."

"Why does she want to meet at the spa?"

"She said she wants to get together in a public location where she can be sure there are a lot of people around. She's very frightened, Jack."

"Why would there be a lot of people at the spa at nine o'clock at night?"

"The spa closes at eight but there are over half a dozen trendy bars and restaurants on that street," Winter said. "There are always a lot of people around on the sidewalks at night in that neighborhood."

"I don't like it."

"Gail Bloom is a very nice person," Winter said, "and what's more, she's seriously scared. If Raleigh Forrester is involved in this thing, we need to know how and why."

"Huh."

"This is a break," Winter said firmly. "We can't ignore it. You're the one who told Gail to get in touch if she had anything she wanted to tell us. Well, now she has gotten in touch. You know as well as I do that we have to follow up."

He thought about it.

"I still don't like it," he said.

Winter cleared her throat. "She, uh, said I'm to come alone."

"Not going to happen."

"I know her, Jack. I could tell she was sincere. She's really worried about me."

"I worry about you, too. That's why you're not going into that spa alone. And just so you know, if I don't like the looks of the setup, neither one of us will be going in tonight."

"Okay, okay," she said. "But I'm telling you, Gail is genuinely frightened. I think she believes that she's in danger."

He gave that some thought. "Was she calling from the spa?"

"No, she was outside on a street somewhere. Jack, I think we need to do some more research on Raleigh Forrester."

"I agree. I'll take a closer look at him after we pay a call to Tazewell Global."

That afternoon they stood in the lobby of the forty-story office tower that housed the headquarters of Tazewell Global. The place was busy because a number of other businesses operated out of the same building.

"I'm sorry," the receptionist said. "But Tazewell Global is closed for a month. Did you have an appointment?"

"Closed?" Jack said. "The entire business just shut down for a month?"

"Tazewell Global is not a huge firm," the receptionist said. "It occupies only half a floor. I was told that the CEO gave the staff a month's vacation—at least what's left of the staff."

"What's left of it?" Jack asked.

The receptionist lowered her voice. "I hear that a lot of people were let go a few weeks ago."

Outside on the street Winter looked at Jack. "You're going to try to get into the Tazewell Global offices, aren't you?"

"Yes," he said.

"You could get arrested, you know."

"Ninety-six percent probability that I won't get caught. I'm not much good with a gun but I do know how to get through locked doors."

"Where did you learn that skill?"

"The Internet."

Winter sighed. "When are you going to do it?"

"First thing in the morning," Jack said. "It will be easier to slip into the crowd of office workers who will be arriving to start the day."

"Maybe we'll get something useful from Gail tonight."

"Maybe," Jack said.

He did not sound hopeful.

"You really don't think Raleigh Forrester is involved in this thing, do you?" Winter asked.

"No," Jack said. "But it's possible that Zane is using him."

CHAPTER FORTY-ONE

⎯⎯⎯≋⎯⎯⎯

The sidewalks on the tree-lined street in front of the Cassidy Springs Wellness Spa were crowded with an assortment of stylishly dressed people coming and going from the various eateries and bars. Music spilled out of the open doors and windows of the establishments.

The only place on the street that was closed was the Cassidy Springs Wellness Spa. The sign was illuminated but the windows were dark.

Winter did her best to stay cool and calm; to stay focused on the coming meeting with Gail, but she could no longer suppress the unnerving frissons of anxiety that iced the back of her neck. The ominous sensation had been growing stronger during the evening. Jack had insisted on keeping an eye on the spa for the past few hours. They had watched the front door from the vantage point of a couple of different cafés.

Gail had not left with the rest of the staff when the spa closed at eight. As far as they could tell she was still inside, but if that was the case, she was waiting for them in the dark.

There were a handful of vehicles parked in the small lot in front. Technically, the lot was reserved for clients of the spa but after it closed people felt free to ignore the posted signs.

Shortly before nine Winter and Jack walked up to the glass doors of the lobby. The shades had been pulled, so it was impossible to see into the darkened space. Jack tried the door. It swung open, revealing a slice of the shadowed lobby.

Winter raised her voice. "Gail?"

The muffled explosion rumbled through the building. Glass shattered somewhere inside.

The screaming started a heartbeat later.

CHAPTER FORTY-TWO

———— ≈ ————

The panic-stricken cries were muffled but Winter recognized the woman's voice immediately.

"Door's locked. I can't get it open. Help me. Someone please help me."

"That's Gail," Winter said. She raised her voice. "It's me, Gail. Winter. Jack is with me. Which room are you in?"

"Women's Retreat." Gail's muffled voice was barely audible. "I can't get the door open. Something is blocking it. Help me, please."

Jack was speaking to the emergency operator, reporting the fire and the fact that there was someone inside the building. He ended the call and looked at Winter.

"Which room is the Women's Retreat?" he asked.

Winter pointed down a shadowy corridor. "Left at the end of the hall. The Women's Retreat chamber is the first door on the right."

"Stay outside on the street," Jack said. "The fire department will be arriving soon. There's a crowd gathering. Make sure you have other people around you at all times."

He did not wait for a response. He started down the hall.

"You might need help," Winter said.

"No. Get out and stay out."

He disappeared into the shadows.

Flames appeared at one of the windows.

Winter wanted to go after him but common sense told her that would be foolish. He needed to stay focused on rescuing Gail.

She retreated into the parking lot where a number of people were already gathered. Others poured out of the nearby restaurants and bars to watch the excitement.

The sirens were closer now. The first fire truck was rolling down the street toward the spa.

Winter edged backward without paying much attention to where she was going. She could not take her eyes off the entrance of the spa. Panic sleeted through her in icy waves. There was no sign of Jack or Gail.

"I wonder what started the fire," a woman said.

"I heard the spa is in financial trouble," a man responded. "What do you want to bet the owner torched the place to collect the insurance?"

Winter focused on the doorway of the spa, willing Jack to reappear. At last there was a shift in the shadows of the entrance and then she saw him emerge from the doorway. Relief soared through her. He had Gail draped in his arms.

A fire truck roared into the parking lot. Firefighters swarmed off the vehicle and took charge. A medic ran toward Jack and Gail.

Winter allowed herself a deep breath. She was vaguely aware of someone moving up behind her.

"Looks like we've got a real hero here," the woman said. "That's our story. See if you can get him on video, Sam."

"On it," a man said.

Winter realized she was standing in front of a reporter and a cameraman. She started to move out of the way but someone slapped a palm across her mouth. Simultaneously she felt a sharp, stinging sensation in the curve of her shoulder. A strange weight settled on her senses, dragging them under.

She tried to struggle; tried to shout for help. But it was too late. The world was already fading.

She thought she heard the reporter say something to some bystanders.

"She's okay. She fainted. Probably shock. We'll take her to the medics' van."

Winter tried to protest; tried to explain that she had not fainted. Tried to tell someone that she had been drugged. But she could no longer summon the energy required for speech.

The night closed in, hard and fast.

CHAPTER FORTY-THREE

———— ≈ ————

"They've got her," Jack said. "That's what this was all about. And I let them do it."

He had a death grip on the cell phone. It was a wonder the device did not crumple in his fist. It took every ounce of control he possessed to fight the hellfire that threatened to sweep through him. If he allowed the rage to consume him, he would be of no use to Winter.

He was sitting behind the wheel of the rental car watching the firefighters extinguish the last of the spa fire. Destroying the business had not been the objective, he thought. The fire was meant to be a distraction. Grabbing Winter had been the goal all along. Maybe they had hoped to take him as well. After all, they'd had no way of knowing that he would go into the building to find Gail.

"You had a decision to make," Anson said. "You made the choice to save a woman who might have died if you hadn't gone in. When it comes to this kind of situation, you don't have a lot of options. You make the decision and you live with it because it was the best decision you could make at the time."

Jack knew Anson had been forced to make his own hard choice on that long-ago night when Zane had torched the cult's compound. There had been no way to save everyone. Anson had made the split-second decision to try to rescue the children in the blazing barn. The mothers, most of whom had been locked inside the women's quarters, had perished.

Anson rarely talked about that hellish night but they all knew that he sometimes relived it in his dreams.

"Okay," Jack said. He took a deep, centering breath. The decision had been made. Now he had to figure it out from here. "Okay."

"You've collected a lot of new information about Quinton Zane in the past couple of days, but you've been running," Anson said. "Now's the time to slow down and put it all together."

That was Anson for you, Jack thought. He didn't dance around the edges of a problem with a lot of false happy talk. He went straight to the bottom line. And he was right. It was time to go down into Ice Town. Time to find the footprints of the killer and follow him into the darkness. Time to think like the human monster who had kidnapped Winter.

Jack used his free hand to open the console. The small slab of black obsidian gleamed in the darkness. He picked up the slice of volcanic glass and held it in his palm. Frozen fire. His key to finding Winter.

"I agree," he said. "But there's something else I have to do first. In the meantime, tell Xavier, Max and Cabot to keep working on the Tazewell Global lead. I need everything they can find on Grayson Fitzgerald Tazewell, his business and his family background. Every single fact. Every rumor. I want it all. Send the data to me as it comes in. Don't wait to verify it."

"I've got everyone on this," Anson said, "including Octavia, Virginia and Charlotte."

Jack didn't say anything. If Anson's lady love and Cabot's and Max's wives were now involved in the investigation, there was nothing else that could be done.

"What is it you have to do before you can focus on the new information you've got?" Anson said.

"I'm going to have a talk with the receptionist, Gail Bloom."

"The woman you were supposed to meet tonight? The one you rescued?"

"Yes. I saw the medics turn her loose a short time ago. She'll be home by now."

"Think she was supposed to survive the fire?"

"No, I think she was supposed to be used and then discarded. Collateral damage."

"In other words, you saved her life."

"If I know Zane, she won't be alive for long. I need to talk to her before he gets to her."

CHAPTER FORTY-FOUR

"What are you doing here?" Gail asked.

Her voice on the apartment building security system phone was breathless with panic.

"I want to ask you a few questions," Jack said.

"Not tonight. Please. I'm exhausted. The medics said I needed rest."

"I think you owe me a few answers, considering the fact that I saved your life tonight."

There was a short pause.

"Look, I really can't deal with this right now. I'll contact you tomorrow."

"They've got Winter," Jack said. "You helped them grab her. How much did they pay you?"

"Nobody paid me anything." Gail's voice was almost a squeak now. "I was just trying to help Winter. What is going on here?"

"I don't have time for games, Gail. Winter has been kidnapped, and if this scenario plays out the way I think it will, you'll be dead within twenty-four hours."

"What are you talking about?"

"What it comes down to is this: if I'm going to have a meaningful conversation with you, it will have to be tonight, before they come for you."

"What do you mean, I'll be dead within twenty-four hours?" Gail's voice rose to a hysterical pitch. "Are you threatening me?"

"Why would I do that?"

"You just said you blamed me for . . . for whatever happened to Winter tonight."

"I don't blame you nearly as much as I blame myself. But we can argue about that some other time, assuming you live long enough."

"You *are* threatening me. I'm going to call the police."

"Right now all I care about is finding Winter before they kill her. Like I said, I don't have a lot of time, because there's a ninety-nine-point-five percent chance that you'll be dead soon."

"Stop saying that," Gail shrieked.

"The only reason I'm not going with a hundred percent is because I have a policy against making one hundred percent predictions about an event until it's in the rearview mirror. There is always some room for uncertainty, at least until the victim is declared dead. When they find your body, I'll go with a one hundred percent prediction."

"You're crazy."

"You're not the first person to mention that possibility."

There was a long pause before Gail spoke again.

"They told me they were undercover detectives," she said. "They said they were investigating you."

"They? How many people are we talking about?"

"Two. A man and a woman." Gail sighed. "You'd better come upstairs. Two-twelve."

The door buzzed. Jack opened it before Gail could change her mind. Ignoring the elevator, he took the stairs two at a time. When he got to 212 he rapped sharply.

Gail opened the door and reluctantly stepped back. He moved in quickly and closed the door. Gail wrapped her arms around her midsection as though to protect herself.

"Tell me what you think is going on here," she said.

She no longer sounded panicked, but anxiety shimmered in every word. He was dealing with a badly frightened woman, Jack thought. He needed to give her a little space. But he also needed answers. He willed himself to exert patience.

"Let's start with one hard fact," he said. "I'm sure it's clear to you now that the two people who told you that they were undercover detectives were lying."

"Yes. I just don't understand any of this."

"I'm ninety-eight percent sure that those two people are working for the man I'm chasing."

Gail stiffened. "Are you a cop?"

"I'm affiliated with a private investigation agency," he said. Technically that was true. He was working with Cutler, Sutter & Salinas. "Here's what I know about my target. He has a habit of getting rid of people who learn too much about him, people he doesn't need anymore. You are now one of those expendable people, Gail. He can't afford to let you live."

"I don't know anything," Gail said. She was trembling.

"You know more than you think. For one thing, you can describe the fake undercover detectives."

"Oh, shit." There was a long pause. "Did they really take Winter? Why?"

"The man I'm after wants her as a hostage. He'll kill her when he doesn't need her anymore."

"Winter trusts you," Gail said finally.

It was a statement, not a question.

"Yes."

"You saved me tonight. I guess I should trust you, too. Right now you're sure a better bet than those two bastards who set me up. Tell me what this is all about. I am really, really scared."

"You've got good reason to be scared," Jack said. "The man I'm hunting is responsible for several murders that happened a little more than twenty-two years ago. There is a very high probability that he is also responsible for at least two more murders that occurred recently. He's been living out of the country for a couple of decades, but now he's back."

"Oh, shit. Oh, shit." Gail hugged herself tighter and rocked back and forth a little. "How is Winter involved?"

"The man who is responsible for kidnapping her is very, very good at manipulating people. He may have planned to grab me tonight, but that didn't work out for him. He got Winter instead. He'll use her to try to control me. And it will work because I'll do whatever he tells me to do if it means buying time for her."

Gail eyed him for a long moment, and then she seemed to fold in on herself.

"I don't understand any of this," she said.

"Start by telling me what those two fake detectives told you that convinced you to make that call to Winter."

"They contacted me the day before you and Winter showed up at the spa. They said they were running a sting operation and that you were the target. They said you were a con artist. They claimed that Winter had recently come into a nice inheritance and that you were trying to get your hands on her money. They told me that Winter was going to lose everything if I didn't help them arrest you. They showed me ID." Gail made a face. "It looked real. I called them after you left. Told them you would be at the self-storage facility that afternoon. I thought they would arrest you there."

"What names did they give you?"

"The man said his name was Knight. Detective Knight. I'm not sure of the woman's name. Sloan, I think. That's all I know, okay?"

"Describe Knight and the woman who was with him."

Gail shrugged. "Both in their thirties. Knight was good-looking in a slick sort of way. Dark hair. The woman was very attractive, too. She was a blonde. Both moved well, and they were both in good shape. I could tell that they work out."

"Accents?"

Gail thought for a beat and then shook her head. "Nothing that sounded unusual."

"How did they get into the spa tonight?"

"They came in as guests earlier this evening but they didn't leave when everyone else did. They stayed out of sight in the pool room. I closed up as usual so I was the last one in the building. I didn't leave."

"At what point did it dawn on you that you'd been conned and that you might die tonight?"

"When that bitch shoved me into the Women's Retreat and pushed something heavy against the door so that I couldn't get out." Gail paused. "What was it, anyway? You must have had to shove it out of the way to get the door open."

"A cabinet."

"Oh, yeah, the big one in the hallway," Gail said. "Well, by then I realized I was in way over my head. I was terrified. The woman warned me not to make any noise. I got the feeling that she would shoot me if I did. I wondered if I had landed in the middle of a drug gang war. A short time later there was a small explosion. Then I smelled smoke coming through the air-conditioning vents. That's when I started screaming."

"Tell me everything you heard them say."

"They didn't do a lot of talking," Gail said. "They were just very efficient about everything. Businesslike."

"Think hard, Gail. What were they driving?"

"Driving? Oh, yeah. A white van."

"Logo on the side?"

"No, I don't think so."

"Figures," Jack said.

"What?"

"White vans are very useful when it comes to kidnapping people."

Gail shuddered. "That's what the serial killers always use on TV."

"Except this isn't TV. They thought you were either going to die in the fire or soon afterward, so they may have gotten careless. Did they say anything about where they were headed or where they had come from?"

"No." Gail frowned. "Wait. I think the man said something about traffic. The woman told him not to worry about it. She said there wouldn't be a problem on I-Five at that hour of the night."

"North or south?"

"What?"

"Interstate Five runs north and south on the West Coast. Do you think the fake cops were headed south? L.A. or San Diego, maybe?"

Gail looked startled by the question and then she shook her head. "No. The woman said that if there was a problem it would be around Portland and Seattle because there would probably be commuter traffic by the time they got there. And then she told Knight to stop fussing. She said he sounded like a little old man."

"Anything else?"

"Well, there was one weird thing but I don't see how it could matter."

"What?"

"I got the feeling that they were having some sort of argument. You know, working together because they had a job to do but bickering with each other. He kept telling her it was a lousy plan and she kept saying it was brilliant. This is going to sound strange, but they sounded like a couple on the brink of a divorce."

"Anything else, Gail? Think hard, because Winter's life depends on it."

"No." Gail burst into tears. "I'm sorry."

It wasn't nearly enough but it was more than he'd had fifteen minutes ago, Jack thought.

"The authorities are probably going to investigate the fire at the spa as an arson-for-hire job," he said. "They'll take a hard look at the owner, Raleigh Forrester, first. But sooner or later they'll circle back to you and they'll have questions. A lot of questions."

"I am so scared. I don't know what to do."

"If I were you I'd leave town. Now. Go somewhere and stay there until this is finished. Pack a bag. I'll wait until you get into your car but that's all the time you get from me. I have other priorities."

"Shit." Gail straightened her shoulders and rushed toward the bedroom. "I should have known they were fake cops."

"What was your big clue?"

"The clothes. How many cops do you know who wear Armani?"

CHAPTER FORTY-FIVE

———— ≈ ————

She floated down an endless corridor on a tide of visions. Occasionally she was aware of being jostled from side to side by the undercurrents of the dreams. Whenever she tried to reach out to steady herself, she discovered that she could not move her hands. Sometimes she tried to surface, to shout for help, but she could not do anything more than make a small croak of sound. She wondered if she was trapped in the terrifying state of sleep paralysis.

It's just a dream, she thought.

But she knew she was lying to herself.

There was a steady rumble in the background. It sounded like a vehicle traveling fast on pavement.

Sometimes there were voices.

"She's waking up," a woman said. "Pull over when you get a chance. I'll give her another injection."

"Be careful with that crap." A man this time. "She's smaller than the other two. An overdose might put her into a coma."

"It's not my fault that she's waking up."

The dreamer went very still and willed herself back into the dream, hoping to feign sleep. Hoping that there would be no more injections.

The woman spoke again. "We're going to have to do something about the receptionist. She wasn't supposed to make it out of the building."

"She doesn't know anything that could hurt us."

"She's a loose end."

"No shit. Don't blame me. I told you and Tazewell that it was a bad idea to use her in the first place."

"Shut up and drive."

"You're fucking him, aren't you?" the man said after a while.

"What are you talking about?"

"You're fucking the client. Tazewell."

"No, I am not fucking the client."

"You want to fuck him," the man said.

"That's not true."

"Shit," the man said again. "I had a bad feeling about this job right from the start."

"This job," the woman said evenly, "is our chance to get out of this fucking business before we get old and slow and dead. Damn it, I'm going to give her another injection."

The dreamer felt another sting. The tide of visions swept over her again. She knew that Jack was somewhere on the distant shore, searching for her. She wanted to call to him but she could not make a sound.

CHAPTER FORTY-SIX

━━━━━━━ ≈ ━━━━━━━

Jack pulled into the empty parking garage of a closed mall and shut down the car engine. He opened the console, took out the chunk of obsidian and held it in one hand while he centered himself. He had a lot to work with now. He just had to step back far enough to be able to analyze the currents.

He took a breath, let it out with control and prepared to visit Ice Town.

. . . He opens the gates of ice and walks into the frozen city. The obsidian in his hand is warm and somehow comforting. It's a talisman he will use to find Winter.

He moves through the maze of streets and alleys until he finds himself in the frozen garden in the center of the town. From there he can observe all that goes on around him.

Zane's footprints burn in the ice of a nearby alley. The alley is in deep shadow but it is no longer uncharted territory. It has a name: Tazewell.

Out of all the hedge funds on the West Coast, what made you go after Tazewell Global? I know why you targeted Jessica Pitt. She had insider information about the fund. But how did you discover that? And how did you learn that she wanted revenge on her ex?

He starts walking toward Tazewell Alley but just as he is about to enter it another set of footsteps catches his attention. Jessica Pitt.

He changes course and follows the dead woman's prints into a narrow lane. At the end of the lane there is a vehicle engulfed in frozen flames. Jessica Pitt is behind the wheel. She looks at him with dead eyes.

"What makes you think that he found me?" she asks.

"Good question," the dreamer says.

And just like that he knows it is the right question, the one he should have been asking all along.

He looks around and, sure enough, there is a name written in letters of frozen fire. He says the name aloud.

"Winter."

Jack surfaced from the waking dream and grabbed his phone.

Anson answered immediately. "What have you got?" he said.

"Jessica Pitt is the key to this thing," Jack said. "I've been assuming Zane used her to get inside Grayson Tazewell's hedge fund business. I'm pretty sure that much is true. But I've been coming at this from the wrong direction."

"What do you mean?" Anson asked.

"I assumed that Zane targeted Jessica Pitt from the outset, that he wanted to find a way into Tazewell's empire and she had the bad luck to be convenient. But that still leaves the question of why he chose Tazewell in the first place. If he just wanted a hedge fund as a cover, why not invent one from scratch online? That's well within his skill set. Why infiltrate an existing fund? That had to be a hell of a lot more complicated, not to mention risky, because he wouldn't be able to control all the moving parts."

"Where are you going with this?" Anson asked.

"What if Zane didn't find Jessica Pitt?" Jack said. "What if Jessica Pitt found Quinton Zane?"

There was a short, charged pause on the other end of the connection.

"Slow down," Anson said. "You and Max and Cabot have been looking for Zane for years. Recently Xavier's been hunting for him, too. The four of you are all pretty damn good when it comes to locating people. What makes you think Pitt could have found Zane when you all couldn't?"

"Maybe Jessica Pitt had information that we didn't have," Jack said. "Very personal information that she got while she was married to Grayson Tazewell."

"Well, damn," Anson said very softly. "Just what kind of information do you have in mind?"

"Thanks to Xavier we know Zane was adopted shortly after he was born. I think there is a possibility that Zane is Tazewell's biological son. What's more, I don't think Zane himself knew that until sometime in the past year. Maybe he found out because Jessica Pitt discovered that her ex-husband had a son he had never acknowledged. After the divorce she went looking for the kid online."

"Because she figured she could use him to get revenge against her ex?"

"Maybe. She might have intended to blackmail Tazewell with the information. Who knows? Whatever the plan was at the start, Zane turned the tables on her."

"That's a reach, Jack. If Jessica Pitt did figure out that Quinton Zane was Tazewell's son and if she searched for him online—a couple of big ifs—she would have run up against the same brick walls that we hit. Officially Zane died over twenty-two years ago. I still can't see how she could have found him if we weren't able to locate him."

"She wouldn't have had to find him," Jack said. "As soon as she started looking for him, he would have been alerted. He's bound to have trip wires out there on the Internet. I'm sure he knows that Max and Cabot and I have been searching for him for the past couple of decades. That's why he's stayed out of the country."

"So Zane is alerted to the fact that someone named Jessica Pitt is looking for him and he gets curious," Anson said, walking through the logic.

"Yes," Jack said. "He's more than curious. It's safe to say he is very worried. After all, it's a threat coming from an entirely unexpected direction. So he starts digging into Jessica Pitt's personal life, trying to find out what set her on his trail. One question leads to another. He wants answers, so he decides to make contact."

"That's when he discovers the truth about his birth?"

"Right. He probably sat on the information for a while, trying to decide how to deal with it."

"Then the Night Watch case goes down here in Seattle and he decides to make his move."

"Yes," Jack said. "The timeline works now. Jessica Pitt is the butterfly that flapped its wings and triggered the hurricane that hit Tazewell Global."

"All right, I'll admit you've got a theory, but it's just a theory. Meanwhile, I was just about to call you. I've got news from this end. Easton and Rebecca Tazewell have disappeared."

"I'm listening."

"Max and Cabot are trying to find them," Anson said. "The Tazewells were last seen late last night. They were leaving a big charity affair here in the city. They got into a limo but they never arrived at their home on Lake Washington."

"Are the cops looking for them?"

"No," Anson said. "Max and Cabot talked to the couple's housekeeper. She told them Mr. Tazewell had sent her a text message saying that he and his wife had decided to slip away for some time together."

"Zane grabbed them."

"Given the timing, I think we have to assume that, yeah. And there's something else. I'll let Xavier tell you."

Xavier spoke, his voice crackling with excitement. "I told you that a few weeks ago, Grayson Tazewell pretty much dropped out of sight. The dude owns five houses—well, one is an apartment in New York. The others are in the Hamptons, Beverly Hills, Hawaii and Sonoma. Sonoma is the closest and I'm pretty sure that's where he went."

"How did you figure it out?" Jack asked.

"Process of elimination," Xavier said. "The Tazewell Global jet is still sitting at the San Francisco airport and the yacht is still in the harbor there. That indicates that wherever Tazewell went, he probably drove."

"And the nearest place he could go where he could be assured of privacy would be his house in Sonoma," Anson concluded.

Jack tightened his fingers around the obsidian. "I was going to pay a visit to Tazewell Global early this morning but I think I'll learn more if I get inside the Sonoma house. I need to choose one or the other, because I can't afford to waste time."

"You really think they're headed toward Seattle with Winter?" Anson said. "And that they're driving?"

"That's the best lead I have at the moment. They've got no choice but to drive. They can't carry a hostage onto a commercial flight and they can't use the Tazewell Global jet because they'd have to explain the hostage to the pilots."

"And even if they came up with a convincing explanation, those pilots would have to file a flight plan," Anson said.

"Why would Zane bring his hostage to Seattle?" Xavier asked.

"Maybe because the other two hostages, Easton and Rebecca Tazewell, were already here," Anson said. "Zane probably figured it would be easier to transport one more here rather than try to move the other two across a couple of states. Besides, he knows the territory up here. Remember, he grew up in the Pacific Northwest."

"Maybe," Jack said. Something did not feel quite right about that theory but he let it go for the moment. "What we do know is that the kidnappers left Cassidy Springs around nine p.m. tonight. Assuming they are driving straight through with no stops except for gas, the earliest they could arrive in the Seattle area is about fourteen hours after they left, depending on traffic. But there is always traffic, so we've got a window of maybe sixteen hours, max."

"That's our clock," Anson said.

"What clock?" Xavier asked.

"That's how long we've got to find the location of the hostages and figure out how to rescue them," Jack said. "Because somewhere between fourteen and sixteen hours from now I'll get a message telling me where I need to be if I want to save Winter and the others. As soon as Zane's got me he won't need the hostages."

"You're sure?" Xavier asked. He sounded stunned.

"One hundred percent probability," Jack said.

CHAPTER FORTY-SEVEN

Jack stood in the shadows of the night-darkened vineyards that surrounded Tazewell's Sonoma estate and studied the gated mansion. A great sense of emptiness shimmered in the atmosphere.

There was no visible security but that didn't mean there wasn't a hell of a lot of the electronic kind, he thought. There was enough light from the full moon to reveal the closed doors of the half dozen garages that lined the courtyard inside the gates. There was no way to know if there were any vehicles inside.

He walked up to the wrought iron gates and examined them closely. There was an electronic security box but the alarm was off. He tested one of the gates. It swung open without protest.

He took out his phone and punched in Anson's number. "The place is deserted. Looks like someone left in a hurry and didn't bother to reset the security system."

"That doesn't sound right," Anson said. "Please tell me you managed to pick up a gun somewhere."

"We both know I'm not a very good shot."

"I've told you before, very few people are good shots, not when they're in a real-world shooting situation. The idea is to scare the hell out of the other guy."

"Under the circumstances I think I can do that without a gun. I am not in a good mood." He walked into the courtyard. "I'm inside the gates. No alarms."

"That doesn't make any sense," Anson said. "Why would a wealthy man leave his house unprotected?"

"I'll find out," Jack said.

He moved across the moonlight-splashed courtyard and tried the front door. It swung open, inviting him into the shadows of the big house.

"I'm in the front hall," he said into the phone. "All the lights are off. I'm going to need my penlight. I'll clip the phone to my belt and put you on speaker."

The rooms on the ground floor resembled a series of elegant hotel lobbies. They were large spaces furnished with oversized chairs, sofas and consoles. They looked like rooms that had been designed to be photographed for spreads in glossy magazines. Everything was on a grand scale. Everything looked expensive. But there was virtually nothing of a personal nature. They were not the sort of rooms that invited you to sit down and read a book. You didn't have a drink with a friend in rooms like these.

He knew all about rooms like the ones he was touring tonight, he thought. They were the glitzy, high-end version of the rooms he had been living in for the past few years. Temporary places. Nothing about them spelled home.

He gave up on the ground floor and climbed the elaborate staircase to the next level.

The scale of the upstairs rooms was somewhat more normal. He sifted through closets and drawers and came across things—a single sock, a tube of toothpaste, a used drinking glass in a bathroom—that told him the spaces had been used by actual humans.

He hit the jackpot when he opened the door of the master bedroom. The clothes in the closet and the array of masculine toiletries in the bath told its own story. Someone had been staying in the big house recently.

"Whoever was here took off in a hurry," he said to Anson. "He left a lot of his stuff behind. There's a third floor in the other wing. I'm going to check it out now."

"I don't like the feel of this."

"I'm pretty sure there's no one here now."

"You never say things like 'pretty sure,'" Anson said. "You always go with precise percentages. Are you telling me you're one hundred percent sure you're alone?"

"No," Jack said.

"Then what the hell are you saying?"

Jack reached the top of the stairs. There was only one room on that floor. The door was closed. He put his back to the wall, wrapped his fingers around the knob and gently opened the door.

The miasma of death wafted out of the opening.

"You asked me if I was sure I was alone," Jack said. "It depends on your definition of alone."

"Body?" Anson asked.

"Yes."

He walked into the room and aimed the penlight down at the face of the man sprawled on a limestone floor that was covered in a spill of dried blood.

"Not Zane," he said. "Not Easton Tazewell and not one of the pros who attacked Winter and me. An older man. Ninety-seven percent probability that it's Grayson Tazewell."

"I'm betting he didn't die of natural causes."

"No, gunshot fired at close range," Jack said. "Looks like there was a struggle. Lot of broken glass. Chair tipped over. Papers on the floor."

Cautiously he nudged the body onto one side and plucked an expensive leather wallet out of a rear pocket. He flipped it open and studied the driver's license.

"ID confirms it's Grayson Fitzgerald Tazewell," he said.

He let the body fall and got to his feet. The flashlight caught the glint of gold on Tazewell's hand. Not a wedding ring, a signet ring. The image carved into it was that of a phoenix rising from the ashes.

Jack speared the light around the office.

"Something went very wrong in this room," he said.

"I'd say so, given that you found a body there," Anson said.

"No, it's more than just the body." Jack paused while he cataloged all of the things that were not right in the space. "Someone didn't just walk in and pull a trigger. This wasn't a professional hit. There was a fight. Grayson Tazewell lost. They tried to set the scene."

"They?" Anson prompted.

"Zane and, very probably, those two bodyguards he's got with him. Tried to make it look like a home invasion."

"Think Zane's security people shot Tazewell?" Anson asked. "Maybe to protect their boss?"

"No. They're pros. This doesn't look like a cold-blooded execution-style killing. Feels like a struggle over the gun." Jack aimed the flashlight at the floor. "And the gun is still here, which means it's probably Taze-well's. This explains why the alarm system was down."

"What do you mean?" Anson asked.

"Whatever occurred here, it wasn't part of the plan," Jack said. "They had to improvise. They switched off the alarm system so that, eventually, when the body was found, the police would assume that someone hacked into it in order to break into the house."

"You need to get out of there, Jack. You can't afford to get arrested, not now. We're on the clock."

"Soon," Jack said.

But he didn't head for the door. There was a very real possibility that Quinton Zane had been in this room; a possibility that Zane had been involved in the struggle that had ended with Tazewell's death. There was information in this office. Impressions. He needed every bit of data he could collect. Winter's life depended on it. So did the lives of Easton and Rebecca Tazewell, assuming Zane hadn't already murdered them.

He forced himself to take the time to go through the desk drawers and then he picked up some of the papers that had fallen onto the floor. For the most part he found himself looking at spreadsheets and other kinds of financial documents.

One file was unlabeled. Jack flipped it open. Inside was a report from a private investigator dated forty-six years earlier. The paper was yellowed with age. Jack read through the details quickly and then summarized them for Anson.

"Forty-six years ago a woman in Seattle tried to blackmail Tazewell," he said. "She claimed to have had his son and she wanted money to keep quiet."

"That wasn't smart," Anson said.

"In the report, the investigator assures Tazewell that the woman is no longer a problem, as she recently died of an overdose."

"What about the baby?"

"The investigator states that shortly before her death the mother evidently sold the baby to another couple. The investigator was unable to confirm the sale but assumes that the infant disappeared into the black market and is unlikely to ever be a problem. That's the end of the report but there's a handwritten note in the file that looks new. It's just a name. Lucan Tazewell."

"Damn," Anson said very softly. "You might be right. Zane may be Tazewell's son. Anything else?"

"Yes. A photo of a woman."

Jack studied the image of a woman with long dark hair and a face that was so spectacularly beautiful as to seem unreal.

"I think I just found a picture of the woman who was Quinton Zane's mother."

"You're sure."

"Zane takes after her, not his father. There's a note underneath the image. Date of death and cause. The woman died forty-six years ago of an overdose." He picked up another page in the folder. "Just came across the results of a DNA test stating that there is a very high probability that subject number one is a close relative or the son of subject number two."

"All right, either Zane really is Tazewell's son or he's managed to convince Tazewell of that. Comes down to the same thing."

"Yes."

Jack put down the folder and prowled the room, searching for additional information.

A glass case that held four bottles of a very exotic and no doubt very expensive hundred-and-fifty-proof brandy was positioned in one corner. The dust marks indicated that two bottles had recently been removed but there was no indication that they had been opened in the study.

The pictures on the walls were mostly photographs of Grayson Tazewell with celebrities and an assortment of VIPs that included a couple of senators. There was also a photo of a sleek, modern-looking yacht. The name on the hull was *The Phoenix IV.*

Jack was about to move on when he noticed the photograph in the center of the display. The mansion in the image was old, a relic of another century's idea of grandeur. It was the kind of over-the-top summer place that established East Coast families had built in the Hamptons or Newport.

But the rugged landscape in the scene did not look like the East Coast. The trees and the cliffs had a Pacific Northwest vibe. There was a dock in front of the mansion. An old-fashioned yacht was tied up at one of the slips. In the beam of the penlight it was just possible to make out the name. *The Phoenix.*

Jack took the picture down off the wall and smashed the glass against the edge of the desk.

"What the hell was that?" Anson asked. "Are you all right?"

"Yes," Jack said. "Looking at another photograph."

He removed the photo from the frame and turned it over. Someone had scrawled the words *Azalea Island House* and a date from nearly four decades earlier.

"Get out of there, Jack," Anson said.

"Heading downstairs now. Tell Xavier I need him to do a property records search."

"What's going on?" Anson demanded.

"Hang on until I get back to the car."

Jack went out of the big, empty house that had never been a home and made his way through the designer-perfect vineyards.

He found the rental car where he had left it on a side road veiled by trees.

"Talk to me, son," Anson said.

"It's okay, Anson, I'm back in the car. Ninety percent sure I know where to look for Zane."

"Listening."

Jack glanced at the photograph sitting on the passenger seat.

"I think he's trying to go home."

CHAPTER FORTY-EIGHT

"You were right," Xavier said. "There was a sixth house and it is in the Pacific Northwest, specifically a private island in the San Juans. Azalea Island. Looks like it was named after Tazewell's first wife. But he sold it over thirty years ago. It's been through three other owners since then."

"What was the date of the last sale and who is the current owner?" Jack asked.

He was sitting in a café near the San Francisco airport, a cup of coffee in front of him, the phone to his ear. He figured there was a ninety-nine percent probability that he would be contacted by Zane in a few hours. He had to be ready with an endgame.

Cabot and Xavier were on the other end of the connection now. Max and Anson were there, too. Virginia and Charlotte were also in the room. The family had gathered together in the offices of Cutler, Sutter & Salinas to face the disaster.

"Turns out it's not easy to unload a private island," Cabot said. "Not a lot of buyers for that kind of property, especially when the island in question is in the cool, damp Pacific Northwest, not the sunny Caribbean. But the current owner is a shell company with so many layers we may never be able to identify the owner. The purchase occurred about five months ago."

"Zane," Jack said. "Ninety-eight percent probability, given the timing."

"Max and I agree that the timing fits," Cabot said. "The purchase took place after Jessica Pitt was divorced from Grayson Tazewell. If she went looking for Zane soon after she and Tazewell separated and if Zane decided that he really was Tazewell's son and that he wanted a piece of family history—yeah, the timing definitely works."

Jack closed his eyes and thought about it. "That feels right. In Zane's view, the Azalea Island house should have been his ancestral home."

"You think Zane took Winter and maybe Easton and Rebecca to the Azalea Island house, don't you?" Cabot asked.

"It fits with everything I know about him," Jack said. "And it's a smart strategy for someone who is holding hostages. He's on ground he believes he controls. If he decides he's losing control he can use a boat to disappear into the San Juans."

"With one of the hostages," Max said, his voice very grim. "He'll keep that hostage alive only as long as he finds it useful. He'll get rid of the others."

No one responded. There was no need. If there was ever a time to stay positive, Jack thought, this was it.

He focused on the logic of a strategy.

"The Azalea Island house was on the market for years," he said. "That means it probably went through a lot of listing agents. There should be photographs of the interiors on the real estate websites. There will also be aerial views of the house and the island. We could really use a floor plan."

"Anson told us to get moving on that angle as soon as you came up with the location of the house," Cabot said. "Virginia and Charlotte are searching the real estate websites for interiors and any architectural details they can find. I've pulled the aerial views. I can tell you one thing already."

"What?" Jack asked.

"That house must have been built for someone with a lot of money back in the day."

"Because of the big dock?"

"No, because there's an old helicopter pad on the roof. You can still see some of the markings."

Jack considered that briefly. "Interesting. But I think there's a very low probability that Zane will be using a helicopter to transport his hostages."

It was Max who answered. "A helo would draw way too much attention out there in the San Juans. Those islands are very, very quiet. People on neighboring islands would notice."

"There's another reason he wouldn't go with a helo," Jack said. "He knows boats. Remember, he used a yacht that he stole to stage his own death years ago. And boats are much quieter and less obvious. A lot of people who live in the San Juans own a vessel of some kind. No one would notice one more."

"I take it you're staying down there in the Bay Area until you hear from Zane?" Max said.

"I don't have any choice," Jack said. "Not if we want him to be convinced that we don't know where he's hiding. If I head north to Seattle before he orders me to get on a plane, he may start to wonder if I've made the connection to Tazewell and Azalea Island."

"There's another reason you need to stay down there," Cabot said. "There's still a possibility that we might be wrong. Maybe Zane is holding the hostages somewhere in California."

"Gotta think positive," Jack said.

CHAPTER FORTY-NINE

———— ≈ ————

She was swimming against the tide again, struggling to surface; dreading the weight that would soon flow through her veins and drag her down.

She was more than a little amazed when she finally got her eyes open and discovered that she was awake. Sort of. The aftereffects of the drug tugged at her senses but this time she was able to overcome the riptide of sleep. She was vaguely aware that the room was illuminated in the glare of a camp lantern.

"You're going to be okay," a woman said. She spoke in low tones, as if she was afraid that someone might be listening. "Here, have some water. We saved one of the sandwiches for you."

She used both hands to hold out a bottle of water. Winter realized that was because the woman's wrists were bound with a zip tie.

"Thanks," Winter said. She realized that she sounded drunk. When she automatically tried to reach for the bottle she discovered that her wrists were bound as well. She swallowed some of the water. After a couple of sips she tried speech again. "Am I hallucinating? You look like a Disney princess."

The woman was dressed in a sophisticated evening gown that rustled a little when she moved. A cashmere stole was draped around her shoulders. A delicate string of diamonds circled her throat. There were more diamonds in her ears.

"If I were a real fairy-tale princess I'd call my fairy godmother and have her wave a wand to rescue us. I'm Rebecca Tazewell. This is my husband, Easton."

Winter scrutinized the man who moved into view. He looked good in his tux, as if he was accustomed to wearing one.

Winter hoisted the water bottle in a small salute. "You must be Prince Charming."

"Not exactly," Easton said. "We were on our way home from a charity event when they grabbed us. Lucan's two bodyguards replaced our usual driver. They used some drug to knock us out. We woke up here. Sorry you got dragged into this. As far as I can tell you're the only one who hasn't got a connection to my crazy half brother. You just happened to be in the wrong place at the wrong time."

"If we're talking about Quinton Zane," Winter said, "and I assume we are, I do have a connection to him." Her voice seemed to be growing stronger. She swallowed some more of the water and lowered the bottle. "He tried to have me killed on at least two occasions. That makes for a unique bond, believe me."

"Try to eat something," Rebecca said. She held out a stale-looking cheese and bologna sandwich that looked as if it had come out of a vending machine. "It will help you get over the effects of the sedative."

Winter examined the sandwich. It did not look particularly appetizing, but she had eaten far less appealing food during the years she and Alice had traveled to far-off research locations with Helen and Susan Riding. She needed her strength. She took a healthy bite.

"What's the setup in this place?" she asked around a mouthful of the sandwich.

"We're in the only house on a private island in the San Juans," Easton said. "My parents bought it back at the start shortly after my father made his first fortune. They never used it much. Turns out most of the people my father wanted to impress weren't interested in spending long weekends on an island where there was nothing much to do except look at the water.

After Mom died he sold it. That was about thirty years ago. There's a new owner now."

"Your crazy half brother?"

"Good guess," Rebecca said.

"How many people does Zane have with him?"

Easton's brows rose. "Why do you call him Zane?"

"Once upon a time he was Quinton Zane. What's his name now?"

"He calls himself Lucan Tazewell," Easton said. "And to answer your question, he's got two so-called security people with him. *Professional thugs* would be a better description. They're both seriously armed. Lucan has a gun, too, although from the way he handled it, I don't think he's familiar with firearms."

"We're on the second floor," Rebecca added. "The door is locked and the windows have been boarded up. Easton has been trying to loosen some of the boards, but no luck so far."

"Even if I do get a few of them free, it's a long drop to the ground," Easton said. "At the very least we will probably break some bones. I'm thinking we might be able to use the drapes to lower ourselves out the window but they're pretty threadbare. Not sure they'll hold our weight."

"Does your half brother ever come up here to check on his hostages?" Winter asked.

"No," Rebecca said. "Lucan or Zane, or whatever he calls himself, doesn't seem particularly interested in us. Haven't seen much of Knight, the male security guy, either. The woman is the one who occasionally checks on us. Her name is Sloan. Victoria Sloan. I think she's more than a little obsessed with Lucan."

Dreamlike memories of a conversation she had overheard while she was fighting the tide of the drug floated through Winter's mind.

A man's voice. "You're fucking the client."

And then a woman. "No, I am not fucking the client."

The man again. "You want to fuck him."

"I might be able to work with that," Winter said. "But first I've really got to pee."

"You're in luck," Rebecca said. "There's a bathroom attached to this room."

"Amenities are important," Winter said.

CHAPTER FIFTY

———— ≈ ————

Juggling a cell phone and a gun, Victoria shoved the ancient key into the equally ancient lock. It was a bit of a struggle. The security in the old house was a bad joke. Lucan had assured her that there was no need to worry about installing a state-of-the-art alarm system because they would not be hanging around for long. He had also told her that no one knew about the island or the house. *Don't worry,* he had said.

That was exactly what he had said when she had confronted him about the other boat, the one she had discovered when she had made a foray outside to identify any potential vulnerabilities. Lucan had assured her that there was only one place on the island where a boat could be docked and that was in front of the house. The remainder of the small islet was protected by walls of rock. The place was a natural fortress, he'd said.

But in the course of doing the recon she had noticed a nearly invisible trail in the woods at the back of the house. She had followed it. When she had emerged from the trees she found herself looking down at a very small pocket beach and what was left of a dock. A sleek little cruiser bobbed gently in the water. She was a professional. She understood the meaning of what she was looking at. Lucan had a backup plan. The question, of course, was why he hadn't mentioned it.

She had confronted him about it but she had been careful to do so in private because she knew that Devlin was already skittish about the job. It wouldn't take much to make him abandon the client. *Don't worry,* Lucan had said. *I didn't tell you because I didn't want to take the risk that you would let something slip to your partner. If we have to leave under less than ideal circumstances, only you and I will be taking the boat. Knight will have to stay behind to cover us.*

It bothered her a little to think that Devlin might not make it off the island. The two of them had been partners for a long time. They had saved each other's lives on more than one occasion. Still, on some level, she had always known that things would probably come to an end one day. You had to make sacrifices when you made the bold decision to adopt a whole new life. Her future was with Lucan, not Devlin.

She pushed the thought aside and opened the door. She was in charge of the hostages and it was time to take a very important picture.

She stopped abruptly on the threshold because the room was unexpectedly drenched in shadows. The only light was the small amount that slanted through the spaces between the boards that covered the windows. It took her a moment to realize that the hostages had turned off the battery-powered camp lantern.

"What the hell?" she said.

"Don't worry, Victoria," Winter said in a calm, soothing, oddly compelling tone. "We just wanted to conserve the battery. Night is coming on fast, isn't it, Victoria? We did not want to be left completely in the dark. I'm sure you know how it feels to be enveloped in darkness, don't you, Victoria?"

You won't have to worry about facing the night without a light because you're going to be dead in a few hours, Victoria thought. But she did not say that aloud. The first rule of hostage-taking was to convince the hostages that there was a chance they would survive as long as they did not cause trouble.

"I've got spare batteries," Victoria said. "Switch on the lantern. I need to take a picture of you. Jack Lancaster will be waiting for it. He'll want proof that you're still alive. Unfortunately, we'll lose some more time because my partner will have to take the boat back to the mainland to send the photo. No cell service on this damned rock."

"All right," Winter said. "I'll turn on the lantern."

The device glowed to life. Victoria realized then that the lantern had been moved from the table in the center of the room. It was now in the far corner. Automatically, she glanced in that direction and saw that Winter was holding the lamp in her bound hands. In the glare, her eyes appeared very deep and mysterious. A shiver of dread whispered through Victoria.

She was vaguely aware that the Tazewells sat in two chairs in the middle of the space, but neither of them spoke or moved. It was as if they had no interest in what was happening.

"This is the darkest place in the room," Winter said. "But the light makes it possible to see into the shadows. It is hard to look away from the light, isn't it, Victoria? You really don't want to look anywhere else. You can't look anywhere else. You need to look at the light. You want to follow it into the darkness . . ."

CHAPTER FIFTY-ONE

The photo of Winter popped up on Jack's phone later that afternoon, some sixteen hours after she had been grabbed. Jack reminded himself that he had been anticipating it since the moment he realized she had vanished. Nevertheless, it sent a shock wave through him.

She sat in a large, ornate chair that looked as if it had once been an expensive piece of furniture. Now it was worn and faded. Her wrists were bound in front with a zip tie. Her ankles were unbound. She wore the clothes she'd had on the night she had been grabbed and a coldly composed expression that gave no hint of any emotion.

The message that accompanied the photo was simple and straightforward. A seat had been reserved for him on a flight that was scheduled to leave in ninety minutes. When he reached Seattle there would be a car equipped with a tracking device waiting for him at a rental counter. He was to drive immediately to a remote location north of Seattle. If he veered off course or if there was any indication that he had been followed, Winter would pay the price.

The only surprising thing was that the captors had sent a photo, not a video, as proof of life. Maybe Zane had been afraid that Winter would figure out how to send a message regarding her whereabouts if she were allowed to speak.

Jack studied every detail of the photograph. He could not afford to overlook even the tiniest, most insignificant bit of data. At first glance it looked as if Winter was clutching her fingers together in a show of anxiety but closer examination showed that her hands were folded together in a way that left only two fingers fully visible. Those two were ever so slightly extended.

"What are you trying to tell me, Winter?"

It seemed likely that she was sending a message about the number of captors who were holding her. But he already knew that there were three, counting Zane. Furthermore, she would know that he knew that.

But the longer he gazed at Winter's two fingers the more he wondered if she was sending a different message.

"Got it," he said. "I'm on the way."

Jack boarded the plane to Seattle a short time later. He shoved his duffel bag into the overhead and stuck the backpack containing Winter's things under the seat.

He nudged the toe of his shoe against the backpack and kept it there, maintaining the small connection to Winter, for the entire flight.

He fastened his seat belt and focused on running scenarios.

Timing, as usual, was going to be everything.

CHAPTER FIFTY-TWO

———— ≈ ————

The man who had once been Quinton Zane waited in front of the massive stone hearth that dominated the far end of the cavernous living room. A lively fire burned in the big fireplace but no amount of warmth could suppress the underlying miasma of damp and decay that permeated the atmosphere.

Some of the windows had a few panes of glass left in them, but most had been boarded up years earlier.

Drapes shredded with age pooled on the scarred hardwood floor. There were a number of area rugs scattered around the room but they were thin and threadbare. The chairs and couches were oversized to suit the grand proportions of the space but the cushions were ripped and tattered, exposing the yellowed innards.

There was no sign of electricity. The only sources of illumination in addition to the fire were a number of battery-operated camp lanterns. No one had bothered to get a generator up and running, a clear sign that Zane didn't plan to hang around long.

Devlin Knight escorted Jack to the far end of the room and stopped a few feet in front of the blazing hearth. Quinton had one hand braced against the mantel. A pistol rested on top of the marble ledge very close to his fingers.

He raised the glass of brandy in his hand. He smiled a cold smile, but there was a feverish excitement in his eyes.

"Jack Lancaster," Quinton said. "It's been a while."

"Twenty-two years, eight months and five days since you torched the California compound, but who's counting?" Jack said. "Where is Winter?"

"Upstairs, at the moment. I can assure you that your little meditation guide is unharmed. My half brother and his wife are with her and they are both still alive, too. No point dumping hostages until it's over. You never know when you might need one."

"Your goons tell me I should call you Lucan Tazewell."

"When we first met you knew me as Quinton Zane. Let's go with that for tonight. But when this is over I will become Lucan Tazewell for real."

Jack angled his head toward the blazing fire. "Nice little Lucifer-reigning-in-hell thing you've got going on here. You always were big on the dramatic touches."

"I enjoy a good fire. I find it soothing. Now, I insist that you join me in a celebratory drink. We have a lot to talk about." Quinton glanced at Devlin. "Untie his wrists so that he can have a drink like a civilized gentleman."

"I don't think it's a good idea to release him," Devlin said. "We made sure he's not carrying any weapons and he's not wearing any communication tech, but just the same—"

"I understand," Quinton said. "You're right. No sense taking chances. But the least you can do is cuff his hands in front so that he can have a drink with me."

"Yes, sir."

Devlin stepped back a couple of paces and leveled his pistol at Jack while Victoria produced a military-grade knife and sliced the zip tie.

"That looks familiar," Jack said. "Same brand of combat knife you gave Kendall Moseley. Speaking of which, that idiotic plan didn't go well, did it? Whose idea was it, anyway?"

Quinton clenched his jaw but he did not say anything.

Jack smiled. "Figures."

"Arms straight out in front, wrists together," Victoria ordered quickly, as if she was worried that if she didn't intervene, there would be a fight.

Jack held out his hands. Victoria cinched a new plastic zip tie around his wrists and stepped back.

"Lancaster is secured as you requested, sir," she announced.

"Excellent," Quinton said. "You and Devlin keep an eye on him but let us have a little space. Jack and I want to have a private conversation. We've got some catching up to do. It's been over twenty-two years since we last saw each other."

Victoria looked at Jack. "Go ahead, but don't try anything. I really can't miss at this distance."

Jack raised his brows. "You do know that Zane has a long history of murdering the women who fall for his con, right?"

Victoria slashed her gun across his face with such speed and force that all he could do was turn his head to the side at the last instant and go with the blow. His glasses flew off. He thought he heard them land somewhere on the wooden floor. He figured he had managed to save his teeth and probably his nose as well, but there was blood. He could feel it dripping down the side of his face.

"Shut up," Victoria snarled.

"Take it easy, Victoria," Quinton said mildly. "Please pick up Jack's glasses and give them back to him. I don't want him to miss a thing tonight."

Victoria did not move. It was Devlin who scooped up the glasses and put them in Jack's hands. Astonishingly, the lenses were still in the frames.

"Jack's opinion of me is somewhat conflicted," Quinton continued. "His mother and I were quite close at one time, but she proved to be . . . untrustworthy."

Jack put on the glasses. "For a while you conned her into thinking you could protect her but she was never one of your women and in the end she knew you for what you are." He glanced at the ring on Quinton's hand. "Family crest?"

Quinton was briefly surprised by the question. He glanced at the ring and then smiled. "Yes. I ordered it made especially for me."

"Can't quite make it out from this distance but I'd say there's a ninety-six percent chance that it's a phoenix rising from the ashes."

For the first time, Quinton looked somewhat less than triumphant. The fever in his eyes got a little hotter.

"That was a very good guess," he said.

"Not really. I just went with the odds."

"What odds?"

"You're a card-carrying pyro. You've always had a thing for fire. It just seemed logical that you'd choose a phoenix for your fake family crest."

Quinton did not rise to the bait.

"Nothing like fire when it comes to erasing the past," he said calmly.

He released his grip on the mantel and crossed the short distance to the tray that held the bottle of brandy. He poured a large glass and set it down on the tray.

"Go ahead," he said. "Help yourself. My security people are very good but it's probably just as well that you and I keep some distance between us. It would be a shame to kill you before we finish our drinks."

"Let's stop playing games," Jack said. "You've got me, Zane. You don't need Winter and the Tazewells."

"You know I can't let any of them go. They've seen too much and they know too much. But if it's any consolation, I'll make sure Victoria takes care of your little meditation guide before I torch the house. It will be quick. Can't guarantee that it will be painless. I've never experienced a bullet in the head. But I'm sure it will be quick. Victoria is an excellent shot."

Jack fought back the tide of rage and resisted the nearly overwhelming urge to hurl himself at Zane. He could do the probability math better than anyone and he knew there was no chance that he would reach Zane before Devlin and Victoria gunned him down.

He crossed the room to the drinks cart, picked up the brandy with his bound hands and took a sip. The stuff burned all the way down. Liquid fire. He glanced at the label.

"This is very good brandy," he said.

"Of course. It belonged to my father. Only the best for dear old dad."

"I know." Jack managed another smile. "I found his body, by the way."

Quinton tensed. So did Devlin and Victoria. Score one for me, Jack thought. None of them had seen that coming. It was time to rattle Zane; time to destabilize the situation.

"I assume your father wised up to the fact that you were going to destroy him so he tried to kill you," he said. "Did the Armani twins stop him or did you shoot him yourself? I could tell there was one hell of a fight in that room at the Sonoma house."

Quinton's jaw flexed. A hot fury flashed through his eyes. "You really are good at reading a crime scene, Professor Lancaster. How did you discover the Tazewell connection?"

"Solved an arson case that was going cold fast," Jack said. "The murder of Jessica Pitt."

"Pitt. How the fuck did you—? Never mind. What's done is done. I always knew you were the dangerous one."

"You must have been severely disappointed when you ended up killing your biological father with a gun. I'm sure you would have preferred to use fire, the way you did with the couple that adopted you."

"Well, shit," Quinton said. Venom dripped on the words. "You discovered my origin story. Congratulations. I thought I had scrubbed my past very clean."

"Murder always leaves a stain."

Quinton got himself back under control with a visible effort. "I will admit I regret that Grayson Fitzgerald Tazewell isn't here to join us for a farewell drink. But he died knowing that I was going to claim his empire and everything that went with it."

"Do you really think you can get away with murdering all of us? Winter, your brother, his wife and me?"

"Give me some credit, Jack. We both know that I can make a fire look good. This is a very old house that hasn't been maintained in decades. The authorities won't be surprised that it burned to the ground."

"Yeah, I figured that was the plan when I saw the stack of one-gallon containers of gasoline out in the hall. But what about all the bodies, Zane? How do you plan to explain them?"

"What bodies? No one knows that the Tazewells and Winter Meadows and you were ever on this island, so it's unlikely that anyone will go looking for bodies in the rubble. But if the bodies do come to light, the explanation is simple. The Tazewells came here with another couple to see about acquiring the old Tazewell family property. Sadly, they tried to start a fire on the old hearth and it got out of control."

"And my brothers?"

"Once you are out of the picture, I can take my time with Cabot Sutter and Max Cutler. There's nothing complicated here. I'll pick them off one by one. When it's over I'll control everything that should have been mine from birth—Tazewell Global, the big houses, the yacht, the corporate jet—all of it. And I will own it all in my real name, Lucan Tazewell."

"Huh." Jack raised his glass in his cuffed hands to examine the brandy in the firelight. The flames rendered the color of the potent spirits a deep amber. "You really must be batshit crazy to think that no one will suspect you're behind the deaths of your whole family, not to mention a few extra people who got in your way."

"You mean Ms. Meadows and yourself."

"Not just us." Jack glanced at Victoria and Devlin. "I was including the Armani twins."

"Shut up," Victoria hissed. She slipped her pistol out of its holster. "You don't know what you're talking about."

"Oh, come on," Jack said. "You're both obviously professionals. You know as well as I do that if Zane is going to make the whole phoenix-out-of-the-ashes thing work, he can't leave anyone behind who knows the truth about what is going to happen here tonight. It would give you too much leverage over him. Talk about blackmail material."

"You don't know what you're talking about," Devlin said. "Tell him the whole plan, Mr. Zane."

Quinton chuckled. "Lancaster is just trying to play you, Devlin. Ignore him. The truth is, you and Victoria are the only ones I can trust. When this is over, you both become partners in the company."

Jack smiled a little and reached for the brandy bottle to top off his glass.

"Isn't it going to look a little odd when everyone finds out that the entire Tazewell clan has been wiped out except for you, Zane?" he asked.

"Don't worry about me, Jack. We both know I can take care of myself. When it's all said and done, I'll have an ironclad alibi—I was on the Tazewell yacht when the tragedy occurred. But I do have a question for you."

"Yeah?" Jack pretended to take a small sip of the brandy. He lowered the glass. "What is it?"

Quinton's eyes tightened. "How did you connect me to Jessica Pitt?"

"Sloppy work on your part. That fire out in the Nevada desert had your fingerprints all over it. One thing led to another. Pretty straightforward stuff, really. Pyros are so predictable."

"You're lying."

"Why would I lie? Jessica Pitt was apparently very good when it came to financial matters. Obviously at some point in her marriage to Grayson Tazewell she discovered that he had gotten a woman pregnant years earlier and that the baby had disappeared in a black market adoption. When Tazewell dumped her, Jessica went looking for the kid. She hit a couple of your Darknet trip wires. You noticed and made contact. It was a match made in hell."

"Thanks to Jessica, I found out that the drug-addicted whore who gave me birth first tried to blackmail Tazewell," Quinton said. "When that failed, she sold me for money to buy another fix, probably the one that killed her. I like to think it was that one, at any rate. Call me sentimental."

"You and Jessica Pitt must have made a good team for a while," Jack said. "She wanted revenge almost as badly as you did. She had all the information you needed to guide Tazewell Global right to the brink of bankruptcy. At which point you stepped in to save the family business."

"Discreetly, of course. I knew I would never be able to move out of the shadows until I got rid of you and Cutler and Sutter."

"Don't forget Anson Salinas."

"Salinas is an old man. He was never anything more than a small-town cop; never a serious threat. But you and your foster brothers are a problem. You have been all along. I also knew that of the three of you, I had to take you out first because you were the one who was most likely to see me coming."

"And I did, because you tried to use Winter Meadows to get to me," Jack said. "Of all the mistakes you've made in this project that was the biggest one."

"I admit a couple of things went wrong early on, but now everything is coming together exactly as I intended."

"I want to see Winter."

"Certainly. In fact, I'll enjoy watching the two of you make your final good-byes. Victoria, go upstairs and get Ms. Meadows. Bring her down here."

Victoria hesitated. "Are you sure that's a good idea, sir?"

"Get her," Quinton snapped.

"Yes, sir."

Zane couldn't resist feasting on the added bit of drama, Jack thought. *So predictable.*

Victoria holstered her pistol and went swiftly out of the room. Jack heard her footsteps echo in the hall and then on the stairs. Devlin did not say anything but something about the set of his shoulders made it clear he was uneasy with the whole situation and growing more so by the minute.

Maybe it was finally dawning on him that his employer was not entirely sane. An obsession with revenge plays havoc with logic and common sense. Devlin had to know that. Given his profession, he had probably worked for more than one obsessed client.

Jack looked at Quinton. "I answered your question. Now it's your turn. Why did you murder my mother that night before you set fire to the compound?"

Quinton was startled. But in the next instant his face was transformed into a mask of rage.

"Your mother was a fucking *magician* when it came to calculating probabilities and odds," he said. "She could have made a fortune for me in the world of online gambling. But she betrayed me."

"You mean she figured out that you were nothing more than a con man. She realized that you had lied to her."

"She tried to kill me."

The words were etched in white-hot fury.

"Wow," Jack said. "I did not see that coming. Unfortunately, she failed."

"The bitch came at me with a fucking kitchen knife." Quinton pulled himself together. "It was pure luck that I survived."

"You murdered her that night. And then you torched the compound."

"I had no choice," Quinton said. "I had begun to suspect that some of the women were plotting against me. After your mother tried to gut me I realized that it was all coming apart. I had no choice but to destroy everything I had built so I could start fresh. I knew I couldn't trust anyone in that compound. They were all witnesses."

"Including the kids you locked in the barn."

"Especially you," Quinton said. "But soon you'll be dead. This time there will be no witnesses left to haunt me."

"Except for the Armani twins, of course," Jack said.

Devlin's face tightened. "Shut up."

Footsteps sounded on the stairs again. A few seconds later they echoed in the hall. Two people this time. Jack looked toward the arched opening. So did Quinton.

Winter came to a halt just inside the cavernous room. Her hair had come undone at some point and now hung in wild, tangled tendrils around her dirt-smudged face. She had every right to looked frantic and desperate—to look like a victim. She was a hostage, after all. But with the exception of her lightning-fierce eyes, everything about her radiated the cool, composed, unnervingly calm expression of a woman who could be killed but never conquered.

She looked magnificent, Jack thought.

"Are you all right, Winter?" he asked quietly.

"The accommodations are less than one-star but, yes, I'm okay. So are Easton and Rebecca."

"Can I assume that you've been reading to Victoria?"

"Yes, as a matter of fact," Winter said. "We've seen a lot of Victoria upstairs. Zane assigned her the job of keeping an eye on the hostages. He probably figured that was women's work. So, yes, she knows the story by heart. Shouldn't be any problem when she takes the test. Didn't get the chance to read to the others, though."

"One down, two to go. That's what I figured when I got your message. Nice work, by the way."

Winter gave him a blazing smile. "Told you I was good."

Quinton moved one hand in a short, chopping action. "Stop the stupid chatter, both of you."

A faint *whop-whop* sounded in the distance.

Devlin glanced toward one of the few uncovered windows. There was nothing to be seen in the deep shadows cast by the trees and the gathering darkness of the September evening, but the whop-whop was getting louder, coming in fast.

"Helo," Devlin announced in grim tones. "What the hell—?"

Quinton spared him a brief, annoyed glance. "It's either a military helicopter from the naval air station on Whidbey Island or the Coast Guard. Just routine maneuvers. Go ahead, Lancaster, say good-bye to your little meditation instructor."

Jack picked up the bottle of hundred-and-fifty-proof brandy.

"Showtime, Winter," he said.

"Victoria," Winter said, "Winnie-the-Pooh."

The effect on Victoria was electrifying.

She froze and gazed into some empty place in the middle of the room.

"We have to leave now, Devlin," she said. Her voice was utterly neutral. "He lied to us. It's a setup. We're here because he needs someone to take the fall."

She turned and started walking quickly toward the hall.

"What the fuck?" Quinton said. "Sloan, come back here, you stupid bitch."

Victoria ignored him. She disappeared into the hall.

"Victoria, what are you talking about?" Devlin called after her. "What do you mean, it's a setup?"

"She's talking about the helo," Jack said. "You were right. It's not military. Cutler, Sutter and Salinas is paying for it."

Lights flashed in the fading daylight outside the windows.

"Shit," Devlin said. "Landing lights. I *hate* the fucking personal jobs."

He broke into a run and took off after Victoria.

"Come back here," Quinton shouted. "Lancaster is bluffing."

Devlin ignored him.

Quinton lunged for the gun on the mantel.

Jack hurled the bottle of brandy into the fireplace. It smashed against the back wall and shattered. The fumes of the hundred-and-fifty-proof spirits exploded in a fireball. Sparks and flaming debris showered the area around the front of the wide hearth.

Jack seized the heavy wooden tray and did a quick calculation to anticipate Quinton's next few moves.

Quinton screamed, a shrill mix of panic and fury. Frantically he scrambled backward, brushing burning bits from his hair and clothing.

It all made for a surprisingly predictable trajectory. When you knew certain things about a man—that he was obsessed with fire and that he was convinced he could control it, for example—you had a lot of data to work with. And then there was the fact that Zane was having trouble grappling with the sudden departure of his security team. His faith in his own ability to manipulate others was his greatest weakness.

Last but by no means least, Zane was right-handed.

Put it all together and it was possible to come up with a fairly accurate prediction of how he would move when he panicked.

"Fuck you, Lancaster," he shrieked.

He somehow managed to grab the gun, but he was off balance and blinded by his panic.

Jack moved in on Quinton's left side, not his dominant side, and slammed the solid wood tray against Quinton's head.

Zane reeled and shrieked again when he realized he was about to stumble into the roaring fire on the hearth. He dropped the gun and grabbed the mantel to keep from plunging into the blaze.

The portion of the frayed carpet nearest the hearth was now in flames.

Jack scooped up Quinton's gun and looked around. He wasn't much of a shot but if he got close enough . . .

Zane had vanished through a dark doorway. There was no time to pursue him. Jack ran toward the front hall.

"We have to get the Tazewells and get to the roof," he said. "This place is going to go off like a bomb when the fire gets to the gasoline in the hall, and that's not going to take long. This whole house is a firetrap."

"Follow me," Winter said.

She ran toward the hall stairs.

The thunder of the helicopter was very loud now. Jack heard a woman's muffled scream for help.

"The helo is coming in on the roof," he said. "Where are Tazewell and his wife?"

"Second room on the next floor," Winter said. She spoke from halfway up the stairs. "I've got Victoria's key."

"Another hypnotic suggestion?"

"Yep."

Jack took one last look at the grand living room. The sofa was now in flames. There was no sign of Zane, but the smoke was starting to thicken at the far end of the room. The only thing that was certain was that Zane had not followed everyone else into the front hall.

Jack glanced at the six containers of fuel stacked beneath the staircase and then he took the stairs two at a time.

"I assume that helicopter is for us?" Winter said over her shoulder.

"There's a helipad on the roof of this place. Rich-guy amenity."

Winter turned the corner at the top of the stairs and vanished. Jack caught up with her in the hallway.

A figure appeared at the far end of the deeply shadowed corridor. He was moving quickly but methodically, checking rooms as he loped down the hall, a gun in one hand.

"Cabot," Jack said, "they're in this room. Winter has the key."

Cabot reached them just as Winter got the door open.

Rebecca Tazewell rushed toward them.

"Winter," she said. "We heard shots. Are you all right?"

Easton looked at Jack and Cabot.

"The roof?" he asked.

"Yes, and fast," Jack said. "Zane has a stash of gasoline downstairs in the front hall."

"I get the picture," Easton said. He grabbed Rebecca's wrist.

"Stairs to the roof are at the end of the hall," Cabot said. He glanced at Jack. "What's the status downstairs?"

"The security people ran, thanks to Winter. They'll be heading for the boat dock. For them it's the only way off the island. Don't know about Zane. He may get caught in the fire when the house blows, but we can't count on it."

"We'll worry about him later," Cabot said.

The four of them pounded down the shadowed hallway and up a flight of stairs. The door at the top was ajar. Cold, damp air blew in through the opening. Easton pushed the door wide and hauled Rebecca out onto the roof. Winter, Cabot and Jack followed.

The sturdy helo was waiting for them, dancing a little on the old landing pad. The thundering rotors sent heavy waves of air washing across the rooftop.

Easton and Cabot got Rebecca and Winter into the helo. The men climbed in behind them.

"This is Sam," Cabot announced, raising his voice to be heard over the rumble and thrash of the blades. He indicated the pilot. "Friend of mine. He did a lot of flying in the desert. He's good."

"Go," Jack said, dropping into the seat next to Sam. "The place is going to blow."

"On our way," Sam said. "Sit back and enjoy the flight."

The helicopter rose and moved forward.

A moment later the mansion exploded in a fireball. The flames leaped and roared, a wild creature born of chaos and hellfire, grasping at escaping prey.

"How did the fire start?" Easton asked. He had to shout to be heard above the noise of the helo.

"A bottle of very expensive, very high-proof brandy," Jack said. "Zane was drinking it when I got there. Figured he might be using it to celebrate his victory."

"Did you know he would have it on hand tonight?"

"I noticed that a couple of bottles were missing from your dad's collection at the Sonoma house," Jack said. "Figured there was an eighty-two to eighty-five percent probability that Zane would want to drink that brandy in your father's first house and that he would want to do it in front of me. He likes drama."

Easton looked at him. "My father is dead, isn't he?"

"I'm sorry," Jack said. "Yes."

Easton looked back at the house in flames. "Rebecca and I knew from the start that it was never going to end well. I tried to tell Dad we couldn't trust Zane but my father was obsessed with saving the company and he believed his long-lost son could do it."

"There was a fight in the Sonoma house," Jack said. "Looked like your father finally realized that Zane was a con and tried to stop him."

Easton nodded. He didn't say anything. Rebecca reached over and took his hand.

"What happens now?" she asked. "Zane might have survived."

"There's a plan B," Cabot said. He flashed a brief grin at Jack. "With my brother there is always a plan B."

"Ninety-nine-point-nine percent sure that Zane has one, too," Jack said.

CHAPTER FIFTY-THREE

———≈———

Zane stumbled through the thick woods. He wanted to howl his rage and frustration to the universe but he knew better than most that the universe did not give a damn about losers. And he had lost everything tonight.

Everything but his life.

He would recover. He was a survivor. He was the smartest man in the room; a phoenix capable of rising once again from the ashes.

He had barely made it out through the old service door at the back of the house. In his blind panic he had not thought to grab a flashlight but he didn't need one. The days were still long in the Pacific Northwest at this time of year. There was enough light left in the September sky to guide him.

He was having trouble processing all the things that had gone wrong—there would be plenty of time for failure analysis later—but one thing was clear. Jack Lancaster had somehow managed to get one step ahead of him. Timing was everything.

He had known from the start that Lancaster was going to be his biggest problem. But in the end the bastard had failed to kill him, just as Lancaster's lying bitch of a mother had failed all those years ago. There would be another reckoning.

Still, he'd never been so terrified in his life as he was when the fire he'd built on the hearth of his ancestral home—the house that should have been his birthright—had exploded out of control.

Because of Lancaster.

He had to concentrate on the path he had marked earlier. Every so often he stopped, gasping for breath, and turned to look back through the trees. He could no longer see the house, but the smoke and the hellfire of the flames told him that the mansion was fully engulfed. He wondered if the surrounding forest would catch fire. Not likely. There had been a lot of rain in the past month, and more was on the way.

The distinctive whop-whop of the helo had faded into the distance. Presumably they had all made it to safety. So many witnesses. No way to get rid of all of them. He had no choice now but to leave the country. Again.

He had made provisions for this eventuality but the truth was that he had never truly expected to have to implement another retreat.

And all because of the sons of Anson Salinas.

He knew the route that he was taking through the woods because escape from the old dock had always been part of the plan. From the beginning he had intended to be the only one who made it off the island. Lancaster had guessed right when he told Devlin and Victoria that they were not slated to leave the Azalea Island house alive. They did, indeed, know far too many of his secrets.

He wondered if they had made it to safety in the cabin cruiser. If so, it meant there were two more witnesses. They didn't know their way around the San Juans. When the authorities picked them up, they'd sell him out in a heartbeat.

Really, you couldn't trust anyone.

A few minutes later he burst through the last of the trees and arrived at the little pocket beach. The old wooden dock extended several feet out into the water. He nearly collapsed in relief when he saw the sleek, fast cruiser still safely secured.

He started toward the dock. In another sixty seconds he would be gone. He knew how to disappear. The authorities would find a capsized boat and conclude that he had gone overboard. Maybe he would make it look like a suicide this time. Change it up a bit.

He stepped onto the dock . . .

. . . and froze when a voice spoke from the trees behind him.

"That's far enough, Zane," Anson Salinas said. "Been watching and waiting for you for over twenty-two years."

Quinton whipped around, stunned.

Anson was not alone. As Quinton watched, shocked, Max Cutler emerged from the trees.

"Jack said that if you made it out of the house alive you'd show up here," Max said. "He was ninety-eight percent certain that you were planning to be the only survivor. He didn't go with a hundred percent because there was a slight possibility that you might die when you set fire to your father's house."

"We could tell from the aerial views of this island that this old dock was the only other place you could tie up a boat," Anson said.

"Jack was right," Max said. "Guys like you are so damn predictable."

Quinton stared at the two men in disbelief. Anson and Max both held guns and, unlike Jack, they knew how to use them. They couldn't miss, not at this distance. All they needed was an excuse to pull the triggers.

He told himself to stay calm. He was smart. He would find a way out. Worst-case scenario, he could go for an insanity plea. Getting out of a hospital for the criminally insane would be a simple matter, given his talent for manipulating others.

He raised his hands, secure in the certainty that Anson Salinas and Max Cutler would not shoot an unarmed man. They were way too old-school for that.

A violent rustling of underbrush, the crunch of leaves and the snapping of twigs underfoot caused all of them to look toward the trees.

"You lying, cheating *bastard*." Victoria stormed out of the woods, gun in hand. "Did you really think you'd get away after what you did? You promised me a whole new *life*."

Quinton stared at her, hope leaping. He knew how to handle Victoria.

"You're safe," he said. "I was afraid they had picked you up. Take care of these two and we'll be on our way."

"Put the gun down," Max said to Victoria.

She ignored him and calmly, coolly pulled the trigger. Twice. Quinton was dimly aware of the crisp, professional shots punching into his chest. The impact slammed him onto his back on the dock.

It took him a couple of seconds to realize what had happened. By that time a cold that was more intense than the waters of the sound was icing his body.

Through the strange fog that was closing in he saw Max take charge of an unresisting Victoria.

And then Anson Salinas was crouching beside him.

"You're bleeding out," Anson said quietly. "Anything you want to say? Any message you want me to give to someone?"

"There isn't anyone."

"Okay," Anson said.

He put his hand on Quinton's shoulder.

"It wasn't supposed to end this way," Quinton whispered.

"You chose the ending, Zane. You made that decision a long time ago."

Quinton wanted to argue, to explain what had gone wrong, why he really was the smartest man in the room, why he was the strong one. But he could no longer fight the fog. It had become too thick, too heavy. It was pulling him under.

The last thing he knew was the feel of Anson's hand on his shoulder. He wondered why, after all that had happened, the old cop would offer the simple comfort of human touch at the end.

And then there was nothing.

CHAPTER FIFTY-FOUR

"The timing of the helo's arrival was the most complicated part," Jack said. "We couldn't risk putting any kind of tracking device on me and, of course, the first thing Knight and Sloan did when I got to the meeting point was smash my phone."

"Not that it would have done any good," Xavier said. "No cell service on that island."

"But we had the advantage of knowing Zane's probable location," Jack said.

They were gathered in the reception area of Cutler, Sutter & Salinas. Investigations. Over the course of the past few hours Winter had met all the various members of Jack's family—Max Cutler and his wife, Charlotte; Cabot Sutter and his wife, Virginia; Xavier, Cabot's nephew; and the patriarch of the clan, Anson Salinas. Octavia Ferguson, Virginia's grandmother, was also present. It was clear that she and Anson had a very personal, very intimate relationship.

They had come together as a family to defeat Quinton Zane and now they were processing the whirlwind of events that had taken place in the last few days.

The agency's offices were located in an older, established neighborhood near the Seattle waterfront. Winter was interested—and rather disappointed—to discover that the interior of a real-world private investigation business looked a lot like the interior of any other service business. The space could have belonged to a small law or accounting firm.

There was a handsome desk for Anson Salinas and some rather stylish leather-and-steel chairs for clients. The wall-to-wall carpeting was a soft gray. A series of opaque glass-paned doors marked the individual offices. There was, she noted, one unmarked door at the end of the hall.

The pictures on the walls featured warm, vibrant Pacific Northwest landscapes. Winter did not consider herself an expert when it came to art but the paintings looked very good to her—interesting and evocative. She suspected they had been selected for the room by Cabot Sutter's wife. Jack had mentioned that Virginia owned an art gallery in Seattle.

All in all, Winter thought, it was a very pleasant, quietly sophisticated space, but it definitely lacked the ambience of a nineteen forties Hollywood version of a private eye's office. There were no wooden venetian blinds on the windows. No well-worn fedoras and trench coats hanging on the coatrack. No sparking red neon sign identifying a low-rent bar outside in the alley. There wasn't even an alley down below the windows. She had checked earlier when they had arrived. It seemed to her that any self-respecting PI needed an alley in which to meet shady informants.

What did look very real were the men of Cutler, Sutter & Salinas. Max Cutler, Cabot Sutter and Anson Salinas were obviously tough, smart and relentless. If you were a bad guy, you would not want any of them looking for you, she thought. And if you needed help, these were the men you could count on.

Although Jack was not officially a member of the firm, he was definitely a member of the family—tough, smart and relentless. In addition, he was going to *look* like a very real, very hard-boiled PI because of the interesting scar he would no doubt have when they took the stitches out of the left side of his face. Victoria had done some damage when she had slashed him with her pistol.

The sons of Anson Salinas did not have a biological relationship, but they were brothers in all the ways that mattered.

"I understand how you figured out where Zane was holding the hostages," Virginia Sutter said. "But how did you deal with the timing of the helicopter?"

"There are a lot of small, uninhabited islands in the San Juans," Jack said. "When I boarded the plane in San Francisco, everyone involved knew that the endgame was on. Anson and Max used a boat to get to one of the little islands that was within eyesight of Azalea Island. They had eyes on the house when Knight and Sloan docked their cruiser with me on board. The only question was whether I would be conscious or unconscious. I was ninety-six percent sure that I would be conscious."

"Why were you so certain of that?" Charlotte asked.

"Two reasons," Jack said. "Zane thought that as long as he had Winter, he could manipulate me. He was right, at least to some extent. I also knew that once I was under his control, he would be eager to prove to me that he was the big winner. He wouldn't want to have to wait for me to come out of a drugged sleep."

Octavia raised her brows. "How could you be so certain?"

Jack hesitated. Winter stepped in to answer the question for him.

"Jack has a talent for being able to predict the actions of the bad guys," she said.

Jack winced.

"I see." Octavia regarded Jack with a thoughtful expression. "You must find that a rather uncomfortable sort of talent at times."

"You have no idea," Jack said. "As I was saying, when Anson and Max saw me walk along the dock and go into the house, they notified Cabot and Sam to get the helo in the air."

Xavier had been lounging against a wall, arms folded in a manner that mirrored Cabot's stance on the opposite wall. He spoke up.

"We figured Zane would move fast once he had Jack," he said. "It was Jack's job to provide some sort of diversion so that Cabot and Sam could extract the hostages."

"He went in knowing he was going to have to improvise," Anson said. "But he also knew approximately how long he had so he could time the distraction."

"I saw the smoke coming out of the chimney when Knight and Sloan brought me to the island," Jack said. "I figured I could work with that."

"From the aerial photos we could tell there were two docks on the island," Anson said, "the big one in front of the old house and another, smaller one hidden in a pocket beach. It seemed reasonable that Zane would have stashed his getaway boat there. When Victoria Sloan snapped out of her trance and went after Zane, Knight jumped into the cruiser at the big dock and made a run for the mainland. But we had alerted the Coast Guard just before it all went down. They picked him up. We gave Sloan to them, as well. I hear both Sloan and Knight are trying to cut deals."

"What shattered the trance that Victoria Sloan was in when she walked out of the house?" Charlotte asked.

Winter looked at her. "I think it was probably the explosion that occurred when the house went up in flames."

"Turns out Sloan had discovered the pocket beach," Max said. "She confronted Zane with it and he assured her that the two of them would escape together, leaving Knight behind. When she came out of the trance she knew exactly where to find Zane."

"I see." Octavia shuddered. "It is frightening to think about how it all could have gone horribly wrong."

Winter smiled at the older woman. "My advice is to focus on how it all went right. That is what I'm going to try very hard to do."

Octavia smiled. "You know, I do believe you make a very good point. I am just glad that Quinton Zane is no longer among the living."

Jack looked at Winter, his gaze icy-hot. "In addition to figuring out where Zane was holding the hostages, we had one other very crucial advantage."

"What was that?" Virginia asked.

"I told Zane he had made his biggest mistake at the beginning when he tried to use Winter to get to me," Jack said. "He had no way of knowing that she was capable of destroying his entire professional mercenary team."

"Well, there were only two of them," Winter said. She knew she was probably blushing. "And I could only get at one of them, Victoria Sloan. Zane and Knight never came upstairs while I was in residence."

Xavier's eyes widened in awed curiosity. "You're a for-real hypnotist?"

Winter glanced at Jack.

"Tell him," he said. "You're among friends here."

He was right, she realized. She was among friends. It felt good.

She turned back to Xavier. "Yes."

"Excellent," Xavier said, waxing enthusiastic. "So what did you do to Victoria Sloan to make her suddenly decide to leave?"

"Gave her a post-hypnotic suggestion," Winter said. "I told her that when I used a certain trigger phrase, she would realize that Quinton Zane was going to betray her and that she and Knight had been set up to take the fall for the murder of the Tazewells and Jack and me. Victoria was in a profession where betrayal is no doubt commonplace. That's what made it easy for me to implant the suggestion."

Winter stopped there and waited because she was pretty sure she knew what was coming.

"You can really hypnotize people?" Xavier said, not bothering to try to conceal his excitement.

"Most people can be hypnotized, at least to some extent," she said.

"Cool," Xavier said. "Go ahead, try to hypnotize me."

"No," Winter said.

"Why not?" Xavier demanded.

"She doesn't do it for fun," Jack said. He did not take his eyes off Winter. "And she doesn't do it to entertain others. She only does it when there is a very good reason to do it."

"Could you teach me how to hypnotize people?" Xavier asked.

"Maybe," Winter said. "If you have an innate talent for it and if you agree to abide by the code."

"What's the code?"

"The code is that you promise to use hypnosis only for a very good reason," Winter said.

"So, what's a good reason?" Xavier demanded eagerly.

"You mean, aside from convincing an armed kidnapper to give her a key and then turn on her employer, thus helping to rescue several people?" Jack asked.

"Yeah," Xavier said, undaunted, "aside from that, what's a good reason to use hypnosis?"

"You'll know," Winter said. "Figuring out your own personal code is part of what being a family is all about."

CHAPTER FIFTY-FIVE

———— ≈ ————

Jack swallowed some whiskey, lowered the glass and gazed into flames on the hearth. "It's been nearly three days now and I'm still having a hard time dealing with the fact that it's over. After more than two decades of watching and waiting for Quinton Zane and all the while knowing that he was probably alive, knowing that he was probably watching and waiting, too, it's difficult to believe that it's finished. Downright surreal."

"You're just not used to the concept of certainty," Winter said. She drank some of the wine she had poured for herself. It was her second glass and she was feeling mellow and wise. "Give it time."

They were back in her cottage in Eclipse Bay. The days since the events on Azalea Island had passed in a blur. They had spent the nights in a hotel room, although Jack's family had offered their spare bedrooms. She and Jack had craved privacy.

That first night they had literally thrown themselves into each other's arms. The lovemaking had been infused with a frantic, adrenaline-fueled intensity. Afterward they had collapsed into an exhausted sleep.

Jack and his brothers and Anson had spent a great deal of time talking to the police and the FBI. On the day after the incidents, Jack had been obliged to fly down to California to give a statement to the cops investigating the death of Grayson Fitzgerald Tazewell. That had involved another conversation with someone from the Securities and Exchange Commission. Evidently the death of a hedge fund founder who had left a company on the brink of bankruptcy had caused a lot of ripples in the financial world as well as in the world of law enforcement.

Cutler, Sutter & Salinas had received some splashy media attention, which had allowed Anson to shine in his role as spokesperson for the firm. Winter suspected that there would be a wave of new business for the agency.

Jack contemplated her words while he swallowed some more whiskey. He set the glass down with great precision and looked at her.

"You're wrong," he said. Behind the lenses of his glasses his eyes heated with the ice-and-fire that indicated he had done some important calculations and come up with even more important conclusions. "I do know what certainty feels like."

"Is that right?" She tucked one jean-clad leg under her thigh and swirled the wine in her glass. "How does it feel, Mr. I-never-go-with-one-hundred-percent-unless-the-situation-is-past-tense?"

"It feels like what I feel for you," he said. "I love you, Winter."

The simplicity of the statement, delivered with complete certainty, stole her breath.

She stared at him, unable to speak because the torrent of joy left no room for words.

She set her wineglass down on the new coffee table and flung herself across the short distance that separated them, straight into Jack's arms. He let the soft weight of her body push him back into the corner of the big chair. He gathered her close against him.

"Does this mean you feel something similar for me?" he asked.

Hope, longing and anticipation blazed in his eyes.

"Yes." She used both hands to carefully remove his glasses and set them on the coffee table. "*Yes*. I love you, Jack Lancaster. I fell in love with you the day you booked your first meditation session with me. One hundred percent."

"Is that so?" He speared his fingers through her hair. "What was it about that first session that made you fall for me?"

"So many things. I loved your passion for your work. I loved your sense of honor. Your integrity. I loved the fact that you were willing to give my meditation therapy a try and that you took my advice about changing your dreamscape. I loved the fact that you love your foster family. I loved knowing that if you ever gave your heart, it would be for real and forever."

Jack's eyes narrowed a fraction. "You really thought you saw all those things in me during that first session?"

"Yep. You're not the only one with pretty good intuition. There was something else I loved about you, too."

"What was that?"

She smiled a wicked smile. "You are incredibly sexy. I knew you'd be a terrific lover. Your turn. What was it about me that made you fall in love?"

"Everything."

She gripped the lapels of his shirt. "I want details. I want a list."

Jack laughed.

It was, she realized, the first time she had ever heard him laugh. The sound was gloriously intoxicating. It was the laugh of a man who has been freed from the past. The laugh of a man who has discovered joy.

After a while he caught her face gently between his hands. "I am one hundred percent certain that I love everything about you."

He brought her mouth down to his and kissed her for a very long time. After a while he pulled her to her feet and drew her down the hall to the shadows of the bedroom.

She forgot about asking for a list detailing all the reasons he loved her. There was no need for one. When Jack was one hundred percent certain, he was one hundred percent certain.

Her future career path came to her on the fragments of a dream. She opened her eyes, absorbing the possibilities and implications. She smiled.

"Jack? Are you awake?"

"I don't think so," he mumbled into the pillow.

"I know what I want to do with the rest of my life."

"How nice for you. Can this wait until morning?"

"No, because this involves you, too."

She told him what she had planned for her new career.

"Huh," Jack said.

"Is that all you have to say?"

"Do I have any options?"

"Well, no."

"I didn't think so." He wrapped an arm around her and pulled her down across his chest. "Why don't you tell me again about how sexy I am?"

"Okay."

"Wait, before we get back to that, I do have a question for you."

"What?" she asked.

"Will you marry me?"

She smiled. "Yes, I will marry you."

"Good. Now we can resume our regularly scheduled programming."

He rolled her onto her back, came down on top of her and kissed her until nothing else mattered.

CHAPTER FIFTY-SIX

———≈———

The wedding was held the following month in Eclipse Bay. The venue was the town library, because that was where other important civic events, such as the celebration of Arizona Snow's birthday, were held.

The bride dressed in the librarian's office. She was not alone. Her sister, Alice, and her parents, Helen and Susan, were with her. For once they were not dressed in trek gear. They were all wearing dresses and heels. Winter felt a rush of pride. Her family cleaned up well. Her family was beautiful.

"What do you mean, you're going into the private investigation business?" Helen said.

She did not sound startled; more like intrigued.

Enthusiasm lit Alice's eyes. "That's so exciting."

Susan got a considering look. "How will you use your hypnosis talent as a private investigator?"

"Jack already specializes in old and very cold cases," Winter explained, slipping one foot into a dainty, high-heeled shoe. "In cases like that memories are vague. The clients themselves have forgotten many of the details. And then there are the small insights they don't bother to mention because it doesn't occur to them that they might be important. By the time people get to Jack they are usually desperate for answers. I can offer my services to help them recall past events and associations."

"Hold still while I adjust your veil," Alice said. "I can see where your talent would be useful in some cases, but is there enough work in the cold case business to keep you busy?"

"Anson says he thinks there will be plenty of work once we do some proper marketing. Until now Jack has never been interested in the promotion aspect of his work. Also, he preferred to specialize in cases involving arson and death by fire. But as his partner I intend to expand the scope of work. Anson agrees with me. I've got his full support."

"Will you run the business out of Eclipse Bay?" Susan asked.

"Eclipse Bay is going to be our home between cases." Winter stepped into the other shoe. "Jack can do his writing here and I've got some meditation students here, as well. But we'll also have an apartment in Seattle. There's an empty office at Cutler, Sutter and Salinas. Anson is having Jack's name and mine put on it this week."

Helen chuckled. "You and Anson Salinas seem to have this all worked out. How does Jack feel about it?"

"Jack seems okay with everything," Winter said. "I've been sort of surprised, to tell you the truth. He's really into the positive-thinking thing these days."

Alice grinned. "That's because he's in love with you."

"And I am in love with him," Winter said. "Everything feels right with Jack."

Tears sparkled in Susan's eyes. She drew Winter into her arms for a careful hug. "It is so good to see you so happy."

Alice gave Winter a knowing smile. "Not just happy. Joyful. You look beautiful, my sister."

Winter felt the moisture well up. "Thank you, my sister."

"Don't you dare cry and ruin my makeup work," Alice said.

Helen gave a little heartfelt sigh. "After all these years, it's wonderful to know you found your passion, Winter. We all love you so much, darling. Never forget that."

"How could I?" Winter said. She felt her own eyes mist up. "I love the three of you, too. My family."

"Always," Alice said.

There was a sharp, warning rap and then the door snapped open. Arizona Snow, dressed in freshly pressed military camo from another era and boots that had been polished to a high gloss, stuck her head into the room.

"Everything good to go in here?" she said.

"Yes, ma'am," Alice said.

She hurried out of the room. Susan followed her. Helen paused at the door to blow Winter a kiss.

"We'll see you at the altar," she said.

She disappeared down the hall.

Arizona gave Winter a head-to-toe survey and nodded once, satisfied.

"You and Jack were made for each other," she announced. "I knew it right off at the start. That's why I made sure you got neighboring cottages."

Winter laughed. "So that was not a coincidence?"

"No such thing as coincidence." Arizona offered her arm. "Ready to do this?"

"Yes," Winter said. "I'm ready."

Arizona walked her down the hall and into the main room of the library, where most of the citizens of Eclipse Bay were gathered. The staff had set up every available folding chair, but the crowd overflowed into the stacks.

Arizona brought Winter to a halt at the top of the aisle created by the rows of seats. Jack, with Anson, Max and Cabot behind him, waited for her at the altar. On the opposite side stood Alice, Susan and Helen.

Arizona raised one hand. The head librarian, Mrs. Henderson, who also happened to be an accomplished pianist, launched into the bridal music.

"Welcome to Eclipse Bay," Arizona said.

It was all Winter could do not to hike up her skirts and run down the aisle. Her family, her future and the love of her life were waiting for her.

A van carrying the groom's gift to the bride arrived during the reception. Arizona Snow took charge of the delivery while the happy couple and their families danced and ate wedding cake and drank champagne at the library.

Winter saw the wedding gift for the first time when Jack opened the door and swept her up into his arms to carry her over the threshold.

She took one look, gave a cry of delight and scrambled out of his arms. He made sure she landed on her feet on the very high heels but he did not try to stop her. He watched, amused, as she dashed across the room.

She stroked a loving hand over the elegantly curved back of the little scarlet sofa.

"Thank you," she said. "It's perfect. Absolutely perfect."

"It's not the original," Jack said. "Figured we could do without the bullet holes."

"Yes," Winter said. "We can definitely do without the bullet holes."

He opened his arms and she flew back across the room to him. He gathered her close and thought about how much he loved her.

"One hundred percent certain," he said.